PENGUIN BOOKS
THE CALCUTTA CHROMOSOME

Amitav Ghosh is one of the most widely known Indians writing in English today. Born in Calcutta in 1956, he studied in Delhi, Oxford and Egypt. He worked for the *Indian Express* newspaper in New Delhi and earned his doctorate at Oxford before he wrote his first novel, *The Circle of Reason*, which won the Prix Medicis Etranger Award. His other books include *The Shadow Lines* (Sahitya Akademi Award), *In an Antique Land*, *The Calcutta Chromosome* (Arthur C. Clarke Award), *Dancing in Cambodia and Other Essays*, *Countdown*, *The Glass Palace* (Grand Prize for Fiction at the Frankfurt International e-Book Awards), *The Imam and the Indian*, *The Hungry Tide* (Best Work in English Fiction, Hutch Crossword Book Award) and *Sea of Poppies*. Amitav Ghosh was also the winner of the 1999 Pushcart Prize, a leading literary award, for an essay that was published in the *Kenyon Review*, and in 2007 was awarded the Grinzane Cavour Prize in Turin, Italy.

He lives with his wife, Deborah Baker, and their children in Brooklyn, USA.

BY THE SAME AUTHOR

The Circle of Reason

The Shadow Lines

In an Antique Land

The Calcutta Chromosome

Dancing in Cambodia and Other Essays

Countdown

The Glass Palace

The Imam and the Indian

The Hungry Tide

Sea of Poppies

The Calcutta Chromosome

A Novel of Fevers, Delirium and Discovery

AMITAV GHOSH

RAVI DAYAL Publisher

PENGUIN BOOKS

PENGUIN BOOKS
Published by the Penguin Group
Penguin Books India Pvt. Ltd, 11 Community Centre, Panchsheel Park,
New Delhi 110 017, India
Penguin Group (USA) Inc., 375 Hudson Street, New York, New York 10014,
USA
Penguin Group (Canada), 90 Eglinton Avenue East, Suite 700, Toronto, Ontario,
M4P 2Y3, Canada (a division of Pearson Penguin Canada Inc.)
Penguin Books Ltd, 80 Strand, London WC2R 0RL, England
Penguin Ireland, 25 St Stephen's Green, Dublin 2, Ireland (a division of Penguin
Books Ltd)
Penguin Group (Australia), 250 Camberwell Ròad, Camberwell, Victoria 3124,
Australia (a division of Pearson Australia Group Pty Ltd)
Penguin Group (NZ), 67 Apollo Drive, Rosedale, Auckland 0632, New Zealand
(a division of Pearson New Zealand Ltd)
Penguin Group (South Africa) (Pty) Ltd, 24 Sturdee Avenue, Rosebank, Johannesburg
2196, South Africa

Penguin Books Ltd, Registered Offices: 80 Strand, London WC2R 0RL, England

First published by Ravi Dayal Publisher 1996
Published in Viking by Penguin Books India and Ravi Dayal Publisher 2008
Published in Penguin Books 2009

ISBN 9780143066552

For sale in India, Nepal and Bhutan only

Typeset in Sabon by InoSoft Systems, Noida
Printed at Gopsons Papers Ltd, Noida

For Koeli

August 20: Mosquito Day

This day relenting God
  Hath placed within my hand
A wondrous thing; And God
  Be praised. At His command,

Seeking His secret deeds
  With tears and toiling breath,
I find thy cunning seeds,
  O million-murdering Death.

Sir Ronald Ross
(Nobel Prize for Medicine, 1906)

~

one

If the system hadn't stalled Antar would never have guessed that the scrap of paper on his screen was the remnant of an ID card. It looked as though it had been rescued from a fire: the plastic laminate had warped and melted along the edges. The lettering was mostly illegible and the photograph had vanished under a smudge of soot. But a four-inch metal chain had somehow stayed attached to the card: it hung down in a rusty loop from a perforation in the top left-hand corner, like a drooping tail. It was the chain that tripped the system, not the card.

The card turned up in one of those routine inventories that went flashing around the globe with metronomic regularity, for no reason that Antar could understand, except that it was what the system did best. Once it got started it would keep them coming, hour after hour, an endless succession of documents and objects, stopping only when it stumbled on something it couldn't file: the most trivial things usually.

Once it was a glass paperweight, of the kind that rain snowflakes if you turn them upside down; another time it was a bottle of correcting fluid, from an irrigation overseer's office just south of the Aral Sea. Both times the machine went into a controlled frenzy, firing off questions, one after another.

Antar had met children who were like that: why? what? when? where? how? But children asked because they were curious; with these AVA/IIe systems it was something else—

something that he could only think of as a simulated urge for self-improvement. He'd been using his Ava for a couple of years now and he was still awed by her eagerness to better herself. Anything she didn't recognize she'd take apart on screen, producing microscopic structural analyses, spinning the images around and around, tumbling them over, resting them on their side, producing ever greater refinements of detail.

She wouldn't stop until Antar had told her everything he knew about whatever it was that she was playing with on her screen. He'd tried routing her to her own encyclopedias, but that wasn't good enough. Somewhere along the line she had been programmed to hunt out real-time information, and that was what she was determined to get. Once she'd wrung the last, meaningless detail out of him, she'd give the object on her screen a final spin, with a bizarrely human smugness, before propelling it into the horizonless limbo of her memory.

That time with the paperweight, it had taken him a full minute to notice what was going on. He was reading: he had been lent a gadget that could project pages from a magazine or a book on the far wall of the room. So long as he didn't move his head too much and hit the right key in a steady rhythm, Ava couldn't tell that she didn't exactly have his full attention. The device was illegal of course, precisely because it was meant for people like him, who worked alone, at home.

Ava didn't notice the first time but it happened again with the correcting fluid: he was reading, staring at the wall when she went deadly quiet. Then suddenly warnings began to flash on his screen. He whisked the book away but she already knew something was up. At the end of the week, he received a notice from his employer, the International Water Council, telling him that his pay had been docked because of 'declining productivity', warning him that a further decline could entail a reduction in his retirement benefits.

He didn't dare take any more chances after that. He took the gadget with him that evening, when he went on his hour-long daily walk to Penn Station. He carried it to the franchise doughnut shop where he was a regular, down by the Long

Island Railroad ticket counters, and handed it back to the Sudanese bank teller who had lent it to him. Antar's retirement was only a year away and if his pension rates went down now he knew he wouldn't be able to work them up again. For years he'd been dreaming of leaving New York and going back to Egypt: of getting out of this musty apartment where all he could see when he looked down the street were boarded-up windows stretching across the fronts of buildings that were almost as empty as his own.

He stopped trying to get the better of Ava after that. He went back to his job, staring patiently at those endless inventories, wondering what it was all for.

Years ago, when Antar was a boy, in Egypt, an archaeologist had turned up at the little hamlet where his family lived—on a strip of land reclaimed from the desert, on the western edge of the Nile Delta. The archaeologist was a woman, a very old Hungarian emigre with skin that was as brittle and closely veined as a dried eucalyptus leaf. No one could pronounce her name so the village children named her al-Magari, the Hungarian.

The Hungarian visited the village several times over a period of a few months. On the first few occasions she brought along a small team of assistants and workers. She'd sit in a canvas-backed chair, under an enormous hat, and direct the excavations with a silver-tipped cane. Sometimes she would pay Antar and his cousins to help, after school, or when their fathers let them off from the fields. Afterwards the boys would sit around in a circle and watch as she sifted through the sand and earth with brushes and tweezers, examining the dirt with magnifying glasses.

'What is she doing?' they'd ask each other. 'What's it all for?' The questions were usually directed at Antar for he was the one who always had the answers at school. The truth was that Antar didn't know, he was just as puzzled as they were. But he had a reputation to live up to, so one day he took a deep breath and announced: 'I know what they're doing: they're counting the dust; they're dust-counters.'

'What?' said the others, mystified, so he explained that the Hungarian was counting the dirt in the same way that old men count prayer beads. They believed him because he was the brightest boy in the village.

The memory stole up on Antar one afternoon, a brilliantly sunlit vision of sand and mud-brick and creaking waterwheels. He'd been struggling to keep himself awake while a particularly long inventory went flashing by. It was from an administrative building that had been commandeered by the International Water Council—some wretched little Agricultural Extension Office in Ovamboland or Barotseland. The Investigation Officers had run everything they could find through Ava, all the endless detritus of twentieth-century officialdom—paperclips, file-covers, diskettes. They appeared to believe that everything they found in places like those had a bearing on the depletion of the world's water supplies.

Antar had never quite understood why they went to so much trouble, but that morning, thinking of the archaeologist, he suddenly knew. They saw themselves making History with their vast water-control experiments: they wanted to record every minute detail of what they had done, what they would do. Instead of having an historian sift through their dirt, looking for meanings, they wanted to do it themselves: they wanted to load their dirt with their own meanings.

He sat up with a start and said, in Arabic: That's what you are Ava, a Dust-Counter, *'Addaad al-Turaab.*

He said it under his breath, but Ava heard him anyway. He could have sworn that she was actually startled: her 'eye', a laser-guided surveillance camera, swivelled on him while the screen misted over with standby graphics. Then Ava began to spit out translations of the Arabic phrase, going through the world's languages in declining order of population: Mandarin, Spanish, English, Hindi, Arabic, Bengali . . . It was funny at first, but when it got to the dialects of the Upper Amazon Antar couldn't bear it any longer. 'Stop showing off,' he shouted. 'You don't have to show me you know everything there is to know. *Iskuti;* shut up.'

But it was Ava who silenced him instead, serenely spitting the phrases back at him. Antar listened awe-struck as 'shut up' took on the foliage of the Upper Amazon.

two

―――――――

Antar was waiting to sign off when the card and chain showed up on Ava's screen. His eyes kept straying to the timeline at the bottom of the screen. He'd been hoping to get off a few minutes early. His neighbour, a young woman who had moved in next door a few months earlier, had invited herself over that evening. She was going to bring dinner. Antar wanted some time to himself before she came: he'd been planning to get a shower and go for his usual evening walk to Penn Station. There was still half an hour to go before he got off, at six.

Restive as he was, Antar probably wouldn't have given the card a second glance; left to himself, he'd have dispatched it with a keystroke, sent it tumbling into the unbounded darkness of Ava's heart. It was only because Ava went into one of her trances of unrecognition over the metal chain that he took a closer look.

The chain was made up of very small, interlocking metal spheres. It was scuffed and rusted with all the nickel-plating gone, but Antar knew what it was the moment he saw it. He'd worn one himself, for years, while he was working at LifeWatch.

LifeWatch was a small but respected non-profit organization that served as a global public health consultancy and epidemiological data bank. Antar had worked there much of his life, as a programmer and systems analyst. In a sense he worked there still except that LifeWatch had long since been absorbed, along with many other such independent agencies, into the mammoth public health wing of the newly-formed International Water Council. Like most of his colleagues, Antar had been assigned to an inconsequential 'At Home' job to see him through to retirement. He was now technically on the Council's payrolls, but he had never set foot in its New York offices. He had not had reason to: they communicated with him through Ava whenever they wanted, which wasn't often.

Antar could remember a time when those little chains had been standard issue at LifeWatch, along with bar-coded identity cards. Some people preferred to wear their cards on clips; he'd always liked the chains himself. He liked the feel of the metal balls, running through his fingernails; they were like miniature worry-beads.

He lingered over the chain for a moment. They hadn't been around for years now and he couldn't quite recall when they were first introduced: probably some time in the 1980s. He had been at LifeWatch for well over ten years by that time. He had joined immediately after graduating from Patrice Lumumba University in Moscow: this was in the days when the Russians were still handing out scholarships to students from poor countries; when Moscow was the best place in the world to study Linear Programming. LifeWatch had advertised internationally for a programmer and analyst, to bring their accounts on line. It was a number-crunching job, not what he had been trained for. But, on the other hand, it was safe, secure, settled, and it offered an American salary and a guaranteed visa. He'd responded immediately without really expecting to get the job: he knew the competition would be fierce. As it turned out, he was third on the shortlist but the two people who were ahead of him got other offers.

Antar rubbed his fingertips, overcome by a tactile nostalgia, recalling the feel of those chains and those laminated plastic ID cards. The chains came in two sizes, he remembered: you could wear them around your neck or thread them through a button-hole. He'd always preferred the shorter chains.

He took his time, keying in answers to Ava's questions. In the meanwhile Ava was toying with the card, flipping it over, blowing up segments in random order.

Suddenly a symbol flashed across the monitor, shooting off at an angle, rotating and diminishing as it went. It caught Antar's eye just before it spun off the edge of the screen. He lunged at the keyboard, and tracked slowly back. When he had the symbol centred he froze the frame.

It was years since he'd seen the once-familiar logo of LifeWatch, a neatly stylized image of two intertwined laurel wreaths. And here it was now, in front of him, plucked out of the bottom of a lost ID card. Antar turned the card over, on Ava's screen, intrigued at the sight of the symbol, so well-known and so long forgotten. He brought the card back on screen, life size, and blew it up, slowly. There couldn't be any doubt about it: it was a LifeWatch ID.

He guessed the card was from the mid-eighties or early nineties or thereabouts—a time when he had spent so many hours with spreadsheets that he'd got to know every name on LifeWatch's payroll. Looking at that grubby old card suspended in front of him he began to wonder whom it had belonged to. He was sure he'd know the name—that at the very least. He might even recognize the face in the picture.

Without thinking, he tapped in a sequence of commands. Ava's screen went momentarily blank as she began reconstructing the card, restoring the original. Almost immediately Antar regretted the command. The process could take a while, and sign-off time was just twenty-five minutes away now. He gave his chair a kick, annoyed with himself. As the chair spun around, he noticed that a word had appeared on the screen, under a line that said 'Point of Origin'. Jamming his foot on the floor, he brought the chair to a halt.

He didn't usually bother to check where the inventories originated: they came through in such quantities it didn't seem to matter much. But he was curious now, especially when 'Lhasa' appeared on his screen. He tried to think back to the eighties and nineties and whether LifeWatch had had an office

Amitav Ghosh

there at the time. Then he noticed that the word 'Lhasa' was prefixed by a symbol which indicated that the item had merely joined the information flow there. It had been found somewhere else.

He looked over his shoulder and discovered that the pale outline of an enormous white triangle had begun to materialize in his living room, a few feet away. Ava had started to create a holographic projection of the reconstructed card: the cloudy triangle represented the top left-hand corner, hugely magnified. He began to drum his fingers on the arms of his chair, wondering whether he had the energy or the inclination to ask Ava where the card had been found. It was always hard to tell when something came through Lhasa.

Lhasa was the International Water Council's continental command centre for Asia. The Council's officers called it the de facto capital of Asia because it had the unique distinction of being the only command centre in the world that was in charge of not one but several major Hydraulic Regions: the Ganges-Brahmaputra, the Mekong, the trans-Yangtze, the Hwang-Ho. The Council's information streams for the eastern half of the continent were all routed through Lhasa. This meant that the card could have entered the system anywhere between Karachi and Vladivostok.

He looked over his shoulder again. Ava was taking longer than he'd thought: she was just getting started on the photograph, at the top right-hand corner of the card. He glanced at the timeline. He really didn't have much time if he was going to walk down to Penn Station before his neighbour, Tara, came over.

Idly, waiting for Ava to put the photograph together, he typed in another command, asking for a follow-up narrative on the card's chain of provenances. Ava took an instant longer than usual, but it was still no more than a couple of seconds before she produced the name of the city where the card had been found.

It was Calcutta.

three
_____

Waiting for Ava to get on with the card, Antar pushed his chair back, on its casters, until he could look into his kitchen, through the door of his living room. There was a window above the sink, and by craning his neck he could just about see the back of Tara's apartment, on the far side of the building's airshaft. He was relieved to see that she wasn't home yet; the apartment was still dark.

He slumped back in his chair, yawning. His eyes began to glaze over at the thought of the steaming cup of sweet, dark tea that was waiting for him at the neon-lit doughnut shop in Penn Station; of the other regulars who occasionally dropped by to sit around the plastic-topped table—the Sudanese bank teller, the well-dressed Guyanese woman who worked in a Chelsea used-clothes store, the young Bangladeshi man from the subway news-stand. Often they just sat in companionable silence around a circular, plastic-topped table at the back of the shop, sipping tea or coffee out of paper cups while watching tapes of Arabic and Hindi films on a small portable monitor. But every once in a while there would be a discussion, or they would exchange tips—about a gadget that was on sale somewhere, or some new scam for saving on subway tokens.

Antar had started going to the doughnut place because the owner of the franchise was an Egyptian, like himself. Not that he missed speaking Arabic: far from it. He got plenty of that all day long, from Ava. Ever since she was programmed to simulate 'localization' Ava had been speaking to him in the appropriate rural dialect of the Nile Delta. Her voice-reproduction capabilities had been upgraded so that she could even switch intonations depending on what was being said—from young to old, male to female. Antar had grown rusty in the dialect; he was just fourteen when he left his village for Cairo and had never been back. At times he had trouble following Ava. And then there were times when he would recognize the authorship of a long-forgotten relative in an unusual expression or characteristic turn of phrase. It was a relief to escape from those voices in the evenings; to step out of that bleak, cold building, encaged in its scaffolding of rusty steel fire-escapes; to get away from the metallic echo of its stairways and corridors. There was something enlivening, magical almost, about walking from that wind-blown street into the brilliantly lit passageways of Penn Station, about the surging crowds around the ticket counters, the rumble of trains under one's feet, the deep, bass hum of a busker's didgeridoo throbbing in the concrete like an amplified heartbeat.

And of course there was the tea. The owner brewed it specially, for himself and Antar, in a chipped enamel pot, thick and syrupy, with a touch of mint—just like Antar remembered from his boyhood.

He ran a finger around his damp collar. It was clammy inside today: too hot if he shut the window and too damp if he left it open. Downstairs, the building's front door was opening and closing in a steady rhythm: he could feel the impact through the floor, every time it slammed shut. The people who worked in the warehouses and storage spaces on the first three floors were on their way home now, a little early because of the long weekend ahead. He could hear them on the street, shouting to each other as they walked towards the subway station on 7th Avenue. He was always relieved when the banging stopped and the building fell silent again.

There was a time when there were nothing but apartments in the building, all rented to families: large, noisy Middle Eastern and Central Asian families—Kurds, Afghans, Tajiks and even a few Egyptians. He had often had to knock on his neighbours' doors, asking them to keep it down. Tayseer, his wife, had become very sensitive to noise after she was confined to bed in the last trimester of her pregnancy. In the past she had never noticed when the neighbours made a racket shouting across the airshaft, or when their kids skateboarded in the corridors. She had grown up within earshot of the canopied souqs around the Bab Zuwayla in Cairo: she liked the bazaarish feel of the building, with everyone dropping in on each other and sitting out on the stoop on summer evenings, while children played around the fire-hydrant. She liked the building, even though the neighbourhood scared her, especially the heavy traffic on either side of it—the West Side Highway at one end and the approaches to the Lincoln Tunnel at the other. But she'd wanted to move there anyway: she thought it would be easier having a baby there, with so many women and children around.

In the end it didn't matter: an amniotic embolism killed her and the baby in the thirty-fifth week of her pregnancy.

They were all gone now, all those noisy, festive families that had so attracted Tayseer. They had been siphoned slowly away into small-towns and suburbs by the demands of their expanding businesses and their ever-growing families. Antar had sometimes thought of moving too, but never with much conviction.

At first he had expected that the building would fill up around him after his old neighbours left—just as it had in earlier generations, with one wave of migrants moving out and another moving in. But somewhere down the line the pattern had changed: an alteration in the zoning regulations had prompted the building's owners to start converting empty apartments into commercial properties.

Soon the only residents left were ageing holdovers like himself: people who couldn't afford to move out of their rent-controlled apartments. Every year the building grew emptier of people, while the storage spaces expanded.

The man in the next apartment had been there since before

Amitav Ghosh

Antar moved in. He was a keen chess player and claimed to be related to Tigran Petrossian. Antar played with him occasionally, losing badly every time.

Then one summer—was it fifteen or twenty years ago?—the chess player began to waste away. He couldn't play chess any more; he barely had the strength to move the pieces.

His nephews drove up from North Carolina, where the rest of his family had settled. They cleared out his apartment and loaded everything into a yellow moving truck. Before they left they gave Antar a gunmetal chess set, as a memento; he still had it somewhere. Antar had watched from his living room window as they carried the chess player away in the truck.

Next it was the woman in the apartment below. She had been in the building since the sixties, when she first came to America from Azerbaijan. She had grown old in that apartment, brought up two children there; she had nowhere to go, especially after her eyesight began to fail. In that familiar space she could still manage on her own; she would have been at a loss anywhere else. Her children had let her stay, giving in to her entreaties against their better judgement. They'd fly in to visit, every other month, from the small mid-Western town where they lived. They arranged to have food delivered to her twice a week, from an uptown grocery.

And one day the delivery boy killed her, battering her head in with a cast-iron skillet. It was Antar who found the body. He had grown accustomed to the rhythm of her movements, and when he didn't hear the familiar tapping of her cane for a whole day, he knew something was wrong.

He'd lived alone on the fourth floor for four years. Then, a few months ago, Maria, the Guyanese woman from the doughnut shop, brought Tara to Penn Station and introduced her to the other regulars. Tara was small and bird-like, with a fine-boned beak of a nose. She was youngish—in her thirties, Antar reckoned—a good deal younger than Maria. He guessed at once that she was from India: the connection was obvious really, because Maria was a Guyanese of Indian origin and he knew she still had relatives there.

The two women made an interesting contrast, although they seemed very easy with each other. Maria was tall, stately, and unfailingly well-dressed, although she barely made minimum wage. Tara on the other hand seemed so uncomfortable in Western clothes that it was clear she'd just arrived: the first time she came to Penn Station she was wearing a loose white shirt that hung halfway down to her knees and a pair of dark trousers that flapped limply above her ankles.

But there was nothing awkward or freshly-arrived about her manner. She gave Antar a smile and a crisp nod when they were introduced and slipped into the chair next to his.

'What's that you're drinking?' she said, tapping his cup.

Mint tea, he explained, the owner of the shop brewed it especially for him, Egyptian-style.

'Splendid!' she said. 'Exactly the kind of thing I had in mind. Would you be good enough to ask him if I might have some too?'

Antar was taken aback by her voice: the plummy accent and the unexpected turn of phrase.

On the way out, walking towards the Broadway exit, Maria took him aside to say that Tara was looking for an apartment; that she had just found a job and needed a place to stay, in Manhattan.

'What does she do?' Antar asked.

'She's in child-care,' said Maria.

'You mean she's a babysitter?' Antar was surprised: somehow Tara didn't strike him as someone who would choose to look after children for a living.

'Yes,' said Maria. She went on to explain that Tara had been brought into the country by a Kuwaiti diplomat and his family, to care for their children. The arrangement hadn't worked out so she'd found another babysitting job, in Greenwich village. But the family she was working for now couldn't give her a place to stay.

Antar nodded. Although Maria didn't say so, he guessed that the change of jobs had made Tara's status illegal and that she needed to find a place where she could pay cash without having to deal with a lot of questions.

He shrugged. 'I'm sorry,' he said. 'There's nothing I can do.'

Maria raised her eyebrows. 'But I've heard there's lots of empty space in your building,' she said. 'Isn't there a vacant apartment on your floor?'

Antar was taken aback. 'How do you know where I live?' he said. One of the unwritten rules of the doughnut shop was that they never enquired too closely into the details of each others' lives.

Maria made a bemused gesture. 'Oh I just heard from someone . . .' she said. Her voice trailed away.

Antar had grown accustomed to having the fourth floor entirely to himself: he baulked at the thought of having a neighbour again. 'It wouldn't be right for her,' he said. 'The building's in terrible shape, and so's the apartment.'

But he gave in when Maria begged him to show Tara the building: the neighbourhood would scare her off anyway, he decided. He was proved wrong: Tara took an instant liking to the apartment and moved in within the month. It still took him by surprise when he went into his kitchen and saw lights blazing across the airshaft. For years he had kept the kitchen window curtained because all there was in the airshaft were dead rats and pigeons. Now he frequently found himself lingering there longer than he needed to.

Antar's eyes strayed to the timeline once again. 'Is it a quarter to six already?' he said out loud, inadvertently.

Instantly Ava bellowed confirmation, calling out the hour in the style of a village-watchman in Egypt, perfect in every detail, down to the tapping of a wooden staff.

four

The photograph on the ID card had begun to take shape in the centre of the living room, top downwards. The first detail to appear was a patch of hair, carefully trimmed, but rather thin and discoloured: definitely a man's hair. Then came a pair of bright black eyes. It occurred to Antar to wonder whether he might be Egyptian, whoever he was: he could have been—but he could just as well be Pakistani or Indian or Latin American. But once the cheeks and nose and mouth appeared, Antar had no doubts left. He'd always been good at placing people, he prided himself on it, it was a talent you developed when you spent a lifetime working for a global agency. The man was Indian, he was sure of that.

The image was huge now, and it was shaking a little, like a banner in the wind. The face was full, moon-like, the cheeks as puffed as a trumpeter's, the aggressively jutting chin ending in a carefully trimmed goatee. It was the nose that gave Antar pause—a boxer's nose, sunken at the bridge. It looked out of place in that well-fed, rounded face. And it also looked somehow familiar.

Antar got up from his chair and stepped back: it was oddly disconcerting to look at a flat, two-dimensional image in a three-dimensional projection. He stepped to one side and then to the other, keeping his eyes on the image's mouth. He noticed that the lips were slightly parted as though in mid-sentence. The beginnings of a memory began to take shape in his mind—

of someone glimpsed in elevators and corridors, a tubby little man with a pot belly, always immaculately dressed—pin-striped suits, razor-edged trousers, starched shirts, always buttoned at the wrist, even on the hottest of summer days. And a hat— he'd always had a hat. That was why it had taken Antar so long to recognize him. He had never seen the man's hair; his head was usually covered—no wonder really, with hair like that.

The image grew clearer in Antar's mind: he remembered seeing the man strutting busily down corridors, shoes clicking on marble, with files tucked under his arm; he had a recollection of an unplaceable accent, neither American nor Indian nor anything else, and a loud, screeching, self-satisfied voice; a voice that would fill crowded elevators and echo through the Trust's polished lobby, leaving behind a trail of amused glances and whispered questions: 'Who the hell is *that*?' and 'Oh, don't you know? That's our own Mr . . .'

He recalled a meeting, a conversation somewhere, years ago, sitting across a table. But just as the memory was beginning to take on an outline, it dissolved.

The name: that was the key. What was his name?

It began to appear, a few seconds later, slowly, letter by letter, and then suddenly Antar knew. Already, when there were no more than four letters in front of him, he had darted over to Ava's keyboard and fed it in, along with a search command.

The name was L. Murugan.

The first search drew a blank, so then Antar took Ava hurrying into the Council's vast archives where the records of all the old global organizations were kept. It took a full ten minutes before the doorkeeper systems allowed him into the stacks, but once he was in, it was a matter of moments.

He smiled when the old-fashioned file turned up in front of him: a tiny little character, the Arabic letter 'ain, blinked at him from the top of the screen, above the heading 'L. Murugan'. He knew that symbol: he had put it there himself. Someone in the office had started a pool, taking in bets to see who used

Spellcheck most often. They'd all devised symbols for themselves, to mark their work. He'd chosen the 'ain because it was the first letter in his name, 'Antar'.

But the file surprised him: he had expected something longer, bulkier; he had a recollection of feeding in a lot of material. He flipped quickly through it, going straight to the end.

On reaching the last line, he sat back, rubbing his chin. He remembered it now—he had typed it in himself, just a few years ago.

'Subject missing since August 21, 1995,' it said, 'last seen Calcutta, India.'

Walking past St Paul's Cathedral, on his first day in Calcutta, August 20, 1995, Murugan was caught unawares by a monsoon downpour. He was on his way to the Presidency General Hospital, on Lower Circular Road, to look for the memorial to the British scientist Ronald Ross.

He had seen pictures of it and knew exactly what to look for. It was an arch, built into the hospital's perimeter wall, near the site of Ross's old laboratory. It had a medallion with a portrait and an inscription that said: 'In the small laboratory seventy yards to the southeast of this gate Surgeon-Major Ronald Ross I.M.S. in 1898 discovered the manner in which malaria is conveyed by mosquitoes.'

He hadn't far to go when the rain caught up with him. He felt the first drops on his green baseball cap and turned to see an opaque wall of rain moving towards him, across the green expanse of the Maidan. He quickened his pace, swearing at himself for having left his umbrella behind at the guest house. The snack vendors at the Fine Arts gallery, racing to cover their baskets with tarpaulin, stopped to stare as he trotted past, in his khaki suit and green baseball cap.

He had packed an umbrella of course, a Cadillac of an umbrella, which opened at the touch of a button: he knew perfectly well what Calcutta was like at this time of year. But the umbrella was still in his suitcase, in the guest house on Robinson Street. He had been so eager to make his pilgrimage to Ross's memorial that he had forgotten to unpack it.

The rain was hard on his heels now. He spotted the gates of the Rabindra Sadan auditorium standing open, a short distance away, and began to run. A honking minibus sent a jet of water shooting up from a puddle as it roared past, drenching his khaki Prado trousers. Still running, Murugan made a forefinger gesture at the conductor, who was hanging out of the door of the bus, watching him. There was a shout of laughter and the bus sped away, spitting parasols of grey-green exhaust.

Murugan turned into Rabindra Sadan just ahead of the rain, and went leaping up the stairs. The outer gallery of the auditorium was brightly lit and hung with posters: he could hear a microphone scratching and humming inside. He could tell that a big event was under way: people were pressing in around the door of the auditorium, trying to push through. A television crew went rushing past, as he watched, carrying cables and cameras. Then the lights dimmed and he was alone in the gallery.

Turning away, he looked out through a window, at the walls of P.G. Hospital, in the distance, hoping to catch a glimpse of the memorial to Ross. But just then the auditorium's loudspeakers came alive and a thin, rasping voice began to declaim. It forced itself on his attention, insistent in its amplified gravity.

'Every city has its secrets,' the voice began, 'but Calcutta, whose vocation is excess, has so many that it is more secret than any other. Elsewhere, by the workings of paradox, secrets live in the telling: they whisper life into humdrum streetcorners and dreary alleyways; into the rubbish-strewn rears of windowless tenements and the blackened floors of oil-bathed workshops. But here in our city where all law, natural and human, is held in capricious suspension, that which is hidden has no need of words to give it life; like any creature that lives in a perverse element, it mutates to discover sustenance precisely where it appears to be most starkly withheld—in this case, in silence.'

Taken by surprise, Murugan looked up and down the glass-fronted hall. It was still empty. Then he noticed two women running up the stairs. They came pelting into the hall and stood by the door, wiping the rain from their hair and shaking it off their sarees. One of them was in her mid-twenties, a thin aquiline woman with a fine-boned face, dressed in a limp, rather bedraggled saree. The other was taller and older, in the beginnings of a youthful middle age, darkly handsome and quietly elegant, in a black cotton saree. She had a broad streak of white running all the way down her shoulder-length hair.

As he made his way across the hall, Murugan noticed that both women had press tags pinned to their shoulders, over their sarees. When he was a few paces away he recognized a familiar logo: both their tags bore the name of *Calcutta* magazine.

It gave Murugan a twinge to see the magazine's Gothic masthead again: his parents had been faithful *Calcutta* subscribers. The sight of that familiar lettering, reproduced in miniature, created an instant sense of connection with the two women.

Craning his neck he saw that the younger woman was called Urmila Roy; the tall, elegant one was Sonali Das.

Murugan stepped up and cleared his throat.

six

Urmila was just about to ask Sonali a question when she was interrupted. She spun around, in annoyance, and discovered a short, odd-looking man standing at her elbow, clearing his throat. Her eyes widened as she took in his green cap, his little goatee, and his mud-bespattered khaki trousers. Then he said something, very fast. It took her a while to work out that he was speaking English: the accent was like none she had ever heard before.

She cast a quizzical, raised-eyebrow glance at her friend, Sonali, but failed to catch her eye. Sonali did not seem in the least bit put out by the man. In fact she was smiling at him. 'I'm sorry,' she said, 'I didn't follow.'

The man flipped his thumb over his shoulder, in the direction of the auditorium. 'What the hell is going on in there?' he said, a little slower this time.

Urmila answered before Sonali could, in the hope that he would go away. 'It is an award ceremony,' she said. 'For Phulboni, the writer—to mark his eighty-fifth birthday.'

Instead of going away, the man now started to introduce himself—muttering a name that sounded like Morgan. Sonali gave him a smile that could easily be mistaken for a sign of encouragement. You could hardly blame him for lingering.

'Phulboni?' said Murugan, scratching his beard. 'The writer?'

'Yes,' Sonali said softly. 'Our greatest living writer.'

Urmila gave Sonali a nudge. 'Sonali-di,' she said. 'There's something I wanted to ask you . . .'

The man went on, without missing a breath, as though he hadn't heard her. 'Yeah,' he said, 'I think I've heard of him.'

Sonali reached into her handbag, took out a cigarette and began to fumble with a lighter. Urmila was mildly shocked: she knew Sonali smoked of course, she had seen her light up in her office. But here, in public?

'Sonali-di!' she said in an undertone. 'Everyone in Calcutta is here; what if someone sees . . . ?'

'It's all right Urmila,' Sonali said wearily, gesturing at the empty hallway. 'No one's looking this way.' She lit the cigarette and blew the smoke into the air, throwing her head back.

'I remember,' Murugan said suddenly. '"Phulboni" is the guy's pen-name, right?'

'That *is* right,' Sonali nodded. 'His real name is Saiyad Murad Husain. He began writing under a pen-name because his father threatened to disown him if he became a writer.'

'That's just a legend,' said Urmila.

'Phulboni would be the first to tell you,' Sonali said with a laugh, 'that legends aren't always untrue.'

Suddenly the writer's voice rose, booming out of a loudspeaker. 'Mistaken are those who imagine that silence is without life; that it is inanimate, without either spirit or voice. It is not: indeed the Word is to this silence what the shadow is to the foreshadowed, what the veil is to the eyes, what the mind is to truth, what language is to life.'

Sonali blew out a cloud of smoke. 'Just listen to him!' she said, cocking her head to catch his voice. 'He's really worked himself up today. He often gets like this nowadays, especially when he's speaking English. You should have heard him the other day at the Alliance Française.'

Urmila noticed, to her dismay, that Sonali was smiling at Murugan again, almost as if she were egging him on. Her heart sank. Sonali was always doing things like this—stopping to talk to strangers, getting into conversations on the lift and missing her floor and so on. As a rule Urmila didn't mind: if anything she thought it endearing that someone as celebrated as Sonali Das should take such evident pleasure in talking to people she didn't know. But today Urmila was in a hurry: she had an assignment to finish and she needed to talk to Sonali.

Earlier in the day she'd dropped in on Sonali, at her fifth-floor office, to suggest that they go over to the ceremony together, hoping to talk to her on the way. But inevitably, they ended up in one of those taxis whose drivers seemed incapable of finding their way from one end of Chowringhee to the other. She and Sonali had spent the entire twenty minutes of the drive from the magazine's Dharmatola office to Rabindra Sadan hanging over the front seat and issuing minute by minute instructions: 'Turn right here . . . look out . . . bus ahead . . . dog there . . . ditch in front.'

And now, just when she had finally got her alone, here was this odd-looking man in the cap and the goatee.

Urmila considered making a more forceful interruption and then decided against it. She was still a little unsure of herself with Sonali: in fact it hadn't been at all easy to go up to her office today, without an invitation.

Urmila had been working at *Calcutta* since she left college, three years ago. She prided herself on dealing with hard news, on being the only woman on the reporting desk. She no longer thought anything of storming into the Home Secretary's office in Building, or of asking pointed questions at the Chief Minister's press conferences. But when it came to Sonali Das she found herself becoming unaccustomedly shy and tongue-tied. Sonali was such a presence in the city, the kind of person you read about in film magazines and newspaper gossip columns; whose name you grew used to hearing on the lips of your aunts and cousins, pronounced with equal measures of censoriousness and admiration, envy and outrage. She was one of those people whom everyone talked about without quite knowing why.

In part, her fame was due to her late mother, a famous stage actress from the forties and fifties. But Sonali had acted in a couple of Bombay films herself while still in her teens. The first one created a sensation, because it wasn't the usual song-and-dance affair. But then, just when she looked set for a big career, she left Bombay and came back to Calcutta. A few years later, she published a wonderful little memoir, funny, but also wistful, even sad. It was mainly about her mother, but also partly about her own childhood—about her mother's friends in the literary world, about the old studios in Tollygunge and Bombay, about accompanying her mother when she acted with jatra companies that travelled the countryside staging vast historical melodramas. A radical young director turned the book into a play; the play, in turn, was filmed, to much acclaim from critics and film societies. From then on, Sonali Das was permanently famous, even though she never did anything else—or at least not until she agreed to join *Calcutta*, at the owner's special request, to look after the women's supplement.

Urmila was intrigued to hear of Sonali's appointment at the magazine, but she hadn't for a moment imagined that they would become friends. And then one day she found herself standing beside Sonali on the lift. She recognized her instantly, even though she'd only set eyes on her once before, years ago. She was much changed, but Urmila decided at once that the changes were all for the better: that white streak in her hair for instance—she was right to let it show. It suited her, marked her out.

After the first quick glance, Urmila kept her eyes carefully on the lift door, determined not to stare. But before she knew it Sonali was talking to her. Within minutes they were sitting in the magazine's grimy little canteen, drinking tea and chatting.

Urmila had broken her watchstrap that morning, while struggling to keep her footing on a crowded minibus. She felt foolish mentioning it: what possible interest could someone like Sonali Das have in a broken watchstrap? But far from being bored, Sonali proved to be very useful: she told her about a stall near Metro Cinema where you could get your watchstrap fixed for a couple of rupees. Urmila was astonished that she should know about something like that.

And now, in the same indiscriminately helpful way, Sonali was telling the stranger with the goatee that the Vice-President had come all the way from Delhi to give Phulboni his award.

Urmila could tell that the only way they were ever going to get rid of the man was by going into the auditorium. 'Come on Sonali-di,' she said jogging her arm. 'Let's go, or we'll miss everything.'

Sonali took a last, long drag on the cigarette and stuck the glowing tip into a sand-filled ashtray. 'I'm afraid we have to go now,' she said flashing Murugan a smile. 'My friend here has work to do.'

Urmila led the way to a door and pushed it open. The auditorium was packed: waves of heads rippled away towards the brilliantly floodlit stage, where a tall, white-haired man was standing at a lectern, wearing a plain white shirt and an old-fashioned, high-waisted pair of trousers of a faded military green. The spotlights above had cast long shadows over his craggy face, but there was no mistaking the dark, glittering eyes beneath the jutting brow. Urmila froze: she had heard so much about him, read so much he had written, but she had never set eyes on him before, not in the flesh.

She took a hesitant step along the darkened aisle. Absently she noted that the Vice-President was swaying sleepily on-stage, behind Phulboni.

The writer was gripping the edge of the lectern, leaning forward, speaking in a low, rasping voice. 'The silence of the city,' he said, 'has sustained me through all my years of writing: kept me alive in the hope that it would claim me too before my ink ran dry. For more years than I can count I have wandered the darkness of these streets, searching for the unseen presence that reigns over this silence, striving to be taken in, begging to be taken across before my time runs out. The time of the crossing is at hand, I know, and that is why I am here now, standing in front of you: to beg—to appeal to the mistress of this silence, that most secret of deities, to give me what she has so long denied: to show herself to me . . .'

Urmila cast a glance over her shoulder, down the aisle. She noticed that Murugan had followed close behind and was standing at her elbow, trying to push his way into the

Amitav Ghosh

auditorium. An usher walked up, torch in hand. He glanced at Sonali's press tag and then at Urmila's and waved them through. Walking down the darkened aisle Urmila looked back again. She was relieved to see that the usher was leading Murugan firmly out of the auditorium.

On the stage there was a minor commotion: the Vice-President's drowsily nodding head had knocked against the back of his chair.

seven

Summoning a dedicated Dåkø´la-class courier signal Antar sent off a message to the Council's headquarters to let them know he had found the ID card of a LifeWatch employee missing since August 21, 1995. Then he settled back in his chair and began to browse through the file that Ava had fetched from the Council archives. They'd want it back in an hour or so, and he knew he ought to go through it, just in case headquarters wanted him to do any follow-up work. From the look of it he estimated it would take him twenty minutes or so—leaving him just enough time for a walk to Penn Station before his dinner appointment with Tara.

In a few minutes he discovered that the file consisted largely of notices and newspaper clippings that had appeared at the time of L. Murugan's 'disappearance'. For the most part they merely reproduced the gossip that had circulated in the office. At the time, Antar remembered, everyone had assumed that 'disappearance' was just a euphemism for suicide.

Some of the clippings referred to the obviously desultory search that had been launched by the Indian police immediately after the 'disappearance': it wasn't hard to see that they, no less than Murugan's colleagues at LifeWatch, had decided on a euphemistic use of the word.

It was the last item in the file that gave Antar pause. It was an article from an unexpected source, LifeWatch's internal newsletter. The piece had the reminiscent, quietly respectful tone of an obituary although the writer was careful to describe Murugan as 'missing' rather than 'dead'. It began on the customary anecdotal note, referring to him as 'Morgan'—'the name by which his friends knew him'. It described him as a 'cocky little rooster of a man'; it talked, not without fondness, of his combativeness, of how he could never resist an argument, of his apparently unstoppable fluency; of the many contributions he had made as LifeWatch's principal archivist. It touched on his 'global' childhood spent wandering between the world's capitals with his technocrat father and spoke briefly of his love of Hollywood 'B' movies and old American TV serials—'the only constant, as for so many, in a peripatetic, internationalized coming-of-age'.

It was as a graduate student at Syracuse, the article said, that 'Morgan' first discovered the great love of his life: the medical history of malaria. He spent several years teaching in a small college in upstate New York, and during this time became to be increasingly interested in one highly specialized aspect of this subject: the early history of malaria research. Later, even while working for LifeWatch he had seized every spare moment to pursue this avenue of research—often to the detriment of his own career. He had published little or nothing in those years, but he had often claimed, in his flippant way, that he enjoyed the happy situation of being pre-eminent in his field by virtue of having it all to himself.

This subject was the research career of the British poet, novelist and scientist, Ronald Ross.

Born in India in 1857, Ross was awarded the Nobel Prize in 1906 for his work on the life cycle of the malaria parasite. At the time it had been widely assumed that this epochal discovery would lead to the eradication of what was possibly the world's oldest and most widespread disease: an expectation, alas, that had been sadly belied, as LifeWatch had discovered to its cost. In occasional moments of seriousness, Murugan had been known to admit that his interest in this rather obscure subject had initially had a biographical origin. The last crucial phase of Ronald Ross's work was done in Calcutta, in the summer of 1898. Murugan was himself born in that city, although he left it at an early age.

Possibly this biographical connection had something to do with the obsessive nature of Murugan's interest in this subject. In 1987 he let some of his friends know that he had finally written a summary of his research in an article entitled 'Certain Systematic Discrepancies in Ronald Ross's account of Plasmodium B'. Although some of his colleagues expressed interest, none of them ever got to see this article. It received such negative preliminary reports at all the journals to which it was submitted that Murugan decided to revise it before putting it in circulation.

As it turned out however, the revised article fared no better than the original. The new piece bore the unfortunate title 'An Alternative Interpretation of Late 19th Century Malaria Research: is there a Secret History?' It met with an even more hostile reception than the earlier version, and it only served to brand Murugan as a crank and an eccentric.

In 1989 Murugan wrote to the History of Science Society proposing a panel on early malaria research for the Society's next convention. When the proposal was rejected he sent pages-long E-mail messages to members of the review committee, jamming their mailboxes. A year later the Society took the unprecedented step of revoking his membership. He was warned that he would face legal action if he tried to attend any further meetings. It was then that Murugan finally gave up trying to argue his case in public.

Generally speaking, Murugan's colleagues at LifeWatch treated his 'research' as a harmless if time-consuming hobby: no one thought the worse of him for it, except when it detracted from his regular work. But it was soon apparent to those who knew him well that he had taken his ostracism from the scholarly community very hard. Indeed, this may well have been the proximate cause of his increasingly erratic and obsessional behaviour. It was at about this time for instance, that he began to speak openly about his notion of the so-called 'Other Mind': a theory that some person or persons had systematically interfered with Ronald Ross's experiments to push malaria research in certain directions while leading it away from others. His advocacy of this bizarre hypothesis gradually led to his estrangement from several of his friends and associates.

Murugan believed that the developments in malaria research that occurred in the early nineteen-nineties—such as Patarryo's immunological work, and the breakthroughs in research on antigenic variations in the plasmodium falciparum parasite—were the most important advances in the subject since Ross's work almost a century before. Murugan persuaded himself (and tried to persuade others) that these developments would have the effect of vindicating his life's work. The turning point came in 1995 when he began to lobby to be sent to Calcutta, the site of Ross's discoveries: he was particularly intent on getting there before August 20, the day that Ross had designated 'World Mosquito Day', to commemorate one of his findings.

Unfortunately LifeWatch had no office in Calcutta: nor would it have been possible to justify the expense of opening one purely for Murugan's sake. However, when it became clear that Murugan was determined to go even if it cost him his job, various people within the organization put their heads together and manufactured a small research project that would allow him to spend some time in Calcutta, although on a greatly reduced salary. To Murugan's great delight, the paperwork was concluded just in time to allow him to reach Calcutta on August 20, 1995.

Later, after Murugan's 'disappearance' there were those who sought to blame LifeWatch for allowing him to go at all. However, the fact was that the organization had done everything in its power to dissuade him. Representatives of the Personnel Department, for example, held several meetings with him in July 1995, shortly before his departure, trying to argue him out of pursuing this project. But by this time the plan had become such an idée fixe that in all likelihood nobody could have dissuaded Murugan from following the course he had decided upon.

'It is unnecessary therefore,' the article continued, 'to seek to blame Murugan's well-wishers at LifeWatch for the sad events of August 1995: it would be more appropriate to join them in grieving for the loss of an irreplaceable friend.'

Amitav Ghosh

eight
_____

The torrential downpour had now thinned to a gentle drizzle.

Murugan made his way quickly out of the premises of Rabindra Sadan, to the traffic-clogged edge of Lower Circular Road. Ignoring the beleaguered policeman on the traffic island, he stepped straight into the flow and marched right through, holding up a hand to ward off the oncoming cars and buses, apparently oblivious to their screeching brakes and blaring horns.

The pavement on the other side was jammed with pedestrians. Murugan was almost swept off his feet by the onrush of people heading towards Harish Mukherjee Road and P.G. Hospital. No sooner had he managed to fall in step with the crowd than he heard a voice calling out to him. He came to a sudden halt only to find himself pushed ahead by the relentless flow of pedestrians.

He threw a quick glance over his shoulder as he was propelled forward. He heard the shout again: 'Hey Mister, where you going?' Sure enough, bobbing up and down in the torrent of people behind him, was the head of a gap-toothed, emaciated boy—a tout of some indeterminate kind, who had accosted him earlier in the day, right outside his guest house.

Murugan quickened his pace and the boy shouted again, at the top of his voice: 'Wait Mister; where you are going?' He was wearing a discoloured T-shirt with a print of a palm-fringed sea and the words 'Pattaya Beach'. Murugan was dismayed to see him again, so close behind: it had taken him the better part of an hour to shake him off earlier.

Murugan fought his way to the wall that flanked the pavement, and waited for the boy to catch up. 'Listen, friend,' he said, first in his half-remembered Bengali and then in Hindi. 'Stop walking behind me: you're not going to get anything out of me.'

The boy bared his teeth in a smile. 'Change dollar?' he said. 'Good rate.'

Murugan exploded. 'Don't you get it?' he shouted. 'How many ways do you want me to say it: no, na, nahin, nyet, nothing, nix. I don't want to change dollars, and if I did you'd be the last person on the planet I'd go to.'

Reaching into his pocket he pushed a handful of coins into the boy's hand. 'That's all you're going to get from me,' he said. 'So take it and shove off.'

He ducked quickly back into the crowd, leaving the boy staring at a palmful of coins. He was at the corner of Harish Mukherjee Road now. Ducking down, Murugan turned the corner and pushed himself flat against the wall. Hidden by the fast-moving crowd, he watched his pursuer running off in the other direction; he saw him looking around, scanning the fast-moving crowd. Then the boy broke away and plunged straight into the traffic, racing towards the Victoria Memorial, in the distance.

'And good night to you too,' Murugan said, stepping back into the crowd.

The crowd thinned out after the corner. The red brick buildings of P.G. Hospital were on his left, well behind the shoulder-high perimeter wall and the narrow ditch that ran along it. He slowed his pace, watching the wall for the memorial arch.

Then suddenly there it was, across the ditch, momentarily spotlighted by the headlights of a passing truck: an arch framing a rusted iron gate. At the apex was a medallion, with Ronald Ross's bearded head in profile. Under it, to the right, was an inscription: 'In the small laboratory seventy yards to the southeast of this gate Surgeon-Major Ronald Ross, I.M.S. in 1898 discovered the manner in which malaria is conveyed by mosquitoes.' On the left, carved in marble, were three verses of Ross's poem, 'In Exile'.

Murugan ran his eyes over the familiar lines:

> This day relenting God
> 　　Hath placed within my hand
> A wondrous thing; and God,
> 　　Be praised. At His command,
>
> Seeking his secret deeds,
> 　　With tears and toiling breath,
> I find thy cunning seeds,
> 　　O million-murdering Death.
>
> I know this little thing
> 　　A myriad men will save.
> O death where is thy sting?
> 　　Thy victory O grave?
>
> 　　　　　　　Ronald Ross

Murugan began to laugh. Turning around he spread his arms out and began to declaim, from the same poem, in a deep, gleefully stentorian voice:

> Half stunned I look around
> 　　And see a land of death—
> Dead bones that walk the ground
> 　　And dead bones underneath;
>
> A race of wretches caught,
> 　　Between the palms of need
> And rubbed to utter nought,
> 　　The chaff of human seed.

He was stopped by the sound of hand-claps from the other side of the wide street. 'Very good Mister,' a voice called out.

Murugan dropped his arms and peered into the tree-shaded darkness on the far side of the road. He caught a glimpse of a printed T-shirt and a grinning, gap-toothed face.

'Are you following me, chaff of human seed?' he shouted, cupping his hands. 'Why? Why, what's in it for you?'

The boy replied with a wave and darted into the traffic. Murugan spotted a truck rumbling towards him, from the direction of the Race Course. He waited until the truck drew alongside, blocking him from the boy's view. Then he turned, pulled himself over the wall, and dropped down on the far side of the arch.

His feet landed in something soft and yielding. At first he thought it was mud; he could feel the dampness soaking through the soft leather of his new loafers. A moment later the smell hit him. 'Shit,' he said, under his breath, looking around.

He was in a narrow, overgrown stretch of waste-land at the back of the hospital's main buildings. Facing him were a few nondescript outhouses and a small cement structure that housed a water-pump. In the reflected light from the hospital's wards, towering above, Murugan could see a pack of dogs scavenging in an open refuse dump close by. Shading his eyes he peered into the shadows: there was no one in sight except for an old man, squatting against the wall, some distance away, washing his buttocks. Heaps of broken masonry lay in front of him. Scattered among them were neat piles of turds, ashen in the reflected light of the neon street lamps.

Murugan clamped a hand over his nose and flattened himself against the wall. He heard footsteps approaching at a run, on the other side; they stopped, receded, came back again. He heard the boy muttering to himself, then walking off, in a hurry.

Breathing again, Murugan began to move sideways, bracing himself against the wall with his open hands. Pushing along the wall, his left hand chanced upon the rim of an opening in the rough brick surface. Murugan leaned over to take a look and discovered that the opening was actually a little alcove: or rather, a gap where a few bricks had been removed from the back of the memorial arch.

He thrust his hand gingerly inside. It brushed against something; a small object. His fingers closed on it and he pulled it out. It was a little clay figurine.

Amitav Ghosh

Murugan held the figurine out at arm's length, into the dim glow of the distant street-lamp. The figure was made of painted clay, and it was small enough to fit quite easily into the palm of his hand. It reminded him of the little images of gods his mother had carried with her on their travels.

The central part of the figurine was a simple, semi-circular mound, crudely modelled and featureless except for two large stylized eyes, painted in stark blacks and whites, on the baked clay. They gave Murugan a momentary start; they appeared luminous in the dim neon glow, staring directly up at him, out of his open palm. They seemed to fix upon his eyes, holding his gaze; he had to blink before he could look away.

He turned the object around in his palm. To the right of the mound was a tiny bird, unmistakably a pigeon, clearly and carefully modelled—feathers, eyes and all. Growing out of the other side of the mound was a little protuberance, like the amputated stub of an arm. The arm had a small metal object attached; Murugan could not tell what it was—all he could see of it was a little metallic cylinder. He brought the figurine closer, examining it carefully, trying to work out what the metal object represented.

Then once again he was interrupted: 'Mister; I find you; what you doing here?' The boy was peering over the wall, his face right above Murugan's head, laughing.

Murugan lost his temper. 'Get out of my sight you son of a bitch,' he shouted.

The boy made a leering face and wagged his head. Then he caught sight of the figurine in Murugan's hand. He shot out an arm and snatched the object from Murugan's hand.

Murugan lunged at the figurine, but his hand caught the boy's fist and knocked it out. It crashed to the ground, on the other side of the wall. The boy dropped off the wall and fell to his knees beside it.

Pulling his head up, Murugan looked over the wall. The boy was on all fours, gathering up the pieces of broken clay. He looked at Murugan over his shoulder and spat out a curse.

'You asked for it,' Murugan said. 'It's not my fault.' Keeping his back to the wall, Murugan began to move to his left, stepping carefully over the excrement and debris. He came to a stop at a dilapidated red-brick outhouse, built so close to the ground that it was almost completely hidden by the boundary wall. The structure seemed like an abandoned shell, with branches of peepul growing out of the cracked plaster and grinning holes marking the old windows and doorways.

Murugan pushed his head gingerly through a gaping window. 'Hello,' he called out. 'Anyone there?'

Suddenly there was a flapping, whooshing sound and he was hit in the face. A flock of pigeons swirled past, brushing his face with their feathers.

Murugan threw himself back and covered his head with his arms. A sound rang in his ears; it was only after a few seconds had passed that he realized he had screamed. Then he heard a pebble strike the ground, beside him. He looked up and saw the boy, hanging over the boundary wall, his arm flexed to throw another stone.

Murugan ducked through a passageway, into the main drive and headed for the hospital's gates, at a run. Several taxis were waiting at the entrance, on Gokhale Road. Murugan jumped into one and slammed the door. 'Let's go,' he cried, 'let's go, move it.'

The Sikh taxi driver turned to look at him, unhurriedly. 'Go where?' he said, in Hindi.

'Robinson Street,' Murugan said, gasping for breath. 'Between Loudon and Rawdon Street.'

The driver turned the ignition key. The old Ambassador started up with a roar and pulled slowly away.

Murugan sat crouched by the window, scanning the road and the pavements. Seeing no sign of the boy, he sank back into the seat. His eyes fell on his shoes; they were covered with brown stains. He caught a whiff of a foul odour and thrust his feet under the front seat, hoping the smell would not reach the driver. But the odour lingered; he couldn't rid himself of it. He wrapped a handkerchief around his hand, took the shoes off and dropped them out of the window.

Amitav Ghosh

He sank into his seat, breathing a sigh of relief. But a moment later there was a thud on the back windshield. He looked around just in time to see his second shoe flying through the air. It struck the window and bounced off, leaving a long brown stain on the glass.

The driver stuck his head out of the window and began to shout at the boy, who was racing towards them through the traffic. Then the lights changed, the cars behind began to sound their horns, and the taxi pulled away.

As the taxi turned into Lower Circular Road, he glanced over at the brilliantly lit façade of the Rabindra Sadan auditorium. He noticed two women hurrying down the stairs, and thrust his head out of the window. The taxi was moving a little faster now and he only had a brief glimpse of them, heading for the gate.

He was almost certain they were the two women he'd spoken to earlier in the evening, at the auditorium.

nine

The article in the LifeWatch newsletter was wrong on one point. There was only one meeting between Murugan and a representative of the Personnel Department before Murugan's departure for Calcutta.

One morning Antar arrived at his cubicle at LifeWatch's headquarters on West 57th Street to find a file waiting on his screen: it contained a complete record of Murugan's requests for re-assignment. Antar was sure that the file had been routed to him by mistake: he was only technically a member of Personnel; he dealt almost exclusively with accounts. He lost no time in shooting off a query to the Director of his department. A couple of hours later the Director sent him a message asking him to drop by.

The Director was a serious and conscientious Swede who never lost an opportunity to remind his staff that their real business was caring. 'Let's get you away from your screen for a bit,' he said to Antar. 'I've got a more human job for you today.' He called up Murugan's file and took Antar through it. 'See if you can't talk some sense into this man Murugan: hard economic sense I mean. Tell him about pension schemes and medical benefits and all that sort of thing. You'll see from the records that this gentleman already pays out a third of his salary in alimony: effectively he's not going to be earning anything if he goes off to Calcutta on this wild-goose chase.'

Antar E-mailed Murugan that very afternoon.

A couple of days later, shortly before the lunch break, Antar heard a loud, screeching voice echoing through the department's open-plan office. He knew at once who it was even though he could not see him from his cubicle.

Murugan was carolling greetings to his acquaintances: 'Hey there, how are you doing on this fine day? Enjoying the low pollen count?'

Antar and his neighbour in the next cubicle exchanged startled glances.

The voice rose several decibels: 'Which one of you is called Ant . . . Ant . . . ?'

'Over here,' Antar shouted, jumping to his feet. He found himself holding his hand aloft, like a schoolboy, so that it peeped out over the plywood top of his cubicle.

'Stay right where you are Ant,' Murugan called out cheerfully. 'I'll find my way to you.'

A minute later he appeared at the entrance to Antar's cubicle; a dapper, pot-bellied man, in a dark three-piece suit and a felt hat. They were about the same age, Antar estimated; both in their early forties.

'Hey there Ant,' Murugan said, beaming at him, holding out his hand. 'This is some heap you've built yourself out here.'

Disconcerted by the man's manner, Antar gave him a thin smile and gestured at a chair. Pulling out a list of figures he plunged straight into the little speech he had prepared, explaining why a move to Calcutta would be a career disaster.

Murugan sat through the monologue in silence, stroking his goatee, his bright, piercing eyes fixed on Antar. When Antar ran out of breath and paused, he gave him a nod of encouragement.

'Go on Ant,' he said, 'I'm listening.'

Antar had saved his trump card for the last. He played it now. 'And have you thought about your payments?' he began. Halted by a momentary twinge of embarrassment, he stopped to clear his throat. 'Your payments to your ex-wife I mean?' he said. 'You'll barely have enough to support yourself if you go ahead with this.'

Suddenly Murugan leaned forward, looking into Antar's eyes. 'You ever been married Ant?' he said.

Startled, Antar fell back in his chair. Without meaning to, he nodded.

'And you're not now?'

'No,' said Antar.

'Yeah.' Murugan pursed his lips, as though confirming something to himself. 'I could tell.'

'How?'

'Just could,' said Murugan. 'So let's hear it Ant: you paying alimony too? You seem to know a lot about the subject.'

'No!' Antar said vehemently. 'My wife died, in her first pregnancy.'

'That's too bad,' said Murugan. 'Were you together long?'

'Yes.' The directness of the question took Antar off guard. 'I was orphaned you see, and her family kind of adopted me when I was in my teens, in Egypt. She was everything to me . . .' He cut himself short, flustered.

Murugan pulled a sympathetic face: 'Shit happens.' He glanced at his watch and pushed his chair back. 'Come on, let's go grab a bite.'

Antar's head was reeling from the barrage of questions. 'Grab - a - bite?' he said, momentarily uncomprehending.

Murugan gave a hoot of laughter: 'Get some lunch, something to eat.'

Antar had brought his lunch with him of course. It was right behind him, in his briefcase; a sandwich and an apple. He liked to have lunch in his cubicle, by himself. But he could not bring himself to say so now.

'All right,' he said. 'Let us go.'

Out in the corridor, on the way to the elevator, Murugan declared cheerfully: 'Sounds like you got a pretty raw deal, huh?'

Trying to turn the conversation away from himself, Antar said quickly: 'And what about you?'

'My divorce was pretty straightforward,' Murugan said off-handedly as they joined the lunchtime queue at the elevator bank. His voice seemed to grow louder as they stepped into the elevator. 'The whole thing was a mistake—arranged by our families. Didn't last but a couple of years. No kids.'

Murugan gave a screech of laughter that went spiralling tinnily around the elevator. 'How did we get on this subject anyway?' he said. 'Oh yeah, you were telling me I'm going to be a deadbeat divorcé if I go to Calcutta.'

Antar intercepted a stare from an acquaintance and dropped his eyes. He kept them down until they stepped off the elevator.

They went to a small Thai restaurant, right around the corner from the building where LifeWatch had its offices. The waiter took their orders, and a moment of constrained silence followed. It was Antar who spoke first. 'Why *are* you so determined to go to Calcutta?' he blurted out suddenly. He regretted it once he'd said it; he was not in the habit of inviting confidences from strangers, especially someone as loud and brash as this. Yet, appalled as he was by the man's voice and manner, he couldn't help feeling an inexplicable sense of kinship with him.

Murugan smiled. 'Shall I tell you why I have to go Ant?' he said. 'It's simple: I don't know how many years I have left, and I want to do something with my life.'

'Do something with your life?' Antar said, on a note of derision. 'What you'll be doing is throwing away all your prospects—at LifeWatch anyway.'

'But look at it this way,' said Murugan. 'You could find a thousand people—no, two thousand . . . maybe ten—who could do what I'm doing now. But you won't find another person alive who knows more than I do about the subject I specialize in.'

'And that is?' Antar asked politely.

'Ronald Ross,' said Murugan. 'Nobel-winning bacteriologist. Take it from me, as far as the subject of Ronnie Ross goes, I'm the only show in town.'

A look of some scepticism must have crossed Antar's face, for Murugan added quickly: 'I know it sounds like I'm bragging, but it's not really that big a claim. Ross wasn't a

Pasteur or a Koch: he just didn't have as much variety to his game. His stuff on malaria was about the only cutting-edge work he ever did. And even that was a freak one-off thing. Do you know how long it took him?'

Antar answered with a polite shake of his head.

'The actual research, the hands-on stuff, took just three years, door to door; three years spent entirely in India. He kicked off in the summer of 1895, in a little hole-in-the-wall army camp in a place called Secunderabad and ran the last few yards in Calcutta in the summer of 1898. And for only about half that time was he actually in the lab. The rest went into cleaning up epidemics, playing tennis and polo, going on holidays in the hills, that kind of stuff. The way I figure it, he spent about five hundred days altogether working on malaria. And you know what? I've tracked him through every single one of those five hundred days: I know where he was, what he did, which slides he looked at; I know what he was hoping to see and what he actually saw; I know who was with him, who wasn't with him. It's like I was looking over his shoulder. If his wife would have asked, "How was your day honey?" I could have told her.'

'And how did you get to learn about all that?' said Antar, raising an eyebrow.

'Look,' said Murugan, 'the great thing about a guy like Ronald Ross is that he writes everything down. You've got to remember: this guy's decided he's going to re-write the history books. He wants everyone to know the story like he's going to tell it; he's not about to leave any of it up for grabs, not a single minute if he can help it. He's figured on a guy like me coming along some day and I'm happy to oblige. If you think about it, it's not a whole lot to know about: five hundred days of a guy's life.'

'Was Ross really that interesting?' Antar said.

'Interesting?' Murugan gave a shout of laughter. 'Yes and no. He was a genius, of course, but he was also a dickhead.'

'Yes,' said Antar, 'go on, I'm listening.'

'Okay,' said Murugan, 'picture this: here's this guy, a real huntin', fishin', shootin' Colonial type, like in the movies; plays tennis and polo and goes pig-sticking; good-looking guy, thick moustache, chubby pink cheeks, likes a night out on the town every now and again; drinks whisky for breakfast some mornings; wasn't sure what he wanted to do with his life for the longest time; sort of thought he'd like to write novels; had a go, wrote a couple of medieval romances; then said to himself, hell, this isn't working out like I thought, let's try writing poems instead. But that didn't pan out either and then Pa Ross who's this big general in the British Army in India, says to him, "And what the fuck do you think you're doing Ron? Our family's been out here in India since it was invented and there's no goddam service here doesn't have a Ross in it, you name it, Civil Service, Geological Service, Provincial Service, Colonial Service . . . I've heard of them all, but no one told me about no Poetical Service yet. You need to dry out your sinuses kid and I'm going to tell you where you're going to do it so listen up. There's this outfit that's short on Rosses right now: the Indian Medical Service. It's got your name on it, written so large you can read it from a space shuttle. So kiss goodbye to this poetry shit, poetry just don't cut it."

'So young Ronnie snaps off a salute and scoots over to medical school in London. He coasts for the next few years, writing a few poems, doing gigs on open-mike nights, dreaming up outlines for his next novel. Medicine is the last thing on his mind, but he gets into the Indian Medical Service anyway and the next thing you know he's back in India toting a stethoscope and carving up vets. So he coasts again, a couple of years, playing tennis, riding, same old same old. And then one morning he gets out of bed and finds he's been bitten by the science bug. He's married, he's got kids, he's about to hit his mid-life crisis; he should be saving for the power lawnmower and what does he do instead? He looks in the mirror and asks himself: what's hot in medicine right now? what's happening on the outer edge of the paradigm? what's going to bag me a Nobel? And what does the mirror tell him? You got it: malaria—that's where it's at this season.

'So the bulbs go off in Ronnie's head until he's strung out like the Brooklyn Bridge on a clear night: sure, he says, why didn't I think of it before? That's the ticket: malaria.'

'Did Ross have malaria himself?' Antar asked.

'He got it about halfway into his work,' said Murugan. He directed a sharply appraising glance at Antar. 'Why'd you ask? Have you ever had it yourself?'

Antar nodded. 'Yes,' he said, 'a long time ago, in Egypt.'

Murugan sat up. 'That's funny,' he said. 'The malaria rates are pretty low in Egypt.'

'I suppose I was an exception,' said Antar.

'So was yours a freak case? Or was there a localized outbreak?'

'I don't know,' said Antar shortly.

'Do you ever get relapses?' Murugan persisted.

'Sometimes,' Antar said.

'That's how it goes,' Murugan said with a wry smile. 'You think it's gone forever and suddenly, it's hey, long time no see.'

'So you get them too!' Antar said, raising his eyebrows.

'Do I ever!' Murugan laughed. 'But you know, I don't worry about it too much. I guess it's because malaria isn't just a disease. Sometimes it's also a cure.'

'A cure?' Antar said. 'For what?'

'Ever heard of Julius von Wagner-Jauregg?'

'No.'

'He won the Nobel too; for stuff he did with malaria. He was even born the same year as Ronnie Ross, but in Austria. He was a psychologist: had a couple of serious run-ins with Freud. But the reason his name is up there in the bright lights is that he discovered something about malaria that Ross couldn't even have begun to guess at.'

'What?' said Antar.

'He discovered that artificially induced malaria could cure syphilis—at least in the dementia paralytica stage when it attacks the brain.'

Amitav Ghosh

'It sounds incredible,' said Antar.

'Sure,' said Murugan. 'But it still got him the Nobel in 1927. Artificially induced malaria was the standard treatment for syphilitic paresis until the forties. Fact is malaria does stuff to the brain that we're still just guessing at.'

'But to come back to Ross,' said Antar. 'You say he didn't catch malaria until he was well into his work? So what got him interested in it then?'

'It was the zeitgeist,' said Murugan. 'Malaria was the cold fusion of his day, the Sunday papers were scrambling to get it on their covers. And it figures: malaria's probably the all-time biggest killer among diseases. Next to the common cold it's just about the most prevalent disease on the planet. We're not talking about a disease which shoots off the charts suddenly some century like the plague or small-pox or syphilis. Malaria's been around since the big bang or thereabouts, pegged at about the same level all along. There's no place on earth that's off the malaria map: Arctic circle, freezing mountaintop, burning desert, you name it, malaria's been there. We're not talking millions of cases here; more like hundreds of millions. We don't even know how many, because malaria's so widespread it doesn't always get on the charts. And besides, it's a master of disguise: it can mimic the symptoms of more diseases than you can begin to count—lumbago, the 'flu, cerebral haemorrhage, yellow fever. And even when it's properly diagnosed it's not like quinine is always going to get you home safe. With certain kinds of malaria you can main-line quinine all the livelong day and come nightfall you'll still be gathering freezer-burn in the mortuary. It's only fatal in a fraction of all reported cases but when you're dealing with hundreds of millions, a fraction adds up to the population of an economy-size country.'

'So when Ross began,' Antar said, 'was there a new interest in malaria?'

'You bet,' said Murugan. 'The mid-nineteenth century was when the scientific community began to wake up to malaria. Remember this was the century when old Mother Europe was settling all the Last Unknowns: Africa, Asia, Australia, the Americas, even uncolonized parts of herself. Forests, deserts, oceans, warlike natives—that stuff's easy to deal with when you've got dynamite and the Gatling gun; chicken-feed compared to malaria. Don't forget it wasn't that long ago when pretty much every settler along the Mississippi had to take time off every other day for an attack of the shakes. It was just as bad in the swamps around Rome; or in Algeria, where French settlers were making a big push. And this was just about the time that new sciences like bacteriology and parasitology were beginning to make a splash in Europe. Malaria went right to the top of the research agenda. Governments began to pour money into malaria research—in France, in Italy, in the US, everywhere except England. But did Ronnie let that stop him? No sir, he just stripped off and jumped right in.'

Antar frowned: 'You mean Ross didn't have any official support from the British government?'

'No sir: the Empire did everything it could to get in his way. Besides, when it came to malaria the British were non-starters: the front-line work was being done in France and the French colonies, Germany, Italy, Russia, America—anywhere but where the Brits were. But you think Ross cared? You've got to hand it to the guy, he had balls that motherfucker. There he is: he's at an age when most scientists start checking their pension funds; he knows sweet fuckall about malaria (or anything else); he's sitting out in the boonies somewhere where they never even heard of a lab; he hasn't set hands on a microscope since he left medical school; he's got a job in this dinky little outfit, the Indian Medical Service, which gets a couple of copies of *Lancet* and nothing else, not even the *Transactions of the Royal Society of Tropical Medicine*, forget about the *Johns Hopkins Bulletin* or the *Annales* of the Pasteur Institute. But our Ronnie doesn't give a shit: he gets out of bed one sunny day in Secunderabad or wherever and says to himself, in his funny little English accent, "Dear me, I don't know what I'm going to do with myself today, think I'll go

Amitav Ghosh

and solve the scientific puzzle of the century, kill a few hours."
Never mind all the heavy hitters who're out there in the ball
park. Forget about Laveran, forget about Robert Koch, the
German, who's just blown into town after doing a number on
typhoid; forget about the Russian duo, Danilewsky and
Romanowsky, who've been waltzing with this bug since when
young Ronald was shitting himself in his crib; forget about
the Italians who've got a whole goddam pasta factory working
on malaria; forget about W.G. MacCallum out in Baltimore,
who's skating on the edge of a real breakthrough in hematozoan
infections in birds; forget about Bignami, Celli, Golgi,
Marchiafava, Kennan, Nott, Canalis, Beauperthuy; forget about
the Italian government, the French government, the US
government who've all got a shitload of money out there
chasing malaria; forget them all. They don't even see Ronnie
coming until he's set to stop the clocks.'

'Just like that?' said Antar.

'That's right. At least that's how it began. And you know
what? He did it; he beat the Laverans and the Kochs and the
Grassis and the whole Italian mob; he beat the governments
of the US and France and Germany and Russia; he beat them
all. Or that's the official story anyway: young Ronnie, the
lone genius, streaks across the field and runs away with the
World Cup.'

'I take it you don't go along with this,' said Antar.

'You said it Ant. This is one story I just don't buy.'

'Why not?'

A waiter appeared at their table and placed bowls of soup
in front of them. Rubbing the palms of his hands together,
Murugan lowered his head into the lemon-scented cloud that
was rising from his soup-bowl.

'I take it,' Antar persisted, 'that you have your own version
of how Ronald Ross made his discoveries?'

'That's certainly one way of putting it,' said Murugan.

'So what's your version of the story?' said Antar.

'I'll tell you what Ant,' said Murugan, picking up his spoon.

'I'll read you all three volumes some day when we're on an around-the-world cruise: you buy, I'll talk.'

Antar laughed. 'All right,' he said. 'What about a couple of pages, just for starters?'

Murugan lifted a long, dripping braid of noodles to his mouth with a pair of chopsticks. He slurped them up with a loud vacuuming sound and sat back in his chair, dabbing a paper napkin on his goatee. There was a brief pause and when he spoke next his voice was soft and matter of fact.

'Can I ask you a philosophical question Ant?'

Antar shifted in his chair. 'Go ahead,' he said, 'although I should tell you I'm not one for big questions . . .'

'Tell me Ant,' Murugan said, fixing his piercing gaze upon Antar's face. 'Tell me: do you think it's natural to want to turn the page, to be curious about what happened next?'

'Well,' said Antar, uncomfortably. 'I'm not sure if I know what you mean.'

'Let me put it like this then,' said Murugan. 'Do you think that everything that can be known, should be known?'

'Of course,' said Antar. 'I don't see why not.'

'All right,' said Murugan, dipping his spoon in his bowl. 'I'll turn a few pages for you; but remember, it was you who asked. It's your funeral.'

ten

_____

Once they were out of the auditorium Urmila thought she had her chance of getting Sonali to herself. 'Do you have a couple of minutes?' she began. But Sonali was already hurrying down the driveway, towards the street.

Urmila caught up with her at the gates, at just the moment when a burst of applause sounded inside the auditorium, signalling the end of Phulboni's speech.

'I'm sorry I had to leave so early,' Sonali said. 'I would have liked to stay for the rest but it's past eight and I really must get home now.'

'Oh,' Urmila made a half-hearted effort to conceal her disappointment. 'You have to go right this minute?'

Sonali paused. 'Yes,' she said. 'I'm expecting someone. Why?'

'It's just that I was hoping to talk to you,' Urmila said.

'About what?'

'About him,' said Urmila, inclining her head towards the auditorium. 'Phulboni.'

'What about him?'

'I've got to write an article about him,' said Urmila. 'And I've been wondering about a couple of things. Someone told me that you might be the person to talk to.'

'Me?' Sonali was taken aback. 'I don't know if I'll be able to tell you very much.'

She stood undecided for a moment. Then with a glance at her watch, she said: 'Well, why don't you come home with me? We can talk until my guest comes.'

Without waiting for an answer Sonali stepped out and flagged down a taxi. Ignoring Urmila's protests, she bundled her in and climbed in after her. 'Alipore,' she said to the driver, and then rolled her window down as the taxi trundled past the cool darkness of the Race Course.

Just before the Alipore Bridge the taxi ran into a traffic jam and came squealing to a halt. Sonali turned to Urmila. 'What was it you wanted to ask me about?' she said, her voice rattling to the rhythm of the idling car.

'About some of Phulboni's early stories,' Urmila said.

Sonali raised her eyebrows. 'But why me?' she said. 'Who told you to ask me, of all people?'

Urmila hesitated. 'Someone I know,' she said.

'Who?' said Sonali.

'You know her too,' said Urmila. 'Or at least you did. She talks about you a lot anyway.'

'Who is it?' said Sonali. 'You're making me curious.'

'Mrs Aratounian.' Urmila said the name with a warm smile.

'Mrs Aratounian?' cried Sonali. 'You mean Mrs Aratounian of Dutton's Nursery on Russell Street?'

'Yes,' said Urmila. 'The same Mrs Aratounian. Do you remember her?'

Sonali nodded, but the truth was that she hadn't seen Mrs Aratounian in years and was just barely able to recall a neat, rather forbidding woman, dressed in a black skirt and gold-rimmed glasses. She'd always reminded Sonali of the Irish nuns at her convent school: she had just that kind of ringing voice and abrupt manner. She was from an Armenian family that had been in Calcutta for generations, Sonali remembered: they'd owned Dutton's Nursery forever.

'My God!' she exclaimed. 'Dutton's! It must be years since I last went there.'

'But you know,' Urmila said, in a rush, 'the first time I ever saw you was at Dutton's.'

'At Dutton's?' Sonali glanced at her in astonishment. 'Why, I didn't know we'd met before I started working at *Calcutta*.'

Amitav Ghosh

'We didn't exactly meet.' Urmila was embarrassed now, she wished she hadn't mentioned it.

It had happened years ago: Urmila was in her last year in school and the reason she was at Dutton's Nursery that morning was that she was the student representative on the Grounds and Gardens Committee. She'd been taken there by the teacher-members of the committee, in the school van.

She was nervous: Mrs Aratounian scared her with her flinty voice and her drill-sharp eyes. The last time she was at the Nursery she'd put out a hand to touch a rose when she felt someone's gaze boring into her. She spun guiltily around, snatching back her hand, and sure enough, Mrs Aratounian was watching her from the far side of the room. 'That's a plant, not a dog,' she said, with a glint of her gold-rimmed bifocals, 'and the reason it has thorns is that it doesn't want to be petted.' Urmila had felt so small she'd wanted to erase herself, like a smudge of chalk.

On this occasion the visit began well. Mrs Aratounian went out of her way to be kind. She pointed to a stand of potted chrysanthemums and said: 'Pick one out dear and I'll let you have it. Just this once.'

Urmila was looking over the chrysanthemums when there was a sudden commotion at the door. She turned to see Sonali Das walking in.

Dutton's was full of people—it was the time of year when everyone was buying seeds and plants. Sonali's entrance created a sensation: she had just published her book and her picture was everywhere. She was dressed in a green and white chiffon saree, with a huge pair of sunglasses pushed back over her hair, looking every bit the film-star.

Urmila had recently seen one of her films: she watched her open-mouthed, shrinking back into the chrysanthemums, mortified at the thought of being seen in her grimy school uniform and her two thin braids.

While talking to Mrs Aratounian, Sonali was joined by a tall, powerfully built man, with a massive, heavy-jawed face. His jaw and eyebrows stood out in sharp outline, under a head that was almost completely bald. It was evident that the two of them had come together.

He seemed old for her, Urmila decided, but he wasn't bad-looking, in a thuggish way. She wondered who he was.

Then the man said something to Mrs Aratounian. To Urmila's utter horror, Mrs Aratounian turned and pointed in her direction, at the chrysanthemums. For a brief moment Urmila stood undecided. By the time she had recovered, it was too late. They were standing right in front of her and Sonali was craning around, reaching for a flower-pot.

Urmila side-stepped quickly, ducking out of her way. But in her hurry she jogged Sonali's hand. The pot fell to the ground and shattered with a terrific crash, showering the floor with leaves, petals and earth.

Aghast, Urmila dropped to her knees. She began to sweep up the scattered earth and pottery, keeping her eyes on the floor, not daring to look up. She was near tears.

Then a very large pair of hands descended to the floor, in front of her, filling her entire field of vision. The hands were matted with thick, curly hair and the knuckles were the size of walnuts. Distracted though she was, Urmila noticed that one of the hands was partly paralysed, with the thumb lying stiffly curled against the palm. Then the hands began to help her, awkwardly sweeping the earth together.

Urmila raised her head and found herself looking at the man who had followed Sonali into the shop. He was staring at her—not angrily, but with a fixed, appraising gaze. Something about his look frightened Urmila and she dropped her eyes.

The next thing she knew, Sonali's arms were around her, helping her up. 'Poor thing,' she was saying to Mrs Aratounian. 'It's not her fault: I'll pay.'

Urmila got a terrific scolding on the way back to school, in the van. But soon enough her teachers lost interest in her and began to gossip about Sonali Das and the man she was with.

Urmila discovered to her surprise that she knew his name: it was Romen Haldar. She'd heard him talked about at home:

Amitav Ghosh

he lived in a huge house just down the road from their flat. She knew he was a wealthy builder and contractor, and that he had a lot of influence in a major club. Her younger brother, who dreamt of playing in the First Division, often talked of him.

Now, recalling the incident, Urmila was able to laugh. 'It was years ago,' she told Sonali. 'I knocked a pot of flowers out of your hand: chrysanthemums.'

'I don't remember,' said Sonali.

'Of course not,' said Urmila. 'But you were very nice about it. So was Mrs Aratounian. She became a real friend after that.'

'So you know Mrs Aratounian well?' Sonali asked.

'I visit her occasionally,' Urmila said, 'at her flat on Robinson Street. She's always been very kind to me. She's very interesting in her own crusty way. Besides, her flat is so peaceful—with all those plants and comfortable chairs and sofas. It's nice to escape from the magazine every once in a while. I drop in whenever I can.'

'I heard Mrs Aratounian retired and sold Dutton's,' Sonali said. 'Must have made a fortune, with that location.'

'I don't know,' Urmila said. 'I never asked. But actually I think she's having trouble making ends meet, now that she's retired. She's always thinking up little schemes for making extra money. "I've been in business all my life," she says—you know how she talks—"and as sure as an egg's an egg, I'm not going to stop now."'

Sonali laughed. 'What are her schemes?' she said.

'Her latest is that she's going to take in paying guests and turn her flat into a businessman's guest house.'

'No!' Sonali exclaimed in disbelief.

'Yes,' Urmila continued. 'She's even stuck a board on her door. The trouble is, no one ever sees it unless they're going up the stairs, so she hasn't had any guests yet.'

'What made her think of it?' Sonali asked.

'I asked her that,' said Urmila. 'And she said she got the idea because an old house on the other side of Robinson Street is being turned into a hotel, by a developer. She said: "The blackguard actually has the cheek to hang a sign on the lawn. Plain as a wart on the nose. 'Site for the Robinson Hotel.' If he can do it, why can't I?'"

And then, suddenly Urmila froze in an attitude of dismay, with her hands clapped over her open mouth.

Sonali smiled, and took a cigarette out of her handbag. 'She meant Romen I suppose?' she said drily, flicking open her lighter. 'Romen showed me that house on Robinson Street the other day. He's very proud of it; he's actually going to rebuild the place.' She puffed at the flame and allowed the smoke to curl slowly out of her pursed lips.

Urmila began to mumble hurried apologies.

Sonali laughed: 'Don't worry. I really don't mind what people say about Romen. You should hear how the wags go on about him at his club. Of course the Calcutta Wicket Club is the last place in the world where wags still survive and live to say waggish things. You should hear them when they start on Romen.'

She gave Urmila a reassuring pat on the arm. 'Have you ever met Romen?' she said.

'No.' Urmila shook her head. 'I just saw him that one time, at Dutton's, with you.'

'I think you'd like him,' Sonali said. 'He's had an extraordinary life you know.'

'Really?' Urmila said in a noncommital voice. She remembered hearing that Romen Haldar had started with nothing; that he'd arrived at Calcutta's Sealdah Station without a coin in his pocket. Sonali nodded. 'You'll see,' she said. 'He's not at all the person people make him out to be. You'll meet him tonight: it's him I'm waiting for. He said he'd come over this evening.'

The taxi stopped at a pair of heavy steel gates. Sonali began to fumble in her handbag, looking for money to pay the driver.

A uniformed chowkidar stepped out of a booth. He took a careful look before allowing the taxi to enter the exclusive residential complex. There were four blocks of flats in the

Amitav Ghosh

estate, set well apart, each at an angle to the other, so that every veranda looked out on its fair share of Alipore's greenery.

As the taxi swung around the complex, Sonali glanced at one of the estate's parking areas. Urmila followed her eyes to a discreet little sign hanging over an empty spot. It said: 'Reserved, R. Haldar'.

Sonali sighed. 'Romen isn't here yet,' she said. 'We can talk until he comes.'

———————

Scribbling a date on the restaurant's brightly coloured paper napkin, Murugan placed it before Antar. 'Here's the deal,' he said. 'It's May 1895. We're in the military hospital in Secunderabad, it's so hot the floors are shimmering, no fans, no electricity, a roomful of jars, all neatly stacked up on shelves, a desk with a straight-backed chair, a single microscope with slides scattered about, one guy in uniform hunched over the microscope and a swarm of orderlies buzzing around him. That's Ronnie and the other guys are the chorus line, or so Ronnie thinks anyway. "Do this" he says and they do it. "Do that" he says and they scramble. That's what he's grown up with, that's what he's used to. Mostly he doesn't even know their names, hardly even their faces: he doesn't think he needs to. As for who they are, where they're from and all that stuff, forget it, he's not interested. They could be buddies, they could be cousins, they could be cell-mates; it would be all the same to Ronnie.'

'Wait a minute,' Antar interrupted. 'May 1895? So Ronald Ross is at the beginning of his malaria research?'

'That's right,' said Murugan. 'Ronnie's just got back from a vacation in England. While he was over there, he met with Patrick Manson, in London.'

'Patrick Manson?' Antar raised an eyebrow. 'Do you mean the Manson of elephantiasis?'

'That's the man,' said Murugan. 'Manson's one of the all-time greats; he's lived in China so long he can skin a python with chopsticks; he's the guy who wrote the book on filaria, the bug that causes elephantiasis. Now he's back in England where he's become the Queen's head honcho in bacteriological research. Doc Manson wants to get the malaria prize—for Britain, he says, for the Empire: fuck those krauts and frogs and wops and yanks. He may be a Scot but come gametime he roots for Queen and country: you don't have to sell him on how no Scotsman ever saw a finer sight than the London turnpike: he's bought it already.'

'If I remember correctly,' Antar said, 'Manson proved that the mosquito was the vector for filaria. Am I right?'

'Right,' said Murugan. 'Now he's got a hunch that the mosquito has something to do with the malaria bug too. He doesn't have time to do the work himself so he's looking for someone to carry the torch for Queen and Empire. Guess who walks in? Ronnie Ross. Trouble is Ronnie's not exactly a front-runner at this point. In fact the century's biggest breakthrough in malaria research has happened recently but it's passed Ronnie by. Way back in the 1840s a guy called Meckel found microscopic granules of black pigment in the organs of malaria patients—black spots, some round, some crescent shaped, tucked inside tiny masses of protoplasm. For forty years no one can figure out what this stuff is. The breakthrough comes in 1880: Alphonse Laveran, a French army surgeon in Algeria, runs out to get some lunch, leaving a plate cooking under his 'scope. He gets back from his hickory-grilled merguez and guess what? One of those crescent shaped granules is moving. He sees it beginning to jive, turning into a miniature octopus, throwing out tentacles, shaking the whole cell.

'So Laveran puts two and two together: hey, this thing moves, it's a bug. He faxes the Academy of Medicine in Paris; tells them he's found the cause of malaria and it's a critter, a protozoan—an animal parasite. But Paris doesn't buy it. Pasteur's the boss out there and he's sent the smart money chasing after bacteria. No one buys Laveran's protozoan critter: it's like he said he found the yeti. Some of the biggest names in medicine get busy refuting "Laveranity". The only converts are the Italians: they become born-again Laveranites. In 1886 Camillo Golgi shows that Laveran's parasite grows inside the red blood cell, eating its host and shitting black pigment; that the pigment collects in the centre while the bug begins to divide; he demonstrates that the recurrence of malarial fevers is linked to this pattern of asexual reproduction.

'Ronnie's a wallflower while this party's heating up. He's on the anti-Laveran bench. He thinks Laveran's bug doesn't exist: he's spent the last several months trying to catch a glimpse of it and hasn't succeeded. He's even published an article trying to prove that Laveran was hallucinating. The first time Ronnie ever sees the bug is in Manson's lab. He converts, and Manson sends him hustling back to India to look for the vector.'

Antar broke in: 'So it was Manson who was responsible for conceiving of the connection between malaria and mosquitoes?'

'It wasn't exactly a new idea,' said Murugan. 'Most cultures that had to deal with malaria knew there was some connection.'

'But,' Antar persisted, 'you're saying it's Manson who first gave Ross the idea?'

'You could say Manson pointed in the general direction,' said Murugan. 'Except that he sent him down the scenic route. He had this screwball theory that the malaria bug was transmitted from mosquito to man via drinking water. His plan was to get Ronnie to do the grunt work on this theory of his.'

'And Ross believed in this theory?'

'You bet.'

'So what happened?' said Antar.

'Okay, we're back in 1895, right? Ross can't wait to get started on Doc Manson's mosquito-juice theory. He gets off the ship at Madras and takes a train up to join his regiment, the 19th Madras Infantry. They're stationed in a neighbourhood called Begumpett in Secunderabad. On his way up Ronnie sticks needles into anything that moves. When he pulls into Begumpett he begins to offer money for samples of malarial blood—real money, one rupee per prick! Think about it. This

Amitav Ghosh

is 1895; one rupee can buy a family of four enough rice to last a month. There's so much malaria in this place, the mosquitoes are doing double shifts and can't keep up. And here's Ronnie willing to pay real money for a few drops of malarial blood, and he can't find a single taker. Someone's put out the word that this weird doctor's blown into town and he gets his rocks off putting naked guys into bed with mosquitoes. No one's going near him; they're crossing the street to get away. Suddenly Ronnie finds himself starring in a bad breath commercial: every time he steps out on Main Street, Begumpett, it's empty.

'Then suddenly his luck changes. On May 17, 1895, just when it begins to look really hopeless, he gets his first perfect case of malaria—a patient called Abdul Kadir. Ronnie goes into high gear: he strips Abdul Kadir, shoves him into a bed, drapes a wet mosquito net over him and releases a test-tube full of mosquitoes into it. Next morning he harvests his crop and suddenly Ronnie's laboratory is the happening place in Begumpett. Until then he's observed only two of the flagellate forms of the parasite. On May 18 he flattens one of Abdul Kadir's mosquitoes (mosquito #18) and he finds sixty parasites in a single field. He's so excited he does back flips all the way to his desk. He's found a "wonder case" he writes Doc Manson. That's just the beginning. The first time Ronnie sees the crescent-sphere transformation of the parasite is on June 26, 1895, in Abdul Kadir's blood. Over the next couple of months Abdul Kadir's blood guides him through all the critical phases of his research.'

'Can a single case make that much difference?' said Antar.

'Ronnie thought so,' said Murugan. 'He was convinced that Abdul Kadir was crucial to his work. He'd looked at a fair number of blood samples already but none of them ever showed him what Abdul Kadir's did. You'd think a bug like the malaria parasite wouldn't look for any teacher's pets, but maybe it doesn't work that way. Maybe it shows itself more clearly in certain cases. That's what Ronnie thought anyway. He became hooked on Abdul Kadir and his blood. Days when Abdul Kadir's parasites went into remission Ronnie was climbing the walls. "Alas! the wonder case which fortune has sent me is *drying up*," he wrote Doc Manson on May 22. The dickhead had an ego so big he thought Fortune was putting him on its cover. He clearly knew that Abdul Kadir was a special case. But he never stopped to ask himself how come this guy just walked through the door when he needed him most. He thought it was just luck.'

'Let me be clear about this,' said Antar. 'Are you suggesting that Abdul Kadir's arrival at the hospital on May 17 wasn't just a coincidence?'

'You've got to wonder,' said Murugan. 'Look at it this way: Ross knows no one else will come near him even when he doubles or triples his one-rupee per prick rate; on July 17 he writes Doc Manson: "The bazaar people won't come to me even though I offer what is enormous payment to them. I offer two and three rupees for a single finger prick and much more if I find crescents—they think it is witchcraft." But Ronnie never stops to ask himself: why's this guy Abdul Kadir here, if no one else is? How come *he* doesn't think this is witchcraft? What makes him so special? Where's he from? What's he doing here? What's his story? We're not talking deep therapy: just plain, everyday curiosity. But Ronnie keeps all his curiosity for the life cycle of the malaria parasite; about the life cycles of its hosts he couldn't care less.'

'So what are you suggesting?' Antar said sharply.

'I'm not suggesting anything at this point,' said Murugan. 'I'm just giving you the facts and the chronology.'

'All right,' said Antar. 'Go ahead.'

'Okay,' said Murugan. 'We fast forward to the week after Abdul Kadir's arrival: May 25, 1895. Doc Manson thinks Ronnie's getting sidetracked, so he's written to remind him of his theory: that "the beast in the mosquito . . . gets to man in mosquito dust". He wants Ronnie to make a cocktail from dead mosquitoes and feed it to someone.

'Ronnie gets out his glasses and starts mixing. Trouble is, he hasn't got anyone to give it to: can't find anyone fool enough to volunteer. Same old story: Ronnie's in his lab in Begumpett, all dressed up and nowhere to go.

'And what do you know? Ronnie gets lucky once again. Or maybe it's not just luck; maybe he left Doc Manson's letter out on his desk and someone read it. Maybe. Anyway, on May 25 1895 at exactly 8 p.m. a guy called Lutchman walks into Ronnie's life. He volunteers to drink Ronnie's cocktail. Ronnie pops the corks and breaks out the mosquito margarita.

'This Lutchman's a "healthy looking young fellow", Ronnie notices: just the guinea pig he's been looking for. He explains the experiment to Lutchman and hands him the dead-mosquito concoction. Lutchman makes like he doesn't already know what it is, and swigs it. Ronnie's a little anxious but he doesn't let on. All he knows about Lutchman is that he's a "dhooley-bearer": in other words the British government pays him to shovel shit. Ronnie knows Her Imperial Majesty wouldn't be too pleased about this little experiment of his if she got to hear of it up in her castle on London Bridge or wherever. Later he covers his tracks by writing Doc Manson: "Don't for heaven's sake mention Lutchman at the British Medical Association . . . he is a government servant. To give a government servant fever would be a crime!"

'Lutchman has a fever next morning: 99.8° at 8 a.m. ("Looking ill", Ronnie notes). Looks like it's time for Doc Manson to jump out of his bathtub; maybe malaria really is spread through mosquito-dust. Ronnie gets ready to pop the corks; he's about to call his agent. But then comes the letdown. Young Lutchman doesn't just look healthy; he *is* healthy. He's allergic to mosquito-dust is all. A day later he's so fit he could run the Begumpett marathon: no sign of malaria in his blood. That's the end of the line for the mosquito-dust theory. Ronnie's free to go back to Abdul Kadir again: he's been headed off at the pass.'

'Wait, wait,' Antar broke in. 'I want to be clear about this. Are you arguing that Lutchman was sent to Ross's lab specifically in order to disprove Manson's theory?'

'I'm not arguing anything,' said Murugan. 'Just taking the

facts as they come. And the facts are these: Ronnie's been working on the malaria bug for about a month when Abdul Kadir and Lutchman walk into his life. Ronnie hasn't made a secret of what he's doing: he's put the word out about needing malaria patients. *If* someone was watching—let's just say *if*—if someone was watching, if someone was looking for a research scientist to do certain kinds of experiments, then this is when they would have picked up the buzz. So this someone, who's watching carefully, maybe reading Ronnie's lab notes and his letters to Doc Manson, this someone decides, okay, it's time to get a new player in place. The first thing they've got to do is to make sure Ronnie doesn't get any patients. So they spread the word about witchcraft; it flies through the bazaar; Ronnie becomes the bogeyman of Begumpett.

'By mid-May they know Ronnie's getting desperate, no patients, no parasites, no nothing. He can't get anyone to come to his parties and he can't figure out why. This is when they send him Abdul Kadir who's got industrial-size parasites; they hold Ronnie's hand as he puts his first twos and twos together; they're happy, everything's on schedule, they're leading Ronnie exactly where they want him to go. And then Ronnie gets his letter from boss-man Manson; suddenly everything flies off track. Ronnie goes off into left field, with this mosquito-powder stuff. They go wild: they know there's nothing at the end of that trail; they have to find a way to turn him back in the right direction. So what do they do? They send him Lutchman.'

'But why Lutchman?' said Antar.

'Let me put it like this,' said Murugan, 'whoever picked Lutchman knew exactly what they were doing. For one thing, they knew enough about microscopy to make sure that he didn't have any malaria parasites in his blood. Ronnie was being second guessed here. Somebody had figured out what was going to happen if Ronnie got a positive result after feeding Lutchman mosquito water. He was going to link the parasites to Doc Manson's theory and bingo! there goes the

Amitav Ghosh

schedule. Months, maybe years could go by while Ronnie chases around Begumpett, making the 19th Madras Infantry drink dead mosquitoes.

'So they stepped in; they sent him someone who didn't have any parasites. Remember that this is a place where the rates of malaria in the general population are so high they're off the charts. It isn't easy to find people who don't have any trace of the parasite in their blood. But these guys reach into their bag, pick out someone who's just right, and then they send him over to Begumpett General. It works: Ronnie's back on track, and right on schedule. And better still they've planted Lutchman exactly where they want him, where he can run interference for the whole team.'

'But,' said Antar, 'wouldn't Ross have noticed something so obvious?'

'Ronnie?' Murugan laughed. 'Ronnie wouldn't have noticed if Lutchman wore it on a T-shirt. If anything but a parasite comes calling, Ronnie's out to lunch. The way Ronnie tells it, he was short of help at the time, so he decided to hire Lutchman as a houseboy-cum-gofer. All that Ron ever knew about him was that his name was "Lutchman" and that he was a "dhooley-bearer" by trade.

'For the next thirty-four months—the entire period that Ron's working on malaria—Lutchman sticks to him like roll-on deodorant. Starting May 1895, until July 1898, when Ron makes his final breakthrough in Calcutta, Lutchman almost never lets Ron out of his sight. He gets pretty good at doing luggage impersonations. "I left Secunderabad with the smallest possible 'kit'," says Ronnie, "my microscope and my faithful Lutchman."

'It gets so that even Ron can't help noticing that Lutchman's making some pretty important connections for him. In April 1897, Ron takes a break in the Nilgiri Hills. He takes Lutchman with him, to Ootacamund—"a bit of England placed on the rounded tops of the Nilgiri Hills", says Ron. But Ron goes down to the Westbury coffee estate in a valley, looking for malaria parasites, and there for the first time in his life, he gets malaria.

'While he's recouping Lutchman succeeds in planting a crucially important idea in his head: that the malaria vector might be one particular species of mosquito. "Oh yeah?" says Ron; he thinks Lutchman's full of shit: he's been getting a lot of negative results but it's never occurred to him that they might have something to do with family differences among mosquitoes. "Tell you what Lutch," says Ron, "next time I want your help I'll ask for it." But after Lutchman plants this little seed something begins to stir in the mud; a creature begins to take shape in Ron's head.

'He starts eyeballing every different species of mosquito he can get his hands on. Trouble is Ron doesn't know a goddam thing about mosquitoes: he's never even heard the word anopheles. He ends up chasing after Culex, Stegomyia—going every which way but ahead. Now Lutchman cuts in once again. On August 15, 1897, he goes into a huddle with the rest of his crew and decides something's got to be done double quick.

'The way Ronnie tells it: "Next morning, 16 August, when I went again to hospital after breakfast, the Hospital Attendant (I regret I have forgotten his name) pointed out a small mosquito seated on the wall with its tail *sticking outwards*." Ronnie kills it with a puff of tobacco smoke and cuts it open: nothing. But at last he's on the right track: Lutchman's got him chasing after the real malaria vector. Ron still doesn't know they're called anopheles: names them "dappled-wing mosquitoes".

'Next day Lutchman makes sure Ronnie gets more of the same: sends him a jarful of anopheles with the same Attendant. "Sure enough," says Ronnie, "there they were: about a dozen big, brown fellows, with fine tapered bodies and spotted wings, hungrily trying to escape through the gauze covering of the flask which the Angel of Fate had given to my humble retainer!—dappled-winged mosquitoes . . ." Angel of Fate my ass! With Ronnie it always has to be some Fat Cat way up in the sky: what's under his nose he can't see.

'On August 20 1897 Ronnie makes his first major breakthrough: he sees the placement of plasmodium zygotes in the stomach sac of Anopheles Stephensii. "Eureka" he says to his diary, "the problem is solved."

'"Whew!" says Lutchman, skimming the sweat off his face. "Thought he'd never get it."

'Later Ron asks him: "Yo Lutch, where'd you get that hot tip about mosquito species?" Lutchman plays dumb: "Oh, some villagers up in them hills happened to mention it one morning while grazing their goats." And you know what? Ron buys it. He thinks Lutchman hit upon this bright idea while gambolling in the hills with happy natives.

'What gets me about this scenario is the joke. Here's Ronnie, right? He thinks he's doing experiments on the malaria parasite. And all the time it's he who *is* the experiment on the malaria parasite. But Ronnie never gets it; not to the end of his life.'

twelve

The taxi slowed to a crawl on Chowringhee. Every time Murugan turned to look back he was certain he'd spot the boy with the printed T-shirt, weaving through the traffic at a run. But there was still no sign of him when the taxi turned on to Theatre Road. Murugan's fingers began to unclench.

Halfway down Theatre Road Murugan spotted a roadside vendor selling rubber slippers and stopped the taxi. He spent several minutes choosing one for himself and felt much better for it. He jumped into the taxi and waved the driver on, impatient to get back to the guest house on Robinson Street.

The guest house was one thing he could congratulate himself on. It was just down the road from where Ronald Ross had lived while he was in Calcutta. Ross had stayed at a 'Europeans only' boarding house at number three; the Robinson Guest House, where Murugan was staying, was on the fourth floor of number twenty-two.

Murugan had found the place entirely by accident, listed in a dog-eared typewritten roster at the airport's tourist information desk. The woman behind the desk had been trying to nudge him towards five-star hotels like the Grand and the Taj. She was doubtful when he picked the Robinson Guest House. It was a recent entry on the list, she told him; she couldn't vouch for it, she didn't know of anyone who'd stayed there. He would do better to go to a hotel.

'But it's exactly where I want to be,' Murugan said in triumph, 'on Robinson Street.'

He had no idea what it would be like of course, and was pleased when Robinson Street proved to be leafy and relatively quiet, lined with large modern blocks of flats and a few old-fashioned colonial mansions. Number twenty-two was one of the older buildings, a massive four-storey edifice, studded with graceful columned balconies: probably once the grandest building on the street, its Doric facade was now much bruised and discoloured, its plaster blackened with mildew.

He went up to the fourth floor in a rattling birdcage of a lift that ascended through the centre of a winding teakwood staircase. When the lift came to a stop Murugan stepped gingerly on to the splintered planks of a wooden landing. A beam of sunlight, shining through a hole in a stained-glass window, revealed a small sign beside the tall door to his right. It said: 'The Robinson Guest House'. Beneath it was a nameplate for 'N. Aratounian'.

Dragging his leather suitcase behind him, Murugan went to the door and rang the bell. Several minutes later he heard footsteps on the other side. Then the door swung open and he found himself looking at an ashen-faced, elderly woman in a frayed dressing-gown and rubber slippers. 'Hi,' said Murugan, sticking out a hand. 'Any vacancies today?'

Ignoring his hand, the woman looked him up and down, frowning through her gold-rimmed bifocals. 'What do you want?' she said, peremptorily.

'A room,' said Murugan. He tapped the sign by the door. 'This is a guest house, right?'

Mrs Aratounian cocked her head so she could examine him through the lower halves of her glasses. 'I don't believe you've introduced yourself,' she said.

'The name's Murugan,' he said. 'But feel free to call me Morgan.'

Mrs Aratounian sniffed. 'You'd better come in Mr Morgan,' she said. 'I don't have much to offer by way of accommodation but I'll show you my spare room. You can decide for yourself whether you want to stay or not.'

She led Murugan through a musty drawing room, cluttered with doilied peg-tables, silver-framed photographs and porcelain statuettes. Pushing open a door, she ushered him into a large sunlit room with very high ceilings. A mosquito-netted bed stood marooned in the centre of the marble floor, like a drifting raft. Directly above it, suspended from an iron hook, hung a bulbous, long-stemmed ceiling fan.

At the far end of the room was a small balcony. Crossing the room, Murugan went out, leaned over the balustrade and looked up and down the street—from the tree-lined cemetery at the Loudon Street end, to the traffic on Rawdon Street, to his right. Shading his eyes, he threw a glance diagonally across at number three Robinson Street. He caught a brief glimpse of a large, old-fashioned colonial mansion, set within high walls and surrounded by ornamental palms. He noticed that the front of the house was covered with bamboo scaffolding and that the driveway was littered with piles of bricks and cement.

Murugan pumped a fist: the location was as good as he could have hoped. 'I'll take it,' he said to Mrs Aratounian. He dumped his luggage on the bed, took a shower and went off to look for the Ross memorial.

That was just a few hours ago, but now, Robinson Street looked quite different. It was packed with cars, all the way down its length: not the usual Ambassadors and Marutis but big expensive Japanese and German cars. The cars were disgorging men in starched dhotis and kurtas and be-diamonded women in dazzling sarees. A wedding was in progress in the compound of a large multi-storeyed block of flats. Music was blaring under the chequered awning of a colourful pandal. A brilliantly illuminated archway over the entrance bore the legend Neeraj weds Nilima', spelt out in flowers. The whole street was lit up—all except number three which seemed, in contrast, to be sunk in a well of darkness although it was right next door to the wedding.

Walking towards the guest house Murugan paused at the

gateway of number three. All he could see of the mansion was the high wall, plastered with handbills and painted slogans; the brilliance of the surrounding lights seemed to have deepened the shadows around the compound. Going over to the steel gates, he saw that they were fastened by a heavy chain. He banged on the gates, just in case there was a watchman inside to let him in. There was no answer. Stepping back, Murugan looked up at the mansion's looming silhouette: it was much more imposing close up than he had expected.

Suddenly, there was a power cut and the lights went out, all the way down the street. There followed an instant of absolute stillness; everything seemed to go quiet, except the chirruping of the cicadas in the nearby trees and the trumpeting of conches in the far distance. In that instant Murugan heard the soft bell-like ringing of metallic cymbals, somewhere within the mansion. He looked up, at the shuttered windows above, and saw a flickering, orange rectangle materialize in the darkness.

He jumped, startled, and looked again. It was merely dim firelight, leaking through the ragged edges of a rotten window-frame. Then with a deafening roar, a generator came on at the wedding next door, and an interrupted film-song screeched upwards through the octaves as a record-player came slowly back to life.

Murugan was certain now that the mansion wasn't empty: from the sound of it there was some kind of ceremony under way inside. He stepped up to the gates and rattled the chains. To his surprise, they fell away from the gatepost: someone had forgotten to lock them.

Murugan pushed the gate open and stepped in. It was dark but his keychain had a small flashlight attached. He took it out, switched it on and shone it ahead. The beam lit upon heaps of bricks and cement, lying in the driveway. There was a colonnaded portico at the apex of the curved drive, covered with a net of bamboo scaffolding. Murugan could see a doorway beyond, leading into the pitch-dark interior of the house.

Bits of grit and cement lodged in Murugan's rubber sandals as he walked up the driveway. He shook them out and went up to the portico. It led into a vast hallway. He pointed his flashlight into the darkness. The beam skimmed over piles of mattresses and mosquito nets, stacked neatly in the corners.

He cupped his hands around his mouth and shouted: 'Anyone in?' His voice was no match for the deafening roar of the nearby generator. He looked around, following the uneasy shadows that skimmed over the cavernous darkness of the hallway. Then his ears picked up a sound, a dull pounding, like a drum. It seemed to be somewhere within the house, but it was hard to be sure because of the generator and the blaring loudspeakers.

He was about to go further into the hallway when a second beam of light appeared in the doorway. He heard an angry voice shouting: 'Who is that? Kaun hai? What are you doing here?'

He spun around and his flashlight fell on a man in a Nepali cap, running towards him, gesturing angrily with a chowkidar's night-stick.

Murugan gave him a two-fingered salute, affecting a cockiness he did not feel. 'Just looking around,' he said.

The Nepali watchman shook his stick under Murugan's nose, turned him around and began to push him down the steps of the portico.

'Just taking a look,' Murugan said mildly. 'I didn't touch a thing.'

The watchman launched into a long tirade; Murugan could only catch snatches of it: he was telling him that no one was allowed in, there was construction going on inside.

Halfway down the driveway, the watchman reached up and pointed angrily at a large tin signboard. It was nailed into the trunk of a tree, beside the driveway. Murugan was surprised that he had missed it on his way in. It said: 'Site for the Robinson Hotel: private property, no trespassing; proprietor and developer Romen Haldar.'

Murugan shook his arm free and went over to take a closer

Amitav Ghosh

look. The watchman followed close behind, his voice growing louder. Murugan turned on him suddenly. 'Who's that?' he said. 'Who is Romen Haldar?'

The watchman paid no attention to his question. He took hold of his elbow, jerked him sideways and began pushing him towards the gate. Murugan caught a glimpse of the hilt of a sheathed khukri, sticking out of the top of his trousers.

As the watchman pulled the gate open, Murugan turned to take a last look, shining the beam of his flashlight into the debris-strewn garden. It fell upon a clothesline, strung between the trunks of two palms. Hanging amongst the dhotis, underwear and sarees was a T-shirt with a print of palm-trees and a beach.

Then the watchman gave him a shove and slammed the gates shut.

thirteen

Antar poured Murugan another cup of the restaurant's hot green tea. 'Do you have any theories about who Lutchman really was?'

'I've got some leads,' said Murugan. 'Too many maybe. As I see it, he was all over the map, changing names, switching identities. My suspicion is that he was the point-man for whoever was the real brain behind the scheme.'

'I see,' said Antar. 'But do you know anything at all about him apart from what Ross had to say?'

'As a matter of fact I do,' said Murugan. 'There's a reference to him in a diary.'

'Whose diary?' said Antar.

'It's like this,' said Murugan. 'There was this one guy we know about who once spent a weekend in the house that Ron lived in, in Secunderabad. Lutchman was part of the household too: in fact he was almost like family for Ron.'

'Go on.'

'Remember,' said Murugan, 'that by the time Ron starts working on malaria he's a happily married man with a couple of kids. But he's also an army officer, working under military conditions of service. That means that while he's frying in the Secunderabad heat, his wife and kids are living up in the hills, with a parallel army of British military wives.

'Ron gives his extra-scientific life in Secunderabad exactly two sentences in his *Memoirs*: "On the 23rd [of April 1895]

I left for Secunderabad . . . and I lived there in a bungalow *en garçon,* with Captain Thomas, the Adjutant, and Lieut. Hole, both first-rate fellows. We had our mess, and there was the Secunderabad Club, where we played golf and tennis; but I kept no ponies, as I expected to be put upon special malaria work at any time."

'You don't have to break a sweat trying to imagine Ron's set-up in Secunderabad: it's straight out of one of those BBC rent-a-serials: sprawling colonial bungalow; white-washed walls, mile high ceilings, cool, dark interiors, elephants parked in the driveway, turbaned servants salaaming the sahibs, doped-out punkahwallahs stirring the air with palm-leaf fans, polo ponies, tennis rackets, cummerbunds, the whole fucking paratha.

'He calls it a bungalow, but don't let him fool you: this place has a couple of dozen rooms, and half an acre of garden. Then there are the servants' quarters, way out back, where you can hardly see them: a long, low line of rooms. The rooms are pretty small, but some of them have six or seven people living inside and some have whole families in residence. This is where Lutchman moves in, exactly a month after Ron arrives in Secunderabad. But Lutchman's quite high up in the pecking order: he's been personally selected by the big doctor sahib. He gets a room to himself. He moves in all his stuff and gets nicely settled in.

'To Ron this bungalow-shit is pretty routine; he hardly notices it: ho hum another day. If he wasn't living like this out here in Secunderabad he would be doing the same somewhere else. Around the world there are thousands of British army officers who are living exactly this way—in South Africa, Malaysia, Singapore, Kenya, you name it. Most of them are dickheads who'd believe you if you told them that Plasmodium was Julius Caesar's middle name. It just so happens that in this particular bungalow in Secunderabad there's this one guy who's doing world-class science, and who's so caught up in what he's doing he hardly notices whether there's anything happening around him—and there is, there's a lot happening around him, only the stupid son-of-a-bitch is such a fucking genius he doesn't know.

'And then one day this other guy arrives to spend the weekend. His name is J.W.D. Grigson; he's just out of Cambridge and he's joined an outfit called the Linguistic Survey of India. Twenty years down the road he's going to write a book called *A Comparative Survey of the Phonetic Structures of the Languages and Dialects of Eastern India.* It won't be a best-seller but in its subject it's going to become the functional equivalent of *Consumer Guide.* This Grigson's quite a character: he's going to die in the forties, in northern Burma, trying to settle a tribal dispute.

'And wherever he goes Grigson takes notes. Boy, does he take notes: he keeps a diary, he keeps a journal. When Ypsilanti College bought his collected papers in 1990 they had to hire an eight-axle truck to ship the stuff out. There's nothing he doesn't make a note of: and that means nothing. For he's not just into languages: he's also seriously into anatomy. He'll hit upon anything that moves: if it can lift a leg he wants to get under it. So Grigson arrives to spend a few days at the bungalow that Ron's living in for the duration. It turns out he went to grade school with one of Ron's room-mates, Lieutenant Hole. They can't stand the sight of each other but their mamas have told them to be neighbourly. So when the Lieutenant hears that Grigson's blowing into town, he asks him if he needs a place to stay; thinks he'll earn a few cheap brownie points. Grigson says, sure, what have I got to lose? He moves into the guest bedroom for a couple of nights.

'It doesn't take Grigson long to figure out that something isn't quite kosher about this Lutchman kid; something doesn't fit, he doesn't know what. All they've said to each other is stuff like, "Like some tea sir?" and "Right on, Lutch, start pouring", but Grigson doesn't miss a trick. Something about the way Lutchman speaks makes him curious: he begins to wonder about this guy.

'He tries a little experiment: instead of calling him "bearer"

Amitav Ghosh

or "boy" or "hey you" or whatever, he suddenly calls out "Lutchman".

'He notes in his diary that there's just this instant's delay before Lutchman responds: just that additional nanosecond it takes when someone responds to a name that's not really their own. Now Grigson's sure his name's not really Lutchman: he's changed it to make it look like he's from the area. Grigson's got it figured that this is one of the commonest names there is, except that what's "Lutchman" in one place is Laakhan somewhere else and Lokhkhon in another place, and Lakshman in still another: depending on which part of the country you're from.

'That evening he asks Ron, "What's the story on this Lutchman? Is he from around here?" Ron's just got in from eight straight hours staring at the lining of mosquitoes' stomachs. He's not in the mood for small talk. He says: "Never asked. Guess he *is* from around here."

'"Is that right?" says Grigson. "But the way he says his unvoiced labials and retroflex dentals, he sounds like he's from much further north."

'"You don't say," yawns Ron: he's asking himself where this nerd blew in from. "Golly gee! Think I'll go and see if I can get a game of tennis." He goes off into the wings yelling "Tennis anyone?"

'By this time it's not just Lutchman's retroflex dentals that Grigson's interested in: he's developing a personal interest in getting behind his labials. Next morning Lutchman brings him his morning cup of tea while he's still in bed. Grigson sees his chance: okay, he says to himself, go for it. He lets his hand linger on Lutchman's arm as he takes his cup of tea; a moment later he's holding Lutchman's hand. And now he notices a cute little detail about Lutchman: his left hand's only got four fingers and no thumb. But it's like he doesn't need one either: he's got his index finger curled around so it functions like a thumb.

'Grigson gets a real rush from the thumb-that-wasn't. He gives it a rub. "Hey there Lutch," he says, patting his bed.

"What's the hurry, sit yourself down here and let's visit for a while." All this time Grigson's making like he can only speak pidgin Hindustani, like every other Englishman in India.

'Lutchman gives him this searching look, like he's trying to suss him out. That's okay with Grigson: he's going wow, this new deodorant really works. Then they hear Ron, shouting from his room: "Hey, you bearer, where's my tea?"

'Lutchman jumps up and sprints off. Grigson decides he'll try again later. He keeps an eye on Lutchman and gets a fix on where he lives: he notes he's got a big metal lantern hanging in his window, back in the servants' quarters.

'That night there's a party at the Secunderabad Club. Grigson goes, but he sneaks away early, says he has a headache; he wants to go back to the bungalow. They arrange a ride for him; he goes back; he stuffs a couple of pillows under his mosquito net and sneaks out.

'It's dark, there's no moon. It's the monsoon: the yard's turned to mud. Grigson sloshes on, towards the servants' quarters. All he can see of the outbuildings is a long, looming shape in the darkness. He curses under his breath but when he's a little closer, he sees a light in a window, a small, bright circle, glowing red. He hitches up his pajamas and tiptoes over to the window and knocks. Lutchman's face appears; he does a double take and his eyes bug out.

'"It's me!" says Grigson. "Just dropped by to see your art collection." Lutchman opens his door and Grigson steps into the room. It's tiny, it smells of clothes and sweat and mustard oil. There's a string bed in a corner, and some clothes hanging from a line. It's very dark. The only light in the room comes from the lamp in the window. Now that he's made it all the way here he wants to get a real eyeful of this dude. But this is no ordinary lamp. It's big, it's strong, it's sturdy, it's got a long handle, and it's got a small circular pane of red glass. Grigson does a double take and then he figures out what it is: it's a standard-issue railway signal lamp. The kind that's used to stop trains at stations. It's not the sort of lamp you can buy

Amitav Ghosh

at a neighbourhood store: come to think of it, it's probably a federal offence to have one hanging in your window.

'By now Grigson's seriously turned on; he's popping his buttons. But at the same time he's also bursting with curiosity. In fact he's not sure which is the bigger turn-on: making out or finding out.

'He says, in pidgin Hindustani, pointing at the lamp: "What's that?"

'Lutchman plays possum. "What's what?"

'"That lamp up there."

'"Oh that: you know what that is."

'"Yeah, but what do you call it?" says Grigson.

'"What's with these questions?" says Lutchman. He's speaking pidgin Hindustani too, so Grigson's having trouble drawing a bead on it.

'"I'm just curious," says Grigson.

'"Why?" says Lutchman. "Did you come all the way out here to ask me these dumb questions?"

'"No," says Grigson. "I'm just curious that's all."

'"Curious about what?"

'"About words."

'"You mean you want to know what it's called?"

'"Yeah," says Grigson. "That's right."

'"Why didn't you say so?" says Lutchman. "It's called a lantern."

'And that was when Grigson knew. He knew because Lutchman didn't pronounce the word as he should have if he really was from where he said he was. What he said was "lalten".

'So Grigson gives him a smile, and says, speaking to him in his own dialect: "So your name is really Laakhan isn't it? Isn't that how they say it where you're from?"

'The minute he says that word, Lutchman's face goes into rigor mortis. But Grigson doesn't notice; he's busy congratulating himself on his infallible ear. He wags a finger at Lutchman: "Can't fool me," he says. "I've got you natives figured: I know exactly where every single one of you belongs. Those loan words will give you away every time."

'Now, suddenly, Lutchman makes his move. He snatches up his lantern and says "Come on, follow me."

'"Where to?" says Grigson, but Lutchman's already out the door. Grigson starts running too.

'Happens that Secunderabad, like many British cantonment towns, is a big railway hub. The station's not far from Ross's bungalow: in fact the shunting yard is just a couple of hundred feet from the bottom of the garden. But Grigson's new in town and he's not wise to this. He's running real hard, chasing after Lutchman's red light. He's panting; endorfins are popping in his head like champagne bubbles. He's not in good shape; he gets more and more disoriented the harder he runs.

'He's giving it everything he's got, but the lantern's always just a little bit ahead, bobbing, turning, twisting: it seems to be leading him somewhere. It's very dark; the glow of the lantern is the only thing Grigson can see. He's not sure where he is, but he knows he's not running on grass any more: this is gravel under his feet. He can hear something ringing on metal. But he can't trust what he hears; he's exhausted, his ears are pounding.

'Then he hears a sound that nearly splits his eardrums: it's a whistle. He looks back and suddenly it's like the movies were just invented and he's sitting in the front row: a locomotive is bearing down on him, snorting clouds of steam. He panics and starts running between the tracks; he's set to become roadkill. But in the last half second he manages to jump: the fenders miss him by a fraction of an inch.

'The red light's gone now. Somehow Grigson manages to find his way back to the bungalow. He's scared: he's sure that Lutchman was trying to stage an accident to kill him. He thinks he should warn Ross that something very weird is going on under his roof. But he chickens out: he doesn't want to explain what he was doing down at the servants' quarters. So what does he do instead? He writes it all down in his diary.

'Next morning Lutchman's waiting at the breakfast table,

just like any other day, looking like there's not a thought on his mind. He's the model servant, as always: smiling, obsequious, attentive. Grigson decides he's not going to lunch in this town any more: he's young, he's got a life to live. He catches the next train out of Secunderabad.'

fourteen

Sonali noticed that Urmila had gone suddenly quiet after stepping into her building; that she didn't say a word while waiting for the lift, just looked around the lobby with her lips pursed, taking in all the details. She could tell Urmila was fighting down an urge to say something disapproving.

Sonali had lived here long enough to forget how strange the place had seemed to her at first, grotesque even: the marble floors, the ornate gilt mirrors on the walls, the tall palms in the corners, in their polished brass planters. It wasn't like anything you expected to see in Calcutta, except in a five-star hotel.

When Romen first showed her the building she'd told him that it didn't seem like a place one could live in—that she, Sonali, could live in, at any rate. One would spend so much time worrying about how to do things: about where to hang one's washing and whether to buy new furniture. But Romen had just laughed, as she knew he would. 'It's just business,' he said, 'all that marble and brass. That's what they pay for, the people who buy these flats. You don't have to take it seriously.'

The lift arrived and Urmila stepped in, still silent. Sonali wished she could think of something to say to put it in perspective: to let her know that this wasn't the kind of place she was used to living in, that she'd spent most of her life following her mother from one poky little flat to another, that her mother was both so used to poverty and so terrified of it that she'd never thought of living in any other way, even when she had money. But then the door of the lift slid open and it was too late.

Sonali opened her front door and was surprised to find her flat in darkness. Switching on the lights, she ushered Urmila in.

'No one at home?' Urmila said, looking around the large, glass-fronted room, with its Kashmiri rugs and its low chairs, upholstered in bright Gujarati mirrorwork.

'There's a boy who cooks and cleans . . .' Sonali said, motioning Urmila to a chair. 'Usually when I get home he's sitting on the carpet watching Zee TV and singing at the top of his voice.'

She tossed her handbag on a chair and walked down the corridor to the kitchen, switching on the lights as she went. The kitchen was tidy, everything in place, the marble counters gleaming clean. She went quickly through, to a room at the back and turned on the naked light bulb that hung from the ceiling on a twisted cord.

The room was empty: the mattress and the bedclothes lay neatly folded, at the foot of the charpai. Everything else was gone: his fearsomely loud transistor radio, his slippers, the printed T-shirts he always wore. She went over to a small desk at the far corner of the room and pulled open a drawer. It was empty too: his books, pencils and ballpoints were all gone.

'Is he there?' Urmila called out.

'No,' said Sonali distractedly. 'I think he's left—all his things are gone.' She switched the light off and walked slowly back to the drawing room.

'Was he your only servant?' Urmila asked.

Sonali shook her head. 'He wasn't really a servant,' she said. 'I don't like to have servants living in the house.'

'So then . . . ?'

'He went to school during the day,' said Sonali. 'But he cooked and cleaned in the evening, when he remembered: that was the arrangement. Romen suggested it. One of his contractors or someone found the boy: he was making a living by performing mathematical tricks for the rush hour passengers on local trains. Romen claimed he was some kind of prodigy and took him under his wing.'

Sonali was absently opening doors, looking into rooms and bathrooms, as though she were half-expecting to find him. 'I can't understand it,' she said. 'Where could he have gone? He doesn't have anywhere to go. He doesn't know anyone except Romen.'

Then the phone rang, in the drawing room. Sonali ran over and picked up the grey cordless handset. With a gesture of apology to Urmila, she unlatched a door and carried the phone out to the balcony.

'Hello,' she said, pressing the 'Talk' button. She lowered her voice to a whisper. 'Romen?'

The phone crackled and a voice came humming over the line. She knew at once it wasn't Romen; it was some other man. Sonali stiffened, embarrassed as well as disappointed.

'Could you please tell me,' the voice said in polite, formal Bengali, 'is Mr Romen Haldar there by any chance?'

'No, he is not,' she said, pitching her voice to a carefully businesslike note, trying to erase every trace of the intimacy that had been in it moments ago. 'Who's speaking?'

'Oh, so he is not there?' came the answer, in muted surprise.

'No,' Sonali answered. She was surprised herself now: the only person who ever telephoned here to ask for Romen was his secretary. That was Romen's rule, not hers, one of his bizarre gestures at domestic propriety. It was to protect her, Sonali, he always said, to keep people from gossiping—as though that would keep people from gossiping.

'Who's speaking?' she said—not harshly, but just a little tentatively.

'It doesn't matter,' said the voice at the other end.

'Wait,' she said quickly. 'Just a minute; who is it? Who's speaking?'

The line had already gone dead.

She sank into a cane chair and dropped the phone on her lap.

Amitav Ghosh

A fluttering curtain caught her eye, somewhere in the building that faced hers. Her suspicions were immediately confirmed: the neighbours were watching her again. She caught a glimpse of a couple of heads just as they were ducking out of sight.

Sometimes she wondered whether they posted lookouts at their windows to keep a watch on her balcony. What did they do when they caught a glimpse of her? Did they go running through their flats shouting: 'Sonali Das is on her balcony again, come out and take a look!'

They always seemed so shy when she ran into them on the lifts or in the parking area—these well-off heart-surgeons and bank managers and their chiffon-wrapped wives. They would smile in acknowledgement and then drop their eyes, as though afraid to be caught staring. Occasionally, they would tell her they liked her films, or her book. Some of the older people would talk about her mother's acting: they'd tell stories about how they had gone all the way to the huge canvas tent at Narkeldanga and bought four-anna tickets to see Kamini-debi performing some of her famous old jatra plays, *Marie Antoinette: Queen of France* or *Rani Rashmoni*.

She knew they gossiped about her and Romen; she often felt a kind of idle curiosity about what they made of her: did they feel sorry for her? contemptuous? outraged? It would have been interesting to know, in an abstract kind of way: not that she cared, really. She'd grown up with gossip: her mother had had to deal with twice as much and she hadn't cared either.

She rose to go inside and then, on an impulse, sat down once more and dialled the number of the Wicket Club. The phone rang several times before the head bartender finally answered.

'Javed?' she said.

'Salaam memsaheb,' he said, recognizing her immediately. 'Romen-saheb left about half an hour ago.'

'Half an hour ago?' said Sonali. 'You mean he was there all evening?'

'Yes,' said the bartender. 'He tried to 'phone you; I heard him asking someone to call you. He waited for a while and then he left.'

'Oh,' said Sonali. She had a sudden vision of Romen standing at the far end of the horseshoe-shaped bar, tall, burly and balding, hunched over the club's telephone, holding the mouthpiece in that awkward fumbling grip of his.

'Do you know where he went?' she asked.

'No,' came the answer. 'But I know he sent the Sierra home with his driver.'

'So how did he go?'

'He took a taxi.'

'A taxi!' Sonali was astonished. 'But Romen always takes his own car. Where was he going? Do you know?'

'No,' said the bartender. But then he added, 'Wait a minute memsaheb.' He put the phone down and she heard him talking to the other bartenders. Then he came back to the phone. 'Memsaheb?' he said. 'The durwan who was on duty at the gate heard Romen-saheb talking to the taxi driver.'

'Did he hear him say where he was going?' Sonali asked.

'Yes. He was going to Robinson Street, but he wanted to stop on the way, at Park Circus.'

'Oh.' Sonali switched the phone off and went slowly back inside.

'What's the matter?' said Urmila, jumping to her feet. 'You look like you've had a shock.'

Sonali fell into a chair. 'Apparently Romen's on his way to Robinson Street,' she said, chewing on her knuckles.

'I see,' said Urmila. 'Did he have an appointment?'

'Not that I know of,' Sonali said. 'And he's going to stop at Park Circus on the way.'

'Why there?'

'I don't have any idea,' said Sonali. 'The only person I know who lives there is Phulboni. But Romen didn't say anything about visiting him: he said he'd come here around nine tonight.'

Urmila gave her arm a pat. 'I'm sure he'll be here soon,' she said in a soothing voice.

Sonali made a distracted gesture. 'I don't know,' she said. 'Everyone seems to be disappearing today. If he doesn't come soon I'll have to go and look for him.'

She laughed, a little nervously. 'Now what was it that you wanted to ask me about?' she said.

Urmila sat up eagerly. 'I was curious,' she said, 'about whether you ever heard Phulboni talk about someone called Laakhan?'

'Someone called Laakhan?' Sonali lowered herself into a sofa. 'That's interesting. Why do you ask?'

fifteen

The crowd in the restaurant was thinning now; the tables were emptying fast as people hurried back to work. Antar glanced from his watch to Murugan, sitting across the table. He was pouring from the restaurant's bamboo-handled teapot, evidently unconscious of the time. Antar decided to stay a few minutes longer.

'What's the joke?' Murugan said sharply, his voice cutting through the buzz.

Antar sat up, startled: 'I'm sorry?'

'Why are you smiling?'

'Was I smiling?'

'You bet you were,' said Murugan.

'Well then,' Antar said. 'I suppose I was smiling.'

'You think this scenario is funny or something?' Murugan asked.

'Frankly, I don't know what to think,' Antar said. 'I've heard you out, and as far as I can see you don't have a shred of real evidence, or proof, or anything . . ."

'And what if I said that's what my proof is?'

'The lack thereof you mean?' said Antar, trying not to smile.

'I mean secrecy is what this is about: it figures there wouldn't be any evidence or proof.'

Antar shrugged. 'But even if I were to grant that,' he said, 'your version still wouldn't make sense. If I followed you correctly, you were suggesting that this other team—to use your phrase—was already ahead of Ross on some of this research. But then why wouldn't they just go ahead with this research themselves? Why wouldn't they publish their findings and put themselves in the running for the Nobel?'

Murugan ran his hand over his chin. 'All right,' he said, after a long pause. 'I'll sketch a scenario for you. I'm not saying that's how it happened: I'm just asking you to hear me out.'

'Go ahead,' Antar said politely.

'Let me put it like this,' Murugan said. 'You know all about matter and anti-matter, right? And rooms and anterooms and Christ and anti-Christ and so on? Now, let's say there was something like science and counter-science? Thinking of it in the abstract, wouldn't you say that the first principle of a functioning counter-science would have to be secrecy? The way I see it, it wouldn't just have to be secretive about *what* it did (it couldn't hope to beat the scientists at that game anyway); it would also have to be secretive *in* what it did. It would have to use secrecy as a technique or procedure. It would in principle have to refuse all direct communication, straight off the bat, because to communicate, to put ideas into language would be to establish a claim to *know*—which is the first thing that a counter-science would dispute.'

'I don't follow,' said Antar. 'What you're saying doesn't make sense.'

'You took the words out of my mouth,' Murugan said. 'Not making sense is what it's about—conventional sense that is. Maybe this other team started with the idea that knowledge is self-contradictory; maybe they believed that to know something is to change it, therefore in knowing something, you've already changed what you think you know so you don't really know it at all: you only know its history. Maybe they thought that knowledge couldn't begin without acknowledging the impossibility of knowledge. See what I'm saying?'

'I'm listening,' said Antar. 'For what it's worth.'

'Maybe none of this makes sense,' said Murugan. 'But let's

just try and take it on its own terms for a minute. Let's look at the kinds of working hypotheses it yields. Here's one: if it's true that to know something is to change it, then it follows that one way of changing something—of effecting a mutation, let's say—is to attempt to know it, or aspects of it. Right?'

Antar nodded.

'Okay,' said Murugan. 'So let's run with this for a bit. Let's say that just about the time that Ronnie's beginning to work on malaria there's this other person—this team—that's also been working with plasmodium falciparum but in a different way; a way so different it wouldn't make any sense to anyone who's properly trained. But let's say that by accident or design, they've made a certain amount of progress; they've taken their work to a certain point and then they've run smack into a dead end: they're stuck, they can't go any further—because of the glitches in their own methods, because they just haven't got the right equipment. Whatever. They decide that the next big leap in their project will come from a mutation in the parasite. The question now is: how do they speed up the process? The answer is: they've got to find a conventional scientist who'll give it a push.

'Enter Ronnie. But what do they do next? They can't tell him what they know because it's against their religion. Besides, they can't exactly walk up to him and say, "Hey there Ron, what's cooking?" To begin with they wouldn't get past the guards of the 19th Madras Infantry. Even if they did, Ronnie wouldn't believe them. They've got to make it look like he's found out for himself. So they go into a huddle and try to think through their next move. Remember that these guys haven't got a whole lot going for them: they're fringe people, marginal types; they're so far from the mainstream you can't see them from the shore. On the credit side, there's a lot of them and they know all about Ronnie, but neither Ronnie nor anyone else knows anything about them. They've also got the best collection of parasites in town. They've just got to play their cards right and they can do it.'

'That's all very well,' said Antar. 'But it still leaves the basic question unanswered.'

'And what's that?' said Murugan.

'Why? Why would anyone go to so much trouble? It's clear enough what's in it for Ross: fame, prospects, promotions, a Nobel. But what could these other people—accepting your premise for a moment—hope to gain from all this?'

'I thought you'd ask,' Murugan said. 'And once again, I don't have the answer. But if I *am* right—and the way this game's set up, there's no way you're ever going to know whether I'm right or not—but if I *am* right, let's just say even fractionally right, then what these guys were developing was the most revolutionary medical technology of all time. Forget about the Nobel, forget about diseases and cures and epidemiology and shit like that. What these guys were after was much bigger; they were after the biggest prize of all, the biggest fucking ballgame any human being has ever thought of: the ultimate transcendence of nature.'

'And what might that be?' Antar asked politely.

'Immortality,' said Murugan.

Antar slapped the table. 'Oh, I see,' he said, with a laugh. 'You mean like Osiris and Horus and Amun-Ra? Were they hoping to grow nice little jackal-heads? Or were they planning to sprout ibis beaks?'

'Maybe I overstated the case a bit,' Murugan said. 'What I'm really talking about is a technology for interpersonal transference.'

'Interpersonal *what*?' said Antar.

Before Murugan could answer, the waiter appeared, and placed the bill between them. He was middle-aged, with a diffident, nervous manner. He looked on, smiling exaggeratedly and rubbing his hands as they counted out their money.

All of a sudden Murugan sat bolt upright in his chair. 'I'll give you an example,' he said. Jumping to his feet, he thrust his face into the waiter's. Then, at the top of his voice he shouted, 'Yo!'

The waiter stumbled back, his mouth open, his eyes dilating.

The plate dropped out of his hands, shattering on the floor. He fell to his knees and began to whimper, in shock, covering his face with his hands.

Antar stared soundlessly, frozen, half in and half out of his chair. There was an absolute hush within the restaurant; several pairs of chopsticks hung in the air as every head turned towards Murugan.

Murugan was watching the waiter with a look of suppressed excitement, his eyes bright with expectation.

'What is the meaning of this?' demanded Antar.

Suddenly Murugan spun around and leapt at him. Thrusting his nose within an inch of Antar's he shouted, 'Boo!'

Antar recoiled, brushing the back of his hand across his face. 'Have you gone out of your mind?' he said angrily.

Murugan stood back, with a smile on his face. 'See,' he said, 'it worked.'

He waved a nonchalant hand at the few remaining diners. 'Relax,' he said, cheerfully. 'Nothing to worry about. Just checking variations in individual motor reactions to stress situations.'

He patted Antar on the shoulder. 'See,' he said. 'Same stimulus, different response: he says tamatar and you say tamatim. Now think, what if the "im" and the "ar" could be switched between you and him? What would you have then? You'd have him speaking, in your voice, or the other way around. You wouldn't know whose voice it was. And isn't that the scariest thing there is Ant? To hear something said, and not to know who's saying it? Not to know who's speaking? For if you don't know who's saying something, you don't know why they're saying it either.'

The hush broke and an indignant, protesting murmur swept through the restaurant. The waiter picked himself slowly off the floor while the manager began to advance purposefully towards their table. Three other waiters followed close behind.

Murugan threw them a hurried glance and pulled out his wallet. 'Now what would you say Ant,' he asked, 'if all of that information could be transmitted chromosomally, from

Amitav Ghosh

body to body?' He shook his wallet under Antar's nose. 'How much do you think you'd pay for that kind of technology Ant? Just think, a fresh start: when your body fails you, you leave it, you migrate—you or at least a matching symptomology of your self. You begin all over again, another body, another beginning. Just think: no mistakes, a fresh start. What would you give for that Ant: a technology that lets you improve on yourself in your next incarnation? Do you think something like that might be worth a little part of your pension fund?'

The waiters converged and Murugan broke off to confront them. 'It's all right,' he said, taking a wad of notes out of his wallet. 'I'll pay for everything.'

Ignoring this, they took hold of his arms and began to push him away from the table.

'Hey guys,' Murugan protested. 'Didn't I say it was an experiment? Where's your spirit of inquiry?'

Lifting him bodily off the floor, the waiters carried him quickly towards the door.

'See why I have to go to Calcutta Ant?' Murugan shouted, as they bore him inexorably towards the entrance. 'If there is a Calcutta chromosome I've got to find it. I guess I need it more than you do.'

sixteen

'I've been doing a little research,' Urmila said to Sonali, 'and I've discovered that when Phulboni was a young man he wrote a set of stories called *The Laakhan Stories*. They were published in an obscure little magazine and have never been reprinted. I managed to find the right issue in the National Library.'

'I've never even heard of them,' said Sonali. 'I was probably too young when they came out.'

'Well, the stories are very short and they all feature a character called Laakhan,' Urmila said. 'In one he's a postman; in another he's a village schoolmaster, something else in another.'

'How odd,' said Sonali.

'Isn't it?' Urmila said. 'When they were first published the critics thought it was some kind of elaborate allegory—with each character being different but also the same and all of them being mixed up and so on. And then of course everyone forgot about them. But I looked them up, and I had the distinct feeling that there was something more to it.'

'More?' said Sonali. 'What do you mean?'

'I couldn't put my finger on it exactly,' said Urmila. 'But I was talking to Mrs Aratounian one day . . .'

'Had she read them?' Sonali interrupted, eyebrows raised.

'Oh no,' Urmila laughed. 'She doesn't have much time for writers. Besides, you know how she is: doesn't know a word of Bengali even though she's been here all her life. But she's very sharp you know and I often find that it helps to talk things over with her. She's given me a lot of good advice over the years: in fact it was she who suggested that I go to the National Library.'

'I see,' said Sonali. 'Go on.'

'So I told her about the stories and she agreed with me at once. "Dust in our eyes, my dear," she said. "Take my word for it."'

'What did she mean?'

'She thought the stories were a message to someone; to remind them of something—some kind of shared secret. You know, like those strange little ads you sometimes see in the Personal columns?'

Sonali's eyes widened. 'That's interesting,' she said. 'It's possible.'

'So you do know something about the stories?' Urmila said eagerly.

Sonali took a sip of her tea. 'I don't know if it has anything to do with the stories you're talking about,' she said. 'But I do know that something very strange happened to Phulboni when he was in his twenties. And it did have something to do with a "Laakhan".'

'Really?' Urmila sat up eagerly. 'What happened?'

'It began with my mother asking him why he'd given up shooting.'

'Shooting?' said Urmila in astonishment. 'You mean Phulboni used to shoot?'

'Yes,' said Sonali smiling. 'He was a very good shot. I'll tell you how I found out.' She curled her legs under her and settled into the cushions that lined the sofa's armrest, her face lit by a fondly reminiscent smile.

'Phulboni was always in and out of our house when I was a child,' she said. 'He was like an uncle to me: I used to call him Murad-mesho. We were living in a tiny flat off Park Circus, just my mother and me. The flat was really very small, but we always had lots of guests—especially writers and artists:

every evening there'd be at least half a dozen people there and Phulboni was one of the regulars. He always came wearing the same old pair of frayed trousers, the same worn leather belt, and starched white shirt. You know how starch always smells a little when you sweat? That's how he smelt: of cigarettes and sweaty starch.

'He was a splendid-looking man: over six feet tall, straight and lean as a lamp-post. He was very poor then and lived all by himself: his wife had left him and gone back to her family. The moment he arrived my mother would whisper to the servants to run down and get some biryani. He'd had a good job once, with a British firm, Palmer Brothers, but he gave it up when he started writing. He wanted to make his living as a writer but his work was just too difficult for the public: all those dialect words from languages no one had ever heard of. His father worked for one of those mountain maharajas in Orissa and he grew up in the jungle, speaking the language of the local people, running wild. That's why he later took the pen-name Phulboni, after the region.

'Living in the forest, he must have learned to shoot very early, but he never told anyone about it. It was quite by accident that I discovered that he was an excellent shot.

'Once, my mother was acting in a jatra somewhere on the outskirts of Calcutta. It was one of those places where the performance is under a huge circus tent. There's a round stage inside and at the same time there is a fair going on outside—you know, with phuchka-stalls and roundabouts and all that.

'I had squeezed into a little space under the wooden stage, and I was watching the crowd, making faces at the children, that kind of thing. The play was *Marie Antoinette: Queen of France*. My mother was playing Marie Antoinette of course: she was getting on then, and if there was a wicked queen or a harridan of a mother-in-law she would invariably get the part. Ma was just launching into her big speech, you know, the famous one: "They don't have any rice? Then let them eat ledigenis."

'Suddenly I looked up and saw Phulboni coming in. I screamed and ran up to him, pushing through the crowd. Both of us had heard the speech a hundred times. I was bored so I didn't let him watch the play. Instead I made him walk around the fair, buying me jhalmuri and mihidana and that kind of thing. Then we came to one of those stalls with an airgun and lots of balloons lined up in rows. I began to tease him, saying why don't you try and shoot some of those balloons: you writers aren't good for anything. He kept saying no, no, no, but in the end he gave in. To my astonishment he didn't miss once in his first ten shots. I said: that was just luck, let's see if you can do it again. He said, All right, and took five steps back, and again he didn't miss a shot. He moved back still further: a whole crowd gathered to watch him. Not a single miss. In the end the stallowner begged him to stop: "Shaheb, please forgive me, but if I let you go on like this, what are my children going to eat?"

'I told my mother about the incident and she was just as surprised as I. Phulboni had never said a word to her about shooting or hunting. She asked him about it and he just laughed it off. But my mother wasn't one to give up. She got to work on him one day after he'd drunk a lot of rum and he told her a story. But he was very upset the next day: he said he didn't want the story to get around and made her promise never to tell anyone.'

'Oh I see.' Urmila could not keep the disappointment out of her voice.

'In fact after that he began to avoid us,' said Sonali. 'In the last years of her life my mother became very worried about Phulboni. His behaviour became stranger and stranger as his fame grew. He'd get drunk and wander the streets all night as if he was looking for something: I've heard he still does. She wanted him to come and live with us but he wouldn't: he stopped seeing his old friends and wouldn't have much to do with anyone. He didn't even come to see her when she was dying. She was convinced that it was because he'd never forgiven her for getting that story out of him and she could never understand why: And I must say I couldn't either.'

'So she told you?' Urmila said.

'Yes,' said Sonali. 'Shortly before she died.'

seventeen

After all these years, Antar still found himself gritting his teeth as he thought back to that day, at the Thai restaurant, remembering how he had sat in his chair, slumped in a stupor of mortification, trying to avoid the stares that were directed at him from the surrounding tables.

On the way out he had plucked up the courage to stutter an apology to the manager. 'I don't really know him at all,' he said. 'I met him for the first time today. The man's clearly mad. I've never had anything to do with him before, and I hope I never will again.' Back at the office he wasted no time in uploading everything he had on Murugan's case and sending the file back to the Swedish Director. 'If this is what it means to deal with the human side of things,' he recalled saying, 'I think I'd rather go back to accounts, thank you.'

By the time he left work, he was confident that he had put the whole business behind him. But he got home to find his answering machine blinking furiously: there were three messages on it. He had a twinge of apprehension: it was rarely that he had so much as a single message; he could not remember an occasion when he had had more. His instincts told him to touch the rewind button, wipe the tape clean. But instead, his hand went out and touched 'Play'—just to make sure, he told himself, just so he would know who it was. His worst fears were instantly confirmed. There was that voice again, blaring out of the machine, the sound of it even more grating now than in real life: 'Listen you fucking jerk: you think this stuff's all just a pie in the sky huh?'

With a jab of his thumb Antar cut the first message short and forwarded to the next one. 'It's me again,' said the same voice, 'your pal Morgan: your dumbass machine cut me off . . .' Antar forwarded to the third and last message and there it was again, that voice: 'Did you know your machine's got the concentration span of a frozen chicken?'

Antar slammed a finger on the Fast Forward button, and kept it there until the tape almost ran out. But he still caught the final sentence: 'there's a document waiting for you right this minute, in your mail-folder . . .' Antar spun around to face his monitor, across the room. Sure enough, the biff was blinking on his screen. He stared unnerved at the blinking elliptical surface of that old-fashioned screen: it was like walking in on a burglar.

He had to make an effort to pull himself together before he could go over to the keyboard. He deleted the entire document without having read a single line.

Now, seating himself on the edge of his bed, Antar tried to think back across the years to 1995. He remembered that he had disposed of the answering machine some time after that incident: he had voice mail at LifeWatch and call-forwarding when he was out, so he didn't really need it anyway. He scratched his head trying to recall what he had done with the machine. He'd meant to sell it or give it away but no one had wanted it. He had a vague memory of putting it in a plastic bag and shoving it into a closet, with his old clothes and shoes.

The closet was in the corridor, between his kitchen and his bedroom, a teeming hollow into which, over the years, he had emptied his life. Rising from his chair he went over and gave its closed door a speculative look. The last time he'd opened it was a few weeks ago, while searching for an old laptop: an avalanche of discarded objects had come tumbling off the shelves. He placed a hand on the knob and prised the door gently open. A tremor ran through the closet, but to his relief everything stayed in place.

He began to empty the shelves, one by one, piling up everything in the corridor: old shoes, timer-less toasters, broken umbrellas, accordion files. And then he spotted it, hidden behind a pile of yellowing Arabic newspapers: a brown rectangular shape, wrapped in transparent plastic.

He took it down and carried it into his bedroom, leaving everything else piled in the corridor. Sitting on the edge of his bed, he unwrapped it, blowing off the dust. He rubbed his finger over the rectangle of clear plastic that covered the machine's microcassette and pushed the eject button. Somewhat to his surprise the mechanism seemed to be in working order. The cassette popped out and he cleaned it carefully, with the corner of his bedsheet.

Slipping the cassette back, he plugged the machine in. The blinking light came on, and the cassette began to turn. And then, punctuated by squeaks from the cassette's dusty wheels, he heard a voice, blunted by the passage of time, but still more or less audible. He turned the volume up.

'Listen you fucking creep,' said the voice, just as he remembered it, 'you think this stuff's all just a pie in the sky huh? You think I don't have any proof? Well let me tell you something: I don't know what they call proof down where you live but I've got something that's good enough for me.

'You remember I mentioned a guy called W.G. MacCallum—a doctor and research scientist who made one of the big breakthroughs in malaria in 1897? Okay, listen to this: what this guy did was he showed that the little "rods" that Laveran had seen coming out of the parasite's hyaline membrane weren't flagellae, like the great man thought. In fact they were exactly what they look like—that is, spunk—and what they did was what spunk does, which is make babies. You wouldn't think it would take a Galileo to figure that out: I mean what did they look like for Pete's sake? But the fact is, that MacCallum was the first to get it. He wasn't the first to see it but he was the first to figure it out. Laveran saw it before him, but he didn't get it: guess Lav-the-Man didn't exactly have sex on his mind. Ronnie Ross saw it about a year before MacCallum did and he thought he'd seen his father. No kidding; he thought the flagella was a kind of soldier, going out to war, like Pa Ross on his white horse. I mean, think about it: Ronnie sees this thing that looks like a prick; it goes swimming across his slide and starts humping an egg, and what does Ronnie make of it? He thinks it's the charge of the Light Brigade. The moral is: just because you take a boy out of Victoria's England, doesn't mean you've got her out of the boy.'

Here there was a beep and the voice was cut abruptly short. A moment later it resumed: 'It's me again, your pal Morgan, your dumbass machine cut me off. Now, where was I? Oh yeah, MacCallum. Anyway, MacCallum was just a kid, and a Yank, stuffed full of pumping red-blooded hormones, and he knew what he'd seen all right. He wrote a paper fast as he could and presented it at a big doctors' convention in Toronto in 1897. It went down so well that he got to go jogging with Mr Germicide himself, Lord Lister.

'Okay, so MacCallum was the first to figure it out. But back when he was getting started on his research, he worked with a whole team down at Johns Hopkins in Baltimore. The other members of the team were Eugene L. Opie and a guy called Elijah Monroe Farley. MacCallum and Opie were the heavies, while Farley was kind of like the water-boy and gofer. He didn't last long. Just when the team was getting started on malaria, Farley got the itch to see the world. He volunteered his services to a missionary group from Boston, and next thing anyone knew he'd shipped out for India.'

Here there was another interruption. With an aggrieved comment, Murugan's voice resumed:

'Okay, so you want to know how I know all this? It happened like this: a couple of years ago I was looking through Eugene L. Opie's private papers in Baltimore. I was checking out his lab notes, and what do you think fell out? A letter from Dr Elijah Monroe Farley addressed to Opie. It was like it had been left there to wait for me. Farley wrote the letter after visiting a lab in Calcutta—a lab run by a guy called D.D. Cunningham. That was the lab where Ross ran the last lap of his race, in 1898. D.D. Cunningham was his predecessor at the lab, and Ross didn't get there until early 1898. But this letter was written in 1894 and it was the last thing Elijah Farley ever wrote.

'To cut to the chase: You know what was in this letter? Well there was a lot of stuff—I mean like pages and pages of stuff—but buried under all the garbage there was this sentence that proves that Farley had already found out about the role of the so-called "flagellae" in sexual reproduction, long before MacCallum. That is, he already knew what MacCallum hadn't yet discovered. And when I worked out the dates and stuff, it was clear that the only place he could have learnt it was in Calcutta. But who could he have learnt it from? D.D. Cunningham didn't know and didn't care, and at this time Ronnie Ross was still in the research equivalent of Montessori school. Fact is, Ronnie *never* managed to work out the stuff about the flagellae for himself: just couldn't bring himself to deal with all that sex happening under his scope. He only found out in 1898, when Doc Manson mailed him a summary of MacCallum's findings.

'And that's not all. Remember Ross's assistant—Lutchman or Laakhan or whatever you want to call him? Well, I have a hunch Farley met him long before Ross did: in fact Farley may have seen too much of him for his own good.

'The trouble is, Farley's letter was uncatalogued, and I only saw it that one time. I put it back, and filled out a form asking for permission to xerox it. But it wasn't there the next time I looked. The librarian wouldn't believe me, because it wasn't on the catalogues. I've never been able to find it again, so strictly speaking I still don't have my smoking gun. But I saw it and I held it in my hands and when I got back to my motel that day I wrote it up, as I remembered it. And guess what? You can have a preview: if you look at your monitor, you'll see there's a document waiting for you right this minute, in your mail-folder . . .'

eighteen

M urugan arrived at the guest house to find Mrs
Aratounian watching TV and drinking pale-yellow
gimlets.

'Why, there you are Mr Morgan,' she said, patting her
fraying, anti-macassared sofa. 'Do sit down. I was just beginning
to worry about you. Can I pour you a gimlet? Are you sure?
Just a chhota—a tiny nightcap to bring you sweet dreams?'

Mrs Aratounian had discarded the blue velvet dressing-gown
she was wearing in the morning, when Murugan arrived; now
she was dressed in a white blouse and severe black skirt. Bottles
of Omar Khayyam Dry Gin and Rose's Lime Cordial stood on
a small carved table beside her, barely visible amongst clumps
of leaves, growing out of ornate brass planters.

She followed Murugan's eyes anxiously as his gaze strayed
to the table. 'No?' she said, squinting at him over her bifocals.
'You don't like Omar Khayyam? I've got a bottle of Blue
Riband gin somewhere; just for special occasions. I could go
and look for it: I know it's here somewhere.'

'Omar Khayyam will do just fine,' said Murugan. 'Thank
you.'

'Good,' said Mrs Aratounian. Reaching for a glass, she
poured out a careful measure of gin, then added a splash of
lime cordial and an ice cube. 'So what did you do with your
day Mr Morgan?' she said, handing the glass to Murugan.

Before Murugan could answer, there was a loud burst of

music from the television set, and a bland voice announced: 'And now we take you to our special newsprogramme . . .'

'News!' Mrs Aratounian said sardonically, settling back into her sofa. 'I get more news from the sweeper-woman than I do from this thing.'

A blandly smiling man in a kurta appeared on the screen, sitting behind a bunch of drooping lilies. 'The Vice-President was in Calcutta earlier today,' he announced, 'to present the National Award to the eminent writer Saiyad Murad Husain, better known by his nom de plume, Phulboni.' Abruptly the newreader's face disappeared from the screen, to be replaced by the Vice-President's, nodding sleepily on the stage of the Rabindra Sadan auditorium.

'Oh no,' groaned Mrs Aratounian. 'It's one of those beastly functions where everybody makes speeches. I really must get cable; everyone in the building has it but I . . .'

The camera swept over a large, packed auditorium, and zoomed in on the front row. Just visible at the corner of the screen were two women standing in the aisle. One of them turned briefly towards the stage before following the other woman down the aisle.

Suddenly Mrs Aratounian sat bolt upright. 'Why,' she cried excitedly, pointing at the TV set with her cane. 'There's Urmila! Imagine seeing Urmila on television! Why, I've known her since she was in school, at St Mary's Convent.'

She turned confidingly to Murugan: 'A scholarship student of course—her family could never have afforded a school like St Mary's. She was the mousiest little thing you ever saw, but lo and behold a couple of years ago she went off and got herself a job at *Calcutta*. What's the world coming to? I said to her, when I have to get my news from a chit of a girl like you?'

The camera panned across the audience again and they had another glimpse of the two women, one a good way ahead of the other.

'Hey!' Murugan thumped his knee. 'I know those two . . .'

'That's Sonali Das,' Mrs Aratounian cried. 'Another of my customers at Dutton's. And such a celebrity too!'

She gave Murugan a speaking look and a half-smile. 'I could tell you a thing or two about *her*,' she said.

Chuckling to herself, she took a sip of her gimlet.

The camera panned to the stage and Phulboni's haggard face appeared, filling the screen. Mrs Aratounian gave a yelp of disgust. 'Oh no,' she said. 'Heaven help us; one of those pompous old windbags is going to make a speech. They're at it all day. I really must get cable; you can even get BBC I'm told . . .'

Suddenly the writer's hoarse, rasping voice filled the room: 'For more years than I can count I have walked the innermost streets of this most secret of cities, looking always to find her who has so long eluded me: Silence herself. I see signs of her presence everywhere I go, in images, words, glances, but only signs, nothing more . . .'

Mrs Aratounian tapped her cane on the floor, in annoyance. 'Didn't I warn you Mr Morgan?' she snapped. 'And I'll wager you tuppence to a groat he'll go on absolutely forever.'

Now Phulboni's eyes filled with tears: 'I have tried, as hard as ever a man has to find my way to her, to throw myself before her, to join the secret circle that attends her, to take the dust of her heels to my head. By every means available, I have sought her, the ineluctable, ever-elusive mistress of the unspoken, wooed her, courted her, begged to join the circle of her initiates.'

Mrs Aratounian slammed her cane on the floor. 'Appalling,' she said. 'The man's making an utter exhibition of himself. Isn't anyone going to do anything?'

'As a tree spreads its branches,' the writer's voice continued, 'to court an invisible source of light, so every word I have ever penned has been written for her. I have sought her in words, I have sought her in deeds, most of all I have sought her in the unspoken keeping of her faith.'

Here, abruptly, the writer's face disappeared from the screen and a slide of a peaceful mountain scene appeared. But the writer's voice continued, eerily disembodied.

Mrs Aratounian gave a yelp of laughter. 'Look at that, Mr Morgan,' she said. 'They're so incompetent they can't even cut him off.'

The voice rasped on: 'If I stand before you now, in this most public of places, it is because I am on the point of desperation and know of no other way to reach her. I know that time is running out—my time and her time. I know that the crossing is nigh; I know it to be at hand . . .'

Even though the writer's face was no longer on the screen, it was evident that he was sobbing: '. . . as the hours run out, when perhaps no more than a few moments remain, knowing of no other means I make this last appeal: Do not forget me: I have served you as best I could. Only once did I sin against the Silence, in a moment of weakness, seduced by the one I loved. Have I not been punished enough? What more remains? I beg you, I beg you, if you exist at all, and I have never for a moment doubted it—give me a sign of your presence, do not forget me, take me with you . . .'

The screen flickered and the newsreader's face reappeared, sweating lightly. Forcing a smile he began: 'We apologize to our viewers . . .'

Mrs Aratounian struggled to her feet, went over to the television set and switched it off.

'This is the kind of nonsense you have to put up with if you don't have cable,' she said in disgust. 'Night after night. You tell me, Mr Morgan, would you ever hear rubbish like that on BBC?'

nineteen

Antar stopped the answering machine and rose to his feet. It was no use regretting the loss of the document that Murugan had posted to his mailbox: if he hadn't deleted it then he would have done so soon afterwards. But possibly, just possibly, it wasn't irretrievably lost. Perhaps Ava could find a trace of it and reconstitute the document: it wasn't inconceivable. Ava knew some pretty good tricks.

Antar started for the bedroom door: there was only one way to find out.

Just as he was about to leave the bedroom, he heard a sound—a muffled sound, like a soft footfall. He spun around to face the wall. Tara's living room lay on the far side, separated only by a couple of inches of plaster and a bricked-in door. It was uncanny how sound carried through that wall.

Perhaps Tara had come home: Antar was sure he'd heard someone. He went to the wall and knocked: 'Tara, are you back?' There was no answer.

He hurried over to his kitchen-window and glanced at Tara's apartment, across the airshaft. The lights were still off: she didn't seem to be home. He shrugged: it must have been a damp floorboard: there was no telling, in a building as old and creaky as this one. He leaned over the sink, splashed water over his face and reached for a kitchen towel.

He went into his living room and seated himself at the keyboard. With a tap of a key he sent Ava shooting off to rummage through the accumulated memories of all his old, superseded hard-disks. It was not unlikely that a binary 'ghost' of Murugan's lost E-mail message had remained somewhere within the system. Even the faintest trace would be enough: Ava would do the rest.

Moments later a hand appeared on Ava's screen, gesturing morosely, fingers half open. Ava had recently begun to learn body-language—in Egyptian dialect of course—and this was her new way of indicating a negative.

Then the gesture changed: the fingers came together, pointing upwards, in a little dipping motion. That meant wait; there's more. Her screen went blank and her voice mechanism clicked on.

The message might still be found, Ava told him. It would just take a while. It had been typed on one of those old-fashioned, contact-based alphabetical keyboards. The electronic signals emitted by the keys were probably still traceable. It was simply a question of matching the electronic 'fingerprint' of Murugan's E-mail message to every electronic signal that was still alive in the ionosphere.

Antar keyed in a query asking how long the whole procedure would take.

Ava took a moment to answer. It would mean sifting through about six thousand eight hundred and ninety-two trillion çuñabytes, came the response, in other words, roughly eighty-five billion times the estimated sum of every dactylographic act ever committed by a human being. It was certain to take at least fifteen minutes.

Antar keyed in two names, Cunningham and Farley, and cut Ava loose.

Suddenly Antar was very tired. He looked down and noticed that there was a mild tremor in his hand. His heart sank as he touched his forehead and cheek. They were hot and clammy: it felt like the start of one of his bouts of fever. Evidently he would have to forgo his walk to Penn Station today.

In a way Antar was almost relieved. He decided to lie down while Ava searched the skies.

Antar had almost drifted off to sleep when Ava began to chirrup a summons twenty minutes later. Heaving off his bedclothes, he rose shakily to his feet and wrapped himself in a dressing-gown. Then he made his way down the corridor to his living room.

A message was waiting for him on Ava's screen: the search had yielded a few traces of Murugan's lost E-mail message. But the signals were faint and possibly distorted. Ava had reconstructed a semblance of a narrative by running the retrieved fragments through a Storyline algorithm. But she was unable to vouch for the authenticity of the restored text.

Antar typed in a query asking if Ava could generate an image-simalcrum of the text with her Simultaneous Visualization program. That way all he'd have to do to review the text was to lock himself into his Sim Vis visor. He could just lie back and watch: Ava would do the rest. His hands felt very unsteady now: he knew he wasn't up to the task of reading through a long document.

A hand appeared on Ava's screen, sketching a gesture of regret. The answer was negative: the text was too corrupt to do a continuous image conversion. The best she could do was provide a verbal rendition.

Antar winced: he hated listening to Ava read, in her flat, uninflected voice. But on the other hand he was in no position to do it himself in his current state.

Reaching for his headphones, Antar snapped them into place.

twenty

It was past eleven when Urmila got home. The flat was in
darkness and everybody was in bed.

She let herself in, as quietly as she could, and stood by the
front-door while her eyes accustomed themselves to the
darkness. Her younger brother was snoring in the sitting room.
He had played in a second-division football match that
afternoon: one of the stringers for the sports page had come
over to the reporting desk to tell her that he'd almost scored.
She tiptoed into the sitting room and found him lying on the
sofa, with the light on. He was barebodied, dressed only in his
team's blue sweatpants, with one foot on the floor and one
arm thrown over the back of the sofa. His head was on the
armrest with his tongue lolling out of his open mouth, trailing
a ribbon of drool.

A plateful of food was waiting for her in the kitchen, under
a net cover. The net seemed to dissolve when she turned the
light on; a swarm of cockroaches melted away into the cracks
and corners. 'Isn't anyone going to be allowed to sleep?' her
older brother shouted, from the bedroom he shared with his
wife and three children. 'Who's turned the light on at this
time of the night?'

Urmila leapt for the switch, almost dropping her plate.
During the day her older brother worked as a salesman for a
company that marketed shares and stock offerings. In the
evenings he earned a little extra by doing tuitions for school-
children. He was always exhausted at night.

She stumbled out of the kitchen in the dark, balancing her plate carefully in her hands. She made her way to the bathroom, edging past the camp-bed where she slept, and half-closed the door before switching on a light. Seating herself on the edge of the bed she began to pick at the plateful of cold dal and chapatis.

There was a rustle and a footstep in the landing and she looked up to see her mother, standing beside the camp-bed, dressed in her white night-time saree. 'When did you get in?' her mother said sleepily. 'I waited and waited . . .'

'Why?' said Urmila. 'You shouldn't stay up so late—you remember what the homoeopath said.'

Motioning to her to keep her voice down, her mother seated herself beside Urmila and put a hand on her knee.

'I had to tell you tonight Urmi,' she whispered. 'There's some good news, some really good news, I knew you would be so happy.'

'What?' said Urmila.

'That's what I was going to tell you: we had a phone call from the Secretary of the Wicket Club at eight o'clock. About your brother, Dinu. I was the one who answered and, let me tell you the first thing I said was: Oh, if only my daughter was here, she would be so happy . . .'

The member-secretary of the Wicket Club had telephoned, she said, to let them know that a senior incumbent of the club's executive committee was going to pay them a call the next day, in person, with a view to discussing Dinu's prospects.

'You know what this means Urmi?' her mother said, glowing with pleasure at the sudden good fortune that had befallen her son.

'What?' said Urmila.

'It means they want to give your brother a First Division contract. Everyone says so—if they're sending an E.C. Member then it means a First Division contract, definitely.'

'Are you sure?' said Urmila. 'We've heard this talk about a First Division contract so many times but nothing ever seems to come of it.'

'But this time's different,' her mother cried. She put an arm around Urmila's shoulders and pulled her close. 'Just think Urmi; a First Division contract—money, maybe a flat. At last you'll be able to give up this stupid job and stay at home. Everything will be paid. Maybe we can even get you married before it's too late. We can put an advertisement in the papers . . .'

'Ma that's enough,' Urmila said wearily, knowing exactly what was to follow: that her time was running out; her hair was thinning; she looked older than she should; the neighbours were talking about how late she got home . . .

Urmila broke in quickly, before the litany could get fully under way. 'Before you start planning my wedding,' she said, 'let's see if we can get the contract signed.'

Her mother did not fail to notice the sceptical note in her voice. 'I thought you would be glad Urmi,' she said with a catch in her voice. 'I thought it would make you happy to hear our news. But instead all you do is pull a long face. You just don't care about us any more; all you think about is that awful job of yours.'

'Ma, if I didn't have the job,' Urmila said wearily, 'how would we get by? How far would Baba's pension go? How would we feed the children? Can you tell me that?'

Her mother paid her no attention; she was dabbing her eyes now. 'That's all you think about,' she said. 'Money, money, money. You have no place in your heart for our joys and sorrows. You should have seen how happy your brother was when I told him about the phone call from the Club: the first person he thought about was you. He said: Didi must cook fish tomorrow, something special like ilish mach so we can ask the Club's representative to stay for dinner.'

Urmila threw her a look of disbelief. 'Ma, I can't cook fish tomorrow morning,' she said. 'I have to be at a press conference at nine—the Communications Minister is arriving on an early morning flight from Delhi. That means I have to leave the house by eight fifteen at the latest—otherwise I'll never get to Dalhousie on time. You know what the traffic is like.'

The first notes of a wail escaped her mother's lips. 'Urmi, what are you saying?' she sobbed. 'Are you saying your job is more important than your brother's life? Are you telling me that some umbrella-head minister from Delhi is more important than us?'

She sobbed on while Urmila sat silent on the edge of the bed. Finally she put her plate down and asked, in exasperation: 'Has someone bought the fish?'

'No,' her mother said. 'There wasn't time and none of us had the money. You'll have to get it tomorrow morning from Gariahat.'

'I can't go to Gariahat in the morning,' Urmila cried, in protest. But she gave up the moment the words were out of her mouth. It was futile to argue; in the end, she knew, she would have to go herself. Her father wouldn't go because it would interfere with his early morning breathing exercises; her brothers wouldn't go because they would be asleep; her sister-in-law wouldn't go because no one would dare ask her. And as for her mother, she wouldn't go either, and if she, Urmila, were to ask her she would burst into tears and say: how could you say this to me? Don't you know the homoeopath told me never to go out early in the morning because of my asthma?

Then Urmila would want to point out that her asthma didn't stop her going to see her guru in Dhakuria every other day when he did his special dawn appearance to show himself to his followers in early morning sunlight. But she knew she wouldn't say it, no matter how much she might want to. Instead of saying it to her mother, she would say it to herself, as she went hurtling towards Dalhousie in a minibus, with elbows digging into her back and her nose stuck in somebody's armpit. She would keep mouthing the words to herself over and over again—but you go to your guru every other morning Ma—and she would get angrier and angrier until finally she did something terrible, as she did the other day, when her mother had made her run down to the ironing-man's stall to fetch her brother's football shorts before catching the minibus: she'd worked herself into such a fury, standing in the bus,

Amitav Ghosh

mouthing her unsaid protests that in the end she picked up her foot and jammed it down on someone's instep. She didn't even know why she'd done that; she just wanted to feel the crunch as the heel of her shoe dug into flesh and bone. And she had enjoyed herself too, exchanging insults with the fat little man whose foot she'd stepped on; they shouted at each other all the way from Lansdowne to Lord Sinha Road, until she finally reduced him to browbeaten silence.

She felt her mother's hands gripping her shoulder. 'Don't fall asleep yet Urmi,' she said. 'Tell me first: will you get the fish and cook it?'

'Maybe I won't have to,' she said sleepily. 'Maybe one of the fish-sellers will come around.'

'But will you do it anyway?' her mother insisted.

'All right,' Urmila said, in resignation. 'I will—now let me go to sleep.'

Her mother gave her shoulder a pat. 'I knew you would,' she said. 'My sweet little Urmi. Oh, your brother will be so happy. You should have seen how excited he was when I told him that Romen Haldar was coming to our house . . .'

It took a moment for the name to filter through and then Urmila sat up, abruptly.

'Who?' she said, in surprise.

'Romen Haldar,' said her mother again. 'He's the one who's coming to visit us, from the Club. You know who he is, don't you?'

'Yes,' Urmila said sleepily. 'Yes I know who he is. It's just a coincidence, that's all.'

twenty-one
_____

Elijah Monroe Farley left for India in October 1893, Ava
began, two years after his departure from the research
laboratories of Johns Hopkins University in Baltimore. Several
friends and acquaintances travelled up to New York to send
him off, including his mentor, the venerable malaria specialist
W.S. Thayer and the two other members of his erstwhile team,
W.G. MacCallum and Eugene L. Opie. By the summer of
1894 the young Reverend Farley was installed in a small
charitable clinic in the remote township of Barich, in the
eastern foothills of the Himalayas. The clinic was run by the
American Ecumenical Mission and its staff were the only trained
medical personnel in the district.

Farley was twenty-six, a tall, lanky man, with ginger hair
and moss-green eyes. Austere and contemplative by nature, he
adapted easily to the rigours of his new calling. If at all he
missed his earlier vocation as scientist, he let no one know: his
every waking hour was consumed by the clinic.

Farley had been at the clinic five months before he had his
first letter. It was from his old friend and colleague, Eugene
Opie in Baltimore. The letter consisted for the most part of
trivialities concerning the weather and the marital and
professional circumstances of common acquaintances. But Opie
also referred, though only in passing, to a research project that
he and MacCallum had recently embarked upon. Writing in
the careless shorthand of a busy research student, Opie did not

take the time to spell out the theoretical implications of this work. But it was immediately clear to Farley that Opie and MacCallum were building on the findings of the Frenchman, Alphonse Laveran.

This unexpected piece of news plunged Farley into a state of perplexity. As a student he had paid little attention to Laveran's work, assuming it to be generally discredited. In this he had taken his lead from no less a person than William Osler, the guiding spirit of Johns Hopkins, who had publicly declared his scepticism of 'Laveranity'. Farley had left for India fully confident that Laveran's theory was headed for medicine's vast graveyard of discredited speculations: his astonishment at the news of its disinterment could not have been greater.

Once introduced, these apprehensions of Laveranity revivified gradually insinuated themselves into the young missionary's mind, creating doubt and disbelief where certainty had reigned before. As the days passed these doubts began to work on him in subtle and unexpected ways, evoking once again the life he had forsaken, giving rise to an overwhelming nostalgia for the half-forgotten habits and routines of the laboratory. He began to bitterly regret the impulse that had caused him to leave his own microscope behind, at his family's New England home: or else it would have been all too easy to set up an improvised laboratory right where he was.

Then, by chance rather than design, he discovered, sandwiched within the pages of a prayerbook, the card of an English doctor, one Surgeon-Colonel Lawrie, of the Indian Medical Service. Farley had met Lawrie on one of his occasional visits to the Mission's headquarters in Calcutta. In the course of their brief meeting, the Surgeon-Colonel had informed him that he was on his way to Hyderabad, to take up an appointment as Professor in the Medical School recently founded by the prince of that state, the Nizam. Fortunately, he had scribbled his new address on the back of his card and Farley lost no time in addressing a letter to him, enquiring into the present state of opinion regarding Laveran's theories.

He had not long to wait: to his great relief Colonel Lawrie wrote back within the month. But the letter, when he read it, only deepened his puzzlement: the Colonel still appeared to hold to the belief that Laveranity was without foundation.

Despite the efforts of certain acolytes, wrote the Colonel, it remained true, so far as rational opinion could discern, that Laveran's speculations were wholly without empirical foundation. He himself had recently been witness to a spectacle that had produced forcible proof of this in a manner that would have been comic, had it not so dramatically shamed its protagonist.

A self-important and opinionated young Army doctor called Ronald Ross had just been posted to the Army hospital at Begumpett, not far from Hyderabad. Having more time on his hands than was good for him, Ross had taken it upon himself to begin an investigation into malaria—a disease of which he had no practical knowledge whatever. The young man had been overheard, not once but several times, at the Secunderabad Club, boasting of his familiarity with Laveran's chimera. Nor had he hesitated to accept an invitation to demonstrate the existence of this creature to the assembled faculty of the Nizam's School of Medicine. To this end, he had actually loaded some poor shivering unfortunate into a bullock cart and brought him rattling over to the School, eleven miles away. But of course when the time came, with everybody gathered in the lecture theatre, there was absolutely nothing to be found in the poor man's blood: not a trace of Laveran's fantastical creature. When asked for an explanation he had come up with some stuttering tale of how the creature had gone into temporary withdrawal: as though the parasite were a sleepy Latin in need of a daily siesta.

As far as he, Surgeon-Colonel Lawrie, was concerned this contretemps put paid to the matter, once and for all. However, the Colonel went on to add, he understood very well that in these matters a man might want to make up his mind for himself. One of his colleagues in the Medical Service, D.D. Cunningham, F.R.S., a very sound man and a scientist of some

Amitav Ghosh

distinction, had the charge of a laboratory, in Calcutta. Although not comparable to the leading laboratories of Europe or America, Cunningham's facilities were certainly the best in India, and possibly within the whole continent of Asia. Cunningham was no more persuaded of Laveran's theory than anyone else, but he was a fair-minded man, and would gladly allow his facilities to be used for a good cause. Should the Reverend Doctor so desire, he, Surgeon Lawrie, would be glad to write a letter of introduction to Cunningham, etc., etc.

Farley wrote immediately to Lawrie, accepting his offer, and it was soon arranged that he would visit Cunningham's laboratory on his next trip to the Mission's Calcutta headquarters.

Farley boarded the train in a state of feverish anticipation. His excitement was in no way diminished when he disembarked at Calcutta's Sealdah Station three days later.

Promptly at five, the next afternoon, Farley presented himself for tea at Dr Cunningham's boarding house. Dr Cunningham proved to be a large man of florid complexion. He greeted Farley with booming goodwill, and enquired in some detail after the health and well-being of his erstwhile mentor W.S. Thayer, whose work he knew and evidently admired.

They conversed for some time about general matters and it soon became clear to Farley that whatever his earlier accomplishments, Cunningham had long since lost interest in research. He was not entirely surprised when Cunningham told him that he was to retire some three years hence, and that with his future leisure in mind, he had been exploring the possibility of establishing a private practice in Calcutta.

When eventually the conversation veered around to the matter at hand, there was a disappointment in store for the young missionary. Cunningham informed him that due to an unforeseen circumstance, he was to leave Calcutta in a day or two: he had been summoned to Assam, by a planter friend who had been taken suddenly ill.

'But don't look so stricken my boy,' Cunningham bellowed, clapping Farley on the back. 'Tomorrow you can look at the all the slides you want. Believe me it won't take you very long to dispose of this Laveran business.'

The next day Farley's duties kept him at the Mission until well into the afternoon. As a result, it was not until four o'clock, when the sun was dipping low over the green expanse of the Maidan, that he arrived at the Presidency General Hospital. Had the circumstances been other than they were, he may well have been tempted to spend a few minutes admiring the restrained elegance of the hospital's red-brick buildings and the well-tended lawns and tree-shaded pathways that surrounded them. But being determined to make good use of such time as he had, Farley quickly ascertained the direction of Dr Cunningham's laboratory from an attendant and set off towards it at a brisk walk.

The laboratory was set well back within the hospital's spacious and thickly wooded grounds. It was screened from the main hospital complex by a tall thicket of bamboo, and upon catching his first glimpse of the building Farley was taken by surprise.

It looked nothing like any laboratory he had ever seen: certainly nothing could have been more unlike the sepulchral chambers of gloom that then served to house the laboratories of most universities in America and Europe. This was just an ordinary bungalow, of a type common to British military installations everywhere.

Standing in the shaded thicket with the bamboo stirring around him, Farley had an unaccustomed sense of unease. Casting a backward glance over his shoulder, Farley saw no one around him, neither in the thicket, nor in the bungalow. Yet he had the distinct feeling that his presence had not gone unnoticed. Within moments, as though in confirmation, the bungalow's front door flew open, and the tall rubicund figure of Dr Cunningham stepped out on the veranda. 'Ah there you are Farley,' he cried, 'they told me you were here. Well, don't just stand there man; come on in. Let's settle this business once and for all.'

Recovering, Farley made his way quickly up the bungalow's steps, and shook Cunningham's large, fleshy hand. After a quick exchange of greetings, the older man put a hand on his shoulder and steered him toward the laboratory's open door. Farley stepped in, only to stop dead in his tracks when he discovered that he was being minutely observed by a saree-clad woman and a young man dressed in pajamas and a laboratory tunic.

The woman was watching him with a look of such piercing enquiry that he could not avert his gaze from her. Dressed in a cheap and brightly coloured cotton saree, she was neither young nor old, perhaps in her late thirties. When she had finished with her examination, she seated herself on the floor, with her knees drawn up in front.

Cunningham must have noticed Farley's discomfiture, for he said: 'Don't pay the slightest attention to her; she loves to stare at people.'

'Who is she?' Farley asked in an undertone.

'Oh, she's just the sweeper-woman,' Cunningham said off-handedly. Only then did Farley notice that she was holding in her hand the mark of her trade, a sweeper's jharu.

'She's a bit of a dragon,' Cunningham continued, 'been here forever. You know what they're like: like to give visitors the once over. Don't let her put you off; there's no harm in her.'

Farley saw her exchanging a glance with the young man who was standing beside her and he had the distinct feeling that a smile and a nod had passed between them, an almost imperceptible gesture of dismissal. Then the woman rose to her feet, turned her back on him and went over to the far corner of the room, as though to indicate that she had exhausted her interest in him.

Farley felt the blood rushing to his face.

'Don't pay her any attention,' Cunningham said to Farley, with a wink, 'she's a little touched . . . you know.'

He motioned to the young man to present himself. 'And this chhokra-boy here,' he said with a loud satirical laugh, 'is a bearer who I've trained to help with my slides. I suppose you could call him my assistant.'

Leading the way between the laboratory's tables, Cunningham pointed to a microscope. 'You can work here,' he said to Farley. 'My bearer will get you your slides.' He allowed himself a snort of laughter as he let himself out: 'I hope you find what you are looking for.'

Farley seated himself at a microscope, and over the next hour and a half the assistant brought him several dozen slides to look at. Since the man was a menial employee Farley was not surprised that Cunningham had not taken the trouble to tell him his name. But now, as he sat watching him work, he was impressed by the young man's deftness: given his circumstances, his efficiency struck him as quite remarkable.

But the slides he presented to Farley held no surprises. They bore dry stains, and were of a familiar kind, with the black pigmented cells of malarial blood much in evidence. He had seen dozens like them as a research student in Baltimore. Of Laveran's parasite, he saw no sign whatever. Indeed, he would soon have abandoned the effort if it were not for an odd little incident.

After he had been looking into the microscope for an hour or so, Farley grew thirsty, and asked the young assistant for water. A tumbler was duly fetched and placed in front of him. He drank half the water and, wanting to save the rest for later, placed it within easy reach, just behind his microscope.

Several minutes later, glancing away from the microscope, he made the discovery that he could see the whole room behind him, mirrored on the convex surface of the glass tumbler. He thought no more of it, but the next time he looked up his eyes were arrested by a scene that was now unfolding behind him.

The assistant, who had gone over to fetch a tray of slides, was whispering with the woman in the saree. It was soon clear that it was he, Farley, they were talking about: the distorted reflections of their faces seemed to take on a grotesque and frightening quality as they nodded and pointed across the room. Farley quickly lowered his head to the microscope, while watching the glass out of the corner of his eye.

What he saw next was even more startling than what had passed before. At the end of the whispered conversation it was not the young assistant but the woman who went over to the stack of drawers by the wall; it was she who selected the slides that were to be presented to him for examination. Watching carefully, Farley saw her picking the slides out with a speed that indicated she was not only thoroughly familiar with the slides but knew exactly what they contained. Farley could now barely restrain himself. His mind began to spill over with questions: how had a woman, and an illiterate one at that, acquired such expertise? And how had she succeeded in keeping it secret from Cunningham? And how was it that she, evidently untrained and unaware of any of the principles on which such knowledge rested, had come to exercise such authority over the assistant? The more he reflected on it, the more convinced he became that she was keeping something from him; that had she wished she could have shown him what he was looking for, Laveran's parasite; and that she had chosen to deny it to him because, for some unfathomable reason, she had judged him unworthy.

Farley would now gladly have walked away from this place, this so-called laboratory, whose all-too-familiar instruments seemed to be turned to purposes as perverse as they were inscrutable. Yet he knew that if he left now he would forever afterwards be tormented by uncertainty and doubt. He had no option but to pursue his enquiry no matter where it led.

And so Farley willed himself to stay where he was, with his eye fixed upon the microscope, staring sightlessly at the meaningless slides that were placed in front of him by the young assistant. After a full half-hour had passed, he said to the young man: 'I have not seen any sign of the parasite today, but I have it on good authority that it does indeed exist. So, I shall have a word with Cunningham-sahib, and with his permission, I shall return tomorrow to continue my researches.'

At this a look of utter consternation descended on the assistant's hitherto smiling face. Farley saw him shooting a glance at the unnamed woman, who was watching them keenly from the other end of the laboratory. Then he launched upon a string of stammering protests: it was unnecessary to return the next day, there was nothing to be seen, it was just a pure waste of time, and anyway Cunningham-sahib would be away; better return later, some other day . . . in a fortnight, or a month hence, perhaps there would be something to see then . . .

The vehemence of his protests were such as to confirm Farley's suspicions: the man could not have indicated more clearly that he, and his silent companion across the room, were keen to rid themselves of him; that his presence the next day would disrupt some previously conceived connivance, some event or events that they had already planned, counting on Cunningham's absence.

Perceiving that he now held the advantage, Farley brushed past the pleading assistant, saying: 'Nevertheless I shall return tomorrow.'

With that he went to find Cunningham.

The Englishman was in the next room, seated on a chaise-longue, puffing dreamily on a long-handled pipe. When Farley asked for his permission to continue the next day, he blew out a plume of sweet-smelling smoke and cried: 'Why, certainly my boy! If you are determined to persist in your quest for this phantom of Laveran's, do come back, as often as you like. I'll tell them to expect you.'

On the point of taking his leave, Farley hesitated. He looked quickly about, to make sure that they were alone, and then, approaching the seated Englishman he dropped to his knees.

'If I may enquire sir,' he whispered in Cunningham's ear, 'under what circumstances did you admit this woman into your laboratory?'

'Mangala?' said Cunningham, pointing his pipe-stem over his shoulder.

'If that is her name, yes.'

'If you're asking me how I found her,' Cunningham said,

Amitav Ghosh

'the answer is I found her where I find all my bearers and assistants: at the new railway station—what do they call it?—oh yes, Sealdah.'

'At the railway station, sir?' gasped the astonished Farley.

'Exactly so,' said Cunningham. 'That's the place to go if you need a willing worker: always said so—it's full of people looking for a job and a roof over their heads. See for yourself the next time you're there.'

'But sir,' Farley exclaimed, 'to take on untrained and uneducated . . .'

'And who better to train one's assistants than oneself, my boy?' Cunningham countered. 'Far preferable, in my opinion, to being surrounded by over-eager and half-formed college students. One is spared the task of imparting much that is useless and unnecessary.'

'So it was you who trained the woman—Mangala?' Farley asked.

'Indeed I did,' said Cunningham, staring hazily into the middle distance. 'And a quicker pair of hands and eyes I had never seen before. But . . .'

Pulling a long face, Cunningham tapped his head with a finger. 'But she's not all there, you see,' he said, 'her mind's been wasted—by disease, or licentiousness or who knows what?'

'And the young man?' Farley asked. 'What about him?'

'He's not been here long,' Cunningham said. 'Mangala brought him here: said he was from her own part of the country.'

'And where is that?'

'Not far from where you are,' Cunningham said. 'I believe the place is called Renupur—you may have passed it on your way here.'

'Why yes,' said Farley. 'I passed through Renupur on my way to Calcutta.'

Farley was just about to ask the assistant's name when he heard a sound behind him. He rose and found himself looking directly at the woman, Mangala. She was glaring at him from across the room, and such was the anger in her gaze that it sent a chill down his back. As he made his way out, he noticed that she was conducting a whispered consultation with the young assistant.

Farley had barely reached the bamboo thicket in front of the laboratory when he heard footsteps racing behind him. Moments later the assistant caught up with him and asked in a voice of polite, almost beseeching enquiry, exactly when it was that he planned to come the next day. Determined to retain the advantage of surprise, Farley gave him a noncommittal reply: 'I shall come when I find myself within the vicinity. My arrival need not interrupt your work for the day.'

With that he turned his back on the crestfallen assistant and walked away.

Through much of the night, for no reason that he could adduce, Farley prayed. Yet he could find no name for what it was that faced him and why he feared it. And this in turn became his very fear, that he could not name what he knew he must confront. All next morning he stayed in his room, touching neither food nor water, and did not emerge from his cubicle until the hour was well past noon.

Thus, once again, it was late afternoon by the time he arrived at the Hospital. But today, unlike the day before, the sky was grey and overcast, and a strong wind was blowing across the Maidan. Approaching the laboratory, Farley had the feeling that the stands of bamboo that separated it from the hospital were alive, astir with movement. And when he stepped into the thicket he saw that there were indeed shadows ahead of him, on the path: three figures, cloaked and swathed, stumbling slowly towards the laboratory. Farley stopped, overcome with misgiving, and then, collecting himself, he went forward again. When he was but a few yards behind the figures, he saw that the little group consisted of a man in a dhoti and a saree-clad woman. They were bearing between them another, almost inert human figure. He approached them boldly, rattling his fob to make his presence known. They stopped and turned to face him.

Farley's eyes went immediately to the figure in the middle. It was a man, possibly young, possibly in middle age, it was impossible to tell, for the hooded face was ravaged beyond description, the eyes turned upwards, showing only the whites, the skin mottled, flecked with scabs, the teeth in the open, drooling mouth sloping towards the throat as though knocked backwards. Farley's glimpse of him was brief, but his diagnostic sense, honed by months of practice in Barich, told him instantly that the man was in the last stages of syphilitic dementia.

Overcome with pity, Farley stretched out a helping hand towards the stricken man. But no sooner had the man's companions caught sight of him, than they fled, melting away into the darkness. Farley stared after them and then headed down the path, to the laboratory.

When he was a few yards from the bungalow an unexpected sound came to his ears: a low chant, sung in unison by a number of voices. Slowing his pace, he listened carefully. It was soon evident that the source of the sound lay not in the bungalow but elsewhere. Looking carefully around, through the trees and bamboo thickets, Farley saw that a number of people had gathered around a low outhouse, a short distance away. They were squatting in a circle, around a fire, chanting to the accompaniment of hand-held brass cymbals, as though in preparation for a ritual or ceremony. Curious now, he hurried towards the outhouse, but just then the main door of the laboratory flew open and the young assistant came running out. Under the guise of an effusive welcome, he ushered Farley quickly towards the laboratory.

Just as he was about to enter the laboratory, Farley noticed that a great deal of activity was taking place in a nearby anteroom. The assistant tried to hurry him past but by dint of dragging his feet Farley managed to steal a quick glance into the room. The sight that met his eyes was so bewildering that he uttered no protest when his guide manoeuvred him through the laboratory door. What he saw was this: the woman Mangala was seated at the far end of the room, on a low divan, but alone and in an attitude of command, as though enthroned. By her side were several small bamboo cages, each containing a pigeon. Yet it was not the birds themselves, but rather the state they were in that amazed him. For they were slumped on the floors of their cages, shivering, evidently near death.

Nor was that all. On the floor, by the divan, clustered around the woman's feet, were some half-dozen people in various attitudes of supplication, some touching her feet, others lying prostrate. Two or three others were huddled against the wall, wrapped in blankets. Although Farley had glanced into their scarred, unseeing faces for no more than an instant, he recognized at once that they, like the man he had seen in the bamboo thicket, were syphilitics, in the final stages of the terrible disease.

Now the young assistant began once again to perform the charade of the previous day, fetching slides, and hurrying back and forth across the room as though egging him on towards some extraordinary discovery. Farley did not demur. He went mechanically about the business of examining the slides they presented him, while his mind remained fixed upon the extraordinary tableau he had glimpsed outside.

If there was much that was bewildering about the strange scenes outside, there was one aspect of it that was perfectly comprehensible to Farley, from his own experience. More than once in Barich he had found himself becoming the reluctant repository of the last despairing hopes of a frantic and fearful family that had arrived at the clinic's doorstep carrying a mortally ill relative through forests and over mountains. He knew the faces of those people, the beseeching supplication in their voices, the waning light of hope in their eyes. His conscience called out to him to go outside and tell them not to waste their hopes on whatever quackery it was that this woman offered; to expose the falsehoods that she and her minions had concocted to deceive those simple people. It was his duty, he knew, to tell them that mankind knew no cure for their condition; that this false prophetess was cheating them of money they could ill afford.

Yet he stayed where he was in the hope that, with some patience, he would be able to see the matter through to the end. Minute followed minute and hour followed hour, and still he kept his eye fixed upon the microscope, pretending to examine everything that was placed in front of him. As the hours wore on, he could feel the impatience growing around him; he could hear it in hurrying footsteps; he could feel it in the eyes that were boring through his back, willing him to leave so they could get on with whatever they had planned. But he stayed at his place, unmoving, immobile, to all appearances utterly absorbed in the slides.

Then at last, when the daylight had nearly faded, Farley called out: 'Bearer, kindly light the gas lamps. I have a great deal more to do.'

At this the assistant began to expostulate: 'But sir, there is nothing here, you will see nothing, you are simply wasting your time, for no reason.'

Farley had been hoping and waiting for precisely such a moment. Now, raising his voice, he said: 'Hear me well: I shall not leave this laboratory until I have seen the transformations that Laveran described. I am willing to stay here all night, if need be: I shall stay as long as I must.'

With that he lowered his head to the microscope once again. But in the meanwhile he had taken the precaution of placing the glass tumbler before him again, and now out of the corner of his eyes he saw the assistant snatching up a set of clean slides and slipping away to the anteroom.

Once he was gone, Farley made his way silently across the laboratory. Flattening himself against the wall, he crept towards the door until he had manoeuvred himself into a position where he could look into the anteroom without himself being detected.

Farley had steeled himself for anything, or so he thought, but he was unprepared for what he saw next. First the assistant went up to the woman, Mangala, still regally ensconced on her divan, and touched his forehead to her feet. Then in the manner of a courtier or acolyte he whispered some word of advice in her ear. She nodded in agreement and took the clean slides from him. Reaching for the birdcages she allowed her hand to rest upon each of the birds in turn, as though she were trying to ascertain something. Then she seemed to come to a decision; she reached into a cage, and took one of the shivering birds into her lap. She folded her hands over it and her mouth began to move as though muttering a prayer. Then suddenly a scalpel appeared in her right hand; she held the bird away from her and with a single flick of her wrist beheaded the dying pigeon. Once the flow of blood had lessened, she picked up the clean slides, smeared them across the severed neck, and handed them to the assistant.

Farley had the presence of mind to go hurrying across the room to his microscope. No sooner had he seated himself than the young man came in.

'Please examine these now sir,' he said with a wide smile. 'Maybe you will at last achieve success in your quest.'

Farley turned the slides over his hand. 'But,' he said, 'these are not properly stained: the blood on them is still fresh.'

'Yes sir,' said the assistant, offhandedly. 'Perhaps that which you are looking for can only be seen in freshly drawn blood.'

Farley placed the slide under the microscope and looked into the instrument. At first he saw nothing unusual; nothing that would have indicated to him, had he not known, that this exhibit came from a pigeon. He noticed the familiar granules of malarial pigment. But then suddenly he saw movement; under his eyes amoeboid forms began to squirm and move, undulating slowly across the glassy surface. Then all at once there was a flurry of movement and they began to disintegrate: it was then that he saw Laveran's rods appear, hundreds of them, tiny cylindrical things, with their pointed, penetrating heads piercing the bloody miasma.

The sweat began to drip off Farley's forehead now, as he watched the horned creatures burrowing, writhing, wriggling in frantic search. His breath grew laboured; his head began to spin. He sat up, gasping, the sight of these wilful, struggling creatures still vivid in his eyes. His gaze strayed to the window, and discovered a row of faces lined up against the glass, watching him, as he squirmed in his seat, mopping his brow. His eyes locked with Mangala's; she was standing in front of all the others, staring at him, smiling to herself. Clutched in her hand, in full view, was the body of the decapitated bird, the blood still oozing from its macabre wound.

'Tell him,' the woman said with a mocking smile, 'tell him that what he sees is the creature's member entering the body of its mate, doing what men and women must do . . .'

And here, at this point of revelation, which shows that Farley had already arrived at the conclusion that was to make his erstwhile team-mate famous, the narrative ends. For now, unable to contain himself any longer, Farley flung the slides at the woman and stalked quickly out of the laboratory.

But before franking the letter for the post, next morning, Farley added a few scribbled lines in the margin: 'In haste: much that I feared has been confirmed in these last hours. Shortly before matins, there was a knock on my door: it was Cunningham's young assistant. He told me—oh so many things—I shall write of them all to you in time. Suffice it to say for the present, that everything is other than what it appears to be, a phantom of itself. The young man has promised to reveal everything to me if I would but accompany him to his birthplace. Fortunately the place of which he spoke is not far from the location of my clinic. We are to leave tomorrow: I shall write again and in greater detail, dear friend, once I know more . . .'

But Elijah Farley never reached Barich: he disappeared during the journey, never to be seen again. The police discovered that he had indeed boarded the train at Sealdah, as scheduled, but had disembarked before his destination—at a remote, rarely used station called Renupur, in severe monsoon weather. A guard was said to have reported later that a young man had been seen carrying his luggage.

Abruptly Ava began to beep: Rest indecipherable, unable to continue . . .

twenty-two

Murugan could not get to sleep.

Sweltering under the mosquito net, he lay awake, watching the ceiling fan beat the heavy monsoon air, its stubbly blades flashing hypnotically in the thin crack of light that was shining through the stubbornly unfastenable balcony door. The bedclothes had bunched up around his waist in moist, sweat-soaked clusters. Taking off his vest, he rolled it into a ball and dropped it out of the mosquitonet. He was naked now, except for his cotton boxer shorts. The generator was still pounding away at the wedding down the road. The music seemed even louder now. But somehow, despite all that noise, he could hear the mosquitoes clearly, droning patiently around the bed, testing for openings, gathering in excitement every time a hand or a foot brushed against the fabric. Soon he couldn't tell whether the buzz was inside the net or outside; whether the tingling in his limbs came from their interrupted probings or the chafing of the moist sheets.

He flattened himself against the mattress and tried to lie still. Spreadeagling his arms and legs he waited—waited to discover whether they were really inside the net; whether his inflamed skin would allow him to discern the feel of their bites.

It was strangely intimate to lie there like that, against damp cloth, spread out in that elementally open posture of invitation, of embrace, of longing. When he looked down at his body, lying flat on the bed, he could not tell whether he was waiting for them to show themselves to him, or whether he was showing himself to them: displaying himself in those minute detailed ways that only they were small enough to see, to understand, because only they had eyes that were designed to see not the whole but the parts, each in their uniqueness. Involuntarily he flexed his shoulders, arching his back, offering himself up, waiting to discover where they would touch him first, where he would first detect the tingling prick of their bites, on his chest or his belly, on the muscle of his forearm or the weathered codpiece of his elbow.

The fan became a blur; the mosquito net melted into a milky fog. He was floating outside it now, looking in, at people he knew, knew very well, even if only through books and papers. And now he was in again, inside the net; he was one of them too, lying on a hard, hospital charpai, stripped, naked, watching the English doctor uncork a test-tube full of mosquitoes into his net. In his fist he still clutched the coins he had been given, at the hospital gates. He held on to them tightly, savouring their feel, their reassurance; they were so cool to the touch, so hard-edged; they made everything so simple, so clean: a handful of coins, a rupee, for handing on the thing that lived in his blood, for safekeeping, to the doctor.

He saw faces around his bed now, rippling, like reeds, beyond the surface of the mosquito net, faces that were watching him, studying his body, as it lay there in its urgent nakedness; faces he knew, or recognized, a grey-haired woman smiling through twinkling bifocals; a gap-toothed boy, grinning, circling the bed; an old man with tears in his eyes, peering at him in the darkness; a thin, young woman, holding hands with her friend. They were standing around his bed in attitudes of concern, like nurses and doctors' assistants, waiting for him to sink into anaesthetized oblivion.

And now the bearded Englishman reappears, dressed in his white coat, smoking a cigar, armed with half a dozen test-tubes; he reaches in, with a little butterfly net, pulls it out and expertly traps an engorged mosquito in a test-tube, covering the opening with a handkerchief-wrapped thumb. He holds up the test-tube and shows it to the others and they clap; they are excited, full of encouragement.

The Englishman draws mightily on his cigar and puffs into the test-tube; the insect dies, the tiny buzzing creature that is carrying his blood inside it. The doctor holds it up and shows it to the others, they reach for it eagerly; they want to see it for themselves; this extrusion of his flesh, and in their eagerness the test-tube slips from their fingers, falls to the floor, shatters, filling the room with a thin tinkle of breaking glass.

Murugan sat suddenly upright, the sweat pouring off his face, not sure whether he was still dreaming or awake. The net was buzzing with mosquitoes; he could see them dancing like motes, in the finger of light that bisected his bed. His whole body was aflame, covered with bites. He had been scratching himself furiously in his sleep; he could see blood on his fingernails, and on the sheets.

He climbed out of the bed and walked around the room, scratching hard. The air was heavy with the smell of his own sweat. He opened the door and stepped out on to the balcony.

The street below was empty now, but the generator was still running in the building down the street. The archway at the entrance to the wedding seemed brighter than ever, flooding the street with light. Relays of workers were running back and forth through the entrance, loading their bamboo hand-carts with stacks of folding chairs and tables.

Suddenly, with a squeal of rubber, a taxi came shooting around the Rawdon Street corner and stopped at the gates of the old mansion at number three. A woman in a saree stepped out. She was too far away for Murugan to get a look at her face, but the light from the wedding arch was just strong enough to give him a glimpse of a streak of white, running through her hair. Taking a key out of her purse, she unlocked the gates and went in.

Murugan waited a minute to see if she would come out again and then went back into the bedroom. He was getting into bed when he heard the click of a closing door somewhere near at hand. Getting out of bed, he stuck his head into the corridor. The flat was dark and still. He fetched a torch and made his way across the drawing room to Mrs Aratounian's bedroom. Lowering himself on one knee, beside the closed door, he put his ear to the crack. He heard a soft, rhythmic sound inside: like gentle snoring—or possibly a fan. It was hard to be sure.

Murugan hesitated, wondering whether he ought to make sure that Mrs Aratounian was all right. He decided against it and tiptoed quickly back to his bedroom. Just as he was about to step through the door he felt a sharp stabbing pain in his right heel.

Swearing softly, he stooped to investigate. There was a small gash on his toe. He had cut it on a sharp object, something that was lying on the floor, glinting in the half-light.

He picked it up and looked at it. It was an inch-long shard of thin glass, probably from some kind of tube.

twenty-three

─────────

It was past one when Sonali decided to go looking for Romen: she couldn't keep still and sleep was out of the question.

Fortunately, at exactly the right moment, one of her neighbours came home from a party, in a taxi. Snatching up her handbag, Sonali ran down and jumped in, without really giving any thought to where she would go. On an impulse, recalling Romen's overheard conversation at the gates of the Wicket Club, she told the taxi driver to go to Robinson Street.

She couldn't think of what Romen might be doing there at this time of the night. Yet somehow, when the taxi stopped at the gates of the old house, she had an inexplicable feeling that Romen was inside. Fortunately he'd left behind a set of keys at her flat a few days ago: she'd put it in her handbag and forgotten to give it back.

She managed to find the key to the gate, but once she was in she wasn't sure of what to do next. She made her way down the gravel path, to the portico and looked in through the door. It was very dark inside; she couldn't see very far. Cupping her hands, she shouted: 'Romen, are you there?'

She wasn't surprised when there was no answer: a generator was making a terrific noise next door. She could hardly hear her voice herself.

She always carried a small torch in her handbag, for power-cuts. She took it out and shone the light into the vast hallway ahead. The beam circled slowly through the darkness, picking out randomly scattered piles of mattresses, charpais and battered cooking utensils.

Romen had brought Sonali to the house once, a few months before, to show off his new acquisition. The hallway was full of people then, cooking, eating, sleeping, feeding their children. The entire construction gang was living in the gutted shell of the house. They were from Nepal and there were about thirty of them altogether, not including the old women who had been brought along to look after the children. They cooked their meals in a paved courtyard at the back and slept in the hallways and under the portico, spreading out their mattresses and charpais wherever they could. They were all related, Romen had told her, sons, grandsons, daughters-in-law, sons' wives, mothers, aunts: a whole village on the move.

She looked around once again, peering into the uneasy shadows that skimmed over the murky gloom of the hallway. Their belongings were all there, just as she remembered, but none of them seemed to be anywhere in sight.

Crossing the threshold, she took a few tentative steps into the hall. Then she caught a whiff of an odd smell and came to a sudden halt. It smelled like smoke at first, and she had a moment of panic, wondering whether there was a fire somewhere within. She sniffed the air again, and was startled to catch the distinctive odour of incense, the sweet, acrid smell of burning camphor. It was sweeping into the hall in clouds, from somewhere at the back.

She took a few more steps into the darkness, and now her ears, growing accustomed to the mechanical roar next door, picked up another sound: a hollow, rhythmic noise just distinguishable from the throbbing of the generator—a sound of drumming, familiar from pujas and festival days, when drums pounded in worship all over the city.

The sound grew louder as Sonali approached the grand, ceremonial staircase that lay at the back of the hall. Suddenly the curved banisters were in front of her, their ragged, splintered rails wreathed in smoke. Shining the torch upwards she saw that smoke was pouring into the stairwell from above. It hung thick around her, diffusing the beam of the torch into a milk-white glow.

The staircase was a rusted shell; the last time she saw it the workers had just begun the job of stripping it down to the steel scaffolding, as a preliminary to restoring it to its original glory, when it had swept upwards in a grand curve of mahogany and wrought iron. 'The structure is still sound,' Romen had told her. She had followed him gingerly, stepping from foothold to foothold, and had counted herself lucky when she made it to the top without a fall. Looking at it now, curling up into the smoke, like a gigantic vine, she shied away, wiping her watering eyes. Then, making up her mind, she took a grip on the banisters and pulled herself up a couple of steps.

She stood on a steel rail and shone the torch ahead until it fell upon a length of rusty metal, lying exposed under a plank of rotten wood, a couple of steps further up. That was what Romen had said to do, she remembered now: don't step on the wood—keep to the steel frame. She leaned forward and jumped. Her foot slipped but she managed to catch hold of the banisters. Trying not to look down, she shut her eyes and breathed deeply, struggling to steady herself. She climbed crablike to the next foothold, biting the torch between her teeth, using her hands as well as her feet. She went up the next few steps the same way, rounding the curve of the staircase. After a few more steps she stopped to catch her breath and pointed the torch ahead. The landing at the top of the staircase was no more than a few yards away now. The drumming seemed very close; she could feel it reverberating in the metal, under her hands and feet. When her hand reached the landing she took the torch out of her mouth and placed it on a ledge. She heaved herself up and collapsed on the floorboards.

The drumming was all around her now, so loud and close that she could not tell which direction it was coming from. As she was turning to look, her saree brushed against the torch and knocked it over. It rolled a couple of inches, eluding her hand, and fell off the edge of the landing. She watched as it

Amitav Ghosh

went spinning down the stairwell, its beam circling around the hall until it hit the floor and went out.

Stifling a sob, she sat up. She began to pat the floorboards around her, trying to orient herself, swivelling all the way around, banging her hands on the splintering wood. Then it dawned on her that she no longer knew which way she was facing—towards the staircase or away from it: her disorientation was complete.

She could feel her chest constricting. She knew she would panic if she stayed on the floor any longer, flailing about, blinded by sweat and smoke, deafened by the noise. She climbed to her feet and saw a dull orange glow somewhere ahead of her, within the whirling clouds of smoke. She took a step towards it and then lowered herself to her hands and knees. She couldn't trust herself to walk on the rotten floor and began to crawl instead, inching slowly towards the glow, shutting her eyes against the stinging smoke.

When she had advanced a couple of yards, she saw that the light was shining out of an arched doorway. Now suddenly she knew where she was: she was facing the entrance to the largest room in the house, a huge wood-panelled, mirrored chamber that had once served as a reception room. Romen had insisted on bringing her up to see it—it was the pride of the house, he said, and he was going to restore it to its former state.

She pushed herself closer to the archway and figures began to take shape in the smoky glow ahead of her. They were sitting cross-legged on the floor, with their backs to her, facing in the other direction. She saw a couple of heads first, and then more, and more, until the whole room seemed to be filled with people. They were chanting something and some were keeping time with drums while others were beating little hand-held cymbals.

She could not bring herself to go forward and there was no going back; she would never be able to find her way down without the torch. Then she remembered something that Romen had showed her on their visit: the reception room had a small raised gallery at the back, a minstrel gallery Romen had called it. He had led her up to it, to show her how immense the room looked from up there. She tried to calm herself now, to think back to that day, several months ago. They had reached the gallery by climbing up a narrow steep staircase, almost like a ladder. Sonali made an effort to calm herself so she could recall where those stairs were.

She crept forward another yard or so and spotted the entrance to a little anteroom to her right. Edging towards it, she drew level with the entrance and glanced in. At the far corner, she spotted the opening that led to the gallery, glowing orange against the velvety darkness of the room. There were no people in the anteroom, so far as she could tell.

She slipped around the corner and rose to her feet. Then she edged along the wall, with one arm stretched out until her hand hit upon the cold metal of the step-ladder. She stepped back and looked at the opening to the gallery: it was directly above her now. All she could see was the flickering orange glow of a fire, reflected through clouds of smoke.

She took a grip on the ladder and climbed quickly up. At the top, the smoke suddenly welled up in her face, forcing itself into her lungs. She stuffed the end of her saree into her mouth, in an effort to choke back a cough and looked in.

The narrow, flimsy-looking gallery was empty. Pulling her feet up, she sank down and flattened herself on the floor of the gallery. She noticed now that the smoke was even thicker here than it was below; trapped by the ceiling, it swirled around the gallery in dense clouds. Lowering her face, she held her saree pressed against her watering eyes. They were smarting so much now that she knew she would not be able to keep them open for more than a few seconds at a time.

When the stinging had dulled a little, she thrust her head to the edge and looked down. She caught a glimpse of the tops of dozens of heads, some male, some female, young and old, packed in close together. Their faces were obscured by the smoke and flickering firelight but she spotted a couple of weatherbeaten Nepali faces that she was sure she had seen before, when Romen last brought her to the house. For the rest it seemed like a strangely motley assortment of people: men in patched lungis, a handful of brightly painted women in cheap nylon sarees, a few young students, several prim-looking middle-class women—people you would never expect to see together.

Narrowing her eyes against the smoke, Sonali followed their gaze to the fire, burning at the far end of the room: a heap of coal-dust was glowing red in a brazier, improvised from a battered cement pan. Then she had a shock: somewhere among the faces around the fire she spotted a face she knew. She looked again: it was a skeletally thin boy in a T-shirt. Sonali reeled: it was the boy who had been living in her servant's room for the last few months, there could be no doubt about it. He was smiling, saying something to the person next to him.

There was a small clearing in front and every now and again the boy and the others around him would reach in and touch something. Sonali could not see what it was: her view was blocked by several closely packed heads. The crowd was hunched thickly around whatever it was that was lying there; everybody in the room seemed to be staring at that space.

Sonali shut her smarting eyes and let her head drop to the floor. Her saree was drenched and she could barely move her limbs. The floor seemed to turn under her: she knew she was very close to losing consciousness.

Then there was a stir in the crowd and Sonali forced herself to look down again. A figure had come out of the shadows: it was a woman and she was dressed very plainly—in a crisply starched saree, with a white scarf tied around her hair. Her figure was short and matronly and Sonali took her to be in late middle age. She looked very familiar, Sonali was certain she was someone she had once known but hadn't seen in years.

She had a cloth bag slung over one shoulder, an ordinary cotton jhola, of the kind that every student takes to college. In her left hand she was carrying a bamboo birdcage. She seated herself by the fire and placed the bag and the birdcage beside her. Then reaching into the bag, her movements brisk and businesslike, she took out two scalpels and a pair of glass plates.

She arranged the plates and the scalpel in front of her, on a piece of white cloth, and reached into her bag again. She took out a small clay figure and touched it to her forehead, before setting it down beside her. Then she reached out, placed her hands on whatever it was that was lying before the fire and smiled—a look of extraordinary sweetness came over her face.

Raising her voice, the woman said to the crowd, in archaic rustic Bengali: 'The time is here, pray that all goes well for our Laakhan, once again.'

Suddenly Sonali was struck by a terrible sense of foreboding. Raising her head as high as she dared she looked again into the space by the fire. She caught a glimpse of a body, lying on the floor.

The drumming rose to a crescendo: there was a flash of bright metal and a necklace of blood flew up and fell sizzling on the fire.

Sonali's head crashed to the floor and everything went dark.

The Day After

twenty-four

It was seven fifteen in the morning and Urmila was nearing the end of her tether. She was in the kitchen, grinding spices, perspiration dripping off her face on to her grease-spotted saree. She had already been up an hour: she had given her parents their breakfast; she had cleaned the kitchen; she had fed and bathed her nephew and niece; she had washed her younger brother's uniform for his afternoon football match. She would have to leave within the hour if she was to be on time for the press conference at the Great Eastern Hotel. But there was still the business of the fish to deal with, and there was no sign of a fish-seller yet.

Urmila looked out of the kitchen window, trying to estimate how long it would take her to run to Gariahat Bazaar and back. She was in trouble, she knew, unless something miraculous happened soon: it would take at least half an hour if she had to go down to the bazaar, what with picking out a fish and bargaining and all the rest—there was no way around that.

The flat was on the third floor, boxed in on every side by other multi-storey buildings. The kitchen window was the only part of the flat that had a view, other than the balcony. It commanded a glimpse of a sliver of the city: she could see the ragged, spreading skyline of south Calcutta stretching away longitudinally, from the park below—a vista of mildew-darkened roofs vanishing into the smudged glow of a lowering, monsoon sky.

Down below, in the park, the usual half-dozen cricket matches were already in progress. She could hear the thud of wood on leather and a few drowsy voices, shouting encouragement. In another corner of the park, half a dozen men were busy swinging clubs and doing push-ups, below the tin roof of a body-building school. Further away, RashBehari Avenue was stirring in anticipation of rush hour. But the roadsides were still relatively empty except for a few shoppers hurrying back from Gariahat Bazaar, along the short-cut, with clumps of vegetables hanging over the tops of their nylon shopping bags.

The short-cut to Gariahat Bazaar curved off from the main avenue a few hundred yards away. It was a long, narrow lane whose principal landmark was a rambling, old-fashioned house, with a gravel driveway, a pillared portico and a well-tended garden. The house was clearly visible from the kitchen: Urmila's eyes often fell on it when she was working there. It was Romen Haldar's residence.

Just then the doorbell rang.

'The bell's ringing Urmi,' her mother called out from her bedroom. 'Can't you hear it?'

Her father was out on the balcony with his paper, going through the 'Announcements' column, a favourite morning pastime. He was reading the entries out aloud to himself, spitting out the names like chewed fish-bones. He put the paper on his knees and looked up. 'Who is it?' he called out. 'Someone go and have a look.'

Almost immediately her sister-in-law's voice came floating out of her bedroom: she was feeding her baby and couldn't get out of bed. Her older brother had already left to catch a morning train. Her younger brother was in the bathroom, snapping his fingers and singing 'Disco diwana'.

Then her mother called out, in her softest, most cajoling voice: 'Go and have a look Urmi, no one will if you don't . . .'

Amitav Ghosh

I'm busy here, she wanted to scream. Can't you see; I'm busy here, trying to get things ready before going to work . . .'

The doorbell rang again and now her six-year-old nephew ran into the kitchen and began to tug at her saree. 'Open the door, Urmi-pishi,' sang the boy. 'Urmi-pishi-kirmi-pishi, open the door, open the door . . .'

She slammed the heavy pestle on the pitted surface of the mortar, brilliantly coloured now with turmeric and chilli, and pushed past her nephew, who was lying flat on the floor. The boy stretched out his hands as she went by and fastened his fingers on the bottom of her saree. She dragged him along for a couple of paces and then slapped his clenched fist.

He erupted into a wail and went racing to his parents' bedroom, crying: 'She hit me, she hit me, kirmi-pishi hit me . . .'

As she undid the doorlatch, Urmila heard her sister-in-law's voice break into a scream: 'How dare you hit my son?'

She flung the door open and found a young man standing outside, beside a large covered basket. She had never seen him before; he looked very young to be a vendor. He was dressed in a lungi and a greying T-shirt.

'You slut,' the voice followed Urmila through the open doorway. 'You think I don't know what you're up to, coming home late every night? I'll teach you a lesson; I'll teach you to hit my children . . .'

Urmila stepped out and slammed the door behind her. Embarrassment lent a note of shrillness to her voice as she snapped: 'What's the matter? What do you want?'

The young man gave her a cheerful grin, exposing a wide gap in his front teeth. Urmila was suddenly ashamed, mortified at the thought that she had allowed her sister-in-law to provoke her in front of a complete stranger. Inadvertently, she drew the back of her hand across her forehead. Her face contorted into a grimace as the ground spices burnt a smarting furrow across her face and brow. She wiped her eyes hurriedly with the end of her saree.

'What do you want?' she said again, more evenly.

The young man was squatting beside the basket now. With another smile he pulled back a layer of paper and plastic to reveal a pile of fish, gleaming silver in the early morning light.

He grinned. 'I just came to ask whether you need any fish this morning didi,' he said. 'That's all.'

twenty-five

―――――――――

'I've never seen you here before,' Urmila said, kneeling beside the basket of fish. She began to examine the fish, pulling back their gills—out of habit, for today she really didn't care what she bought or for how much.

The young fish-seller gave her a cheerful smile, bobbing his head. 'I'll be coming regularly now,' he said. 'Buy one and see: I have the best fish in the market, fresh out of the water.'

'Every fish-seller says that,' said Urmila. 'It doesn't mean a thing.'

The fish-seller bristled. 'If you don't believe me, go and ask around,' he said. 'I sell to all the best houses. Why, do you know Romen Haldar's house, in the next lane?'

Urmila looked up, raising an eyebrow.

'Let me tell you,' he said proudly. 'They buy all their fish from me. Only from me: you can go and ask if you like.'

Reaching into the basket he moved a couple of fish out of the way. 'Here, let me show you something,' he said. 'Do you see this one here, this big ilish? I'm keeping that for them. I'm on my way there right now. I told them I'd bring them something special this morning.'

'I'll take it,' said Urmila.

The fish-seller shook his head. 'No,' he said, grinning. 'I can't give you that one: that's for them. But I'll give you this other one, it's just as good—here, look.'

Urmila gave him a perfunctory nod. 'All right,' she said, 'that one.' She told him to cut it up and went in to fetch her purse. By the time she came back, the fish-seller had a packet ready for her: he had wrapped the fish in bits of paper and stuffed it into a plastic bag.

Urmila clicked her tongue in annoyance when she saw the packet. 'You shouldn't have wrapped it up,' she said.

The fish-seller mumbled an excuse and began counting his money. Urmila went inside. She had no time to lose now. Hurrying into the kitchen she tipped the contents of the packet into a plastic plate, in the sink. The chunks of fish fell out with a thump, scattering all over the sink. Urmila grimaced: the paper in which the fish was wrapped had turned into a soggy mess. She touched a piece of fish gingerly and the tip of her finger came away with a bit of paper attached. She had trouble shaking it off; it had dissolved into a wad of sticky glue.

Wrinkling her nose in disgust, she stole a quick glance out of the window. RashBehari Avenue was jammed with buses and minibuses, all belching thick clouds of smoke. She had no more than half an hour to spare if she was to get to the Great Eastern Hotel in time for the press conference. She began to scrub furiously.

After a few minutes she realized that her scrubbing was only making matters worse by working the paper deeper into the chunks of fish. She threw up her hands, thoroughly irritated now, and peeled a scrap of paper off her fingers. It was thin, cheap xerox paper: the kind that accumulated in vast quantities in the *Calcutta* copying room.

So this is where it all ends up, she thought, as fish-wrapping.

She glanced at the plastic bag again and saw that it was still full of paper. A few bits and pieces were dry, the blood hadn't seeped through to them yet. She tipped the paper out on the counter and held a sheet flat with the back of her hand.

It was a large, legal-size photocopy of a page of very fine English newsprint. The typeface was unfamiliar, old-fashioned: she knew at a glance that the page wasn't from any of the current English-language papers printed in Calcutta. She made space for it on a shelf and spread it out.

The print was so fine she had trouble reading it. She turned on a light and looked at it again, turning instinctively to the top margin to look for the paper's name. The masthead said, *The Colonial Services Gazette*, in beautiful Gothic characters. Beside the name was a dateline: 'Calcutta, the twelfth of January, 1898.' The page was divided into eight columns, each containing dozens of announcements of a routine kind: 'D. Attwater Esq. transferred to Almora as Deputy Magistrate, Revenues', 'So-and-so to quit his post in the Port Authority, Calcutta, in order to become Assistant Harbourmaster in Singapore', and so on. Urmila skimmed quickly through it. She could not see why anyone would go to the trouble of copying something like that, a record of old bureaucratic appointments. She was about to sweep it into the wastebin when she noticed that one of the announcements had been underlined, in ink.

Squinting at the page she read: 'Leave approved for Surgeon-Colonel D.D. Cunningham, Presidency General Hospital, Calcutta, January 10-15 . . .'

Urmila cast a quick glance at the clock above the dining table. She really had no time to lose now, not a minute; if she didn't get the fish done in the next ten minutes she would be late for the press conference.

She knew she ought to get on with the cooking. But instead she found herself pulling out the two other bits of paper left in the plastic bag.

The next page was even more puzzling than the first. It was a copy of a sheet of paper with a list of names under an elaborate and unfamiliar logo. Holding the logo up to the light, she saw that it said 'South-Western Railways'. Handwritten beneath it were the words: 'January 10, 1898, Passenger list, Compartment 8'. Under this was a list of names. Urmila looked quickly through them; they seemed like British names. She read a couple of them to herself, spelling them out slowly: 'Major Evelyn Urquhart, D. Craven, Esq., Sir Andrew

Acton, C.I.E. . . .' Then she noticed that a name at the bottom of the list had been underlined. It was: 'C.C. Dunn, Esq'.

That's strange, she thought. The other name was D.D. something.

She didn't bother to look. She pushed the page aside and spread out the only remaining sheet.

It was a copy of another page of *The Colonial Services Gazette*. This one was dated January 30, 1898. She cast a quick glance over it: another long list of transfers, leaves approved, positions filled. Again one of the announcements was underlined. It read: 'The public is notified that Surgeon-Colonel D.D. Cunningham is currently on leave pending his retirement. He will be replaced by Surgeon-Major Ronald Ross of the Indian Medical Service.'

'Haven't you started cooking yet Urmi?' her mother called out from the bedroom. 'It's getting late.'

Urmila started. She was furious with herself now for wasting so much time staring at used xerox paper. She snatched the sheets off the shelf, flung them aside and hurried over to the sink.

The paper-wrapped fish had turned into a stinking, glutinous mess. It was all she could do not to vomit into the sink.

twenty-six

Suddenly Urmila found herself shaking with indignation. She knew she was on the verge of one of those periodic seizures of outrage, which sometimes gripped her when she was working on her investigative articles. She was so angry now that she stopped caring about the time—about the press conference at the Great Eastern, the news editor, even the Minister of Communications from Delhi. She stuffed the pieces of fish back into the plastic bag and marched to the door. On her way out she snatched up the sheets of xerox paper, crumpling them into a ball, in her fist.

Her mother had come out of her bedroom to see what the matter was. Her mouth fell open, seeing Urmila marching out of the flat in her grease-spattered saree, clutching a ball of paper and a bag of fish. 'Where are you going Urmi?' she cried.

'I'm going to return this fish,' Urmila said, letting herself out. 'We can't eat this: it'll kill us. Look at this filthy paper it's wrapped in. I'm going to make that man take it back: I paid more than a hundred rupees for this fish. I'm not going to be cheated like this.'

The front door of their flat opened on a narrow, corridor-like veranda that served three other apartments beside their own. Urmila was certain she would find the fish-seller outside, knocking on the doors of the other flats. But the veranda was empty: she looked to her right and then to her left. There was no sign of the young man with the basket of fish.

Urmila stood undecided for a moment and then she went to the neighbouring door and rang the bell. Several minutes later the door opened and a middle-aged man dressed in pajamas and a cotton vest looked out suspiciously. 'Yes?' he said. 'What do you want?'

Urmila was momentarily at a loss for words: a long history of disputes and quarrels lay between this family and hers. Trying to smile, she said: 'Did a fish-seller ring your bell this morning? A young man in a T-shirt and a checked lungi?'

The man looked her over sardonically, his eyes travelling slowly from the plastic bag stuffed with fish, to her crumpled spice-stained saree.

Urmila held her ground. 'Did you see him?' she said again.

'No,' said the man. 'We were asleep until you rang the bell.'

'What?' said Urmila. 'The fish-seller didn't come here? With the basket . . .'

'What did I tell you?' the man snapped. 'Didn't I tell you we were fast asleep?' He slammed the door on her.

Urmila ran up one flight to the fourth floor, the highest in the building. The floors in their building were exactly alike, each with four identical flats, lined up next to each other along an open veranda. There was no sign of the fish-seller on the fourth floor. She turned and went pelting down, stopping at each landing to look up and down the long verandas. The man wasn't anywhere in the building so far as she could tell. She checked the veranda on the ground floor twice, and then ran out to the small paan shop on the pavement, near the entrance to the building.

The stall-owner was sitting cross-legged on the counter, saying a prayer before starting the day's work. She had to wait until he opened one eye. 'What's this?' he said, in surprise, staring at her dishevelled hair and her crumpled night-time saree. 'Why are you outside in this state?'

She asked him about the fish-seller, and he shook his head: 'No, I haven't seen anyone; I've just got here as you can see.'

She turned on her heel and headed down the road.

'Where are you going?' the paan-wallah called after her.

'I'm not going to let that man rob me in broad daylight,' she said. 'I'm going to find him and get my money back.'

The paan-wallah gave a derisory laugh. 'It's no use,' he said. 'Those vendors are too clever for the likes of you.'

'We'll see,' Urmila shouted back, over her shoulder.

RashBehari was thronged with its usual morning crowd of pedestrians, some hurrying towards Lansdowne, some towards Gariahat. People turned to stare at Urmila as she went marching along swinging her clenched fists. There were a few jeers and catcalls from loiterers, standing against the railings and squatting by the road. Urmila walked on, oblivious of her soiled saree and her soggy bag of fish.

She turned into a lane, off RashBehari, and almost before she knew it she was standing before a pair of tall, wrought-iron gates. A portly chowkidar in khaki uniform was on guard at the gate. Right above him was an elaborately carved marble name-plate, set deep in the wall. It bore the name 'Romen Haldar' written in richly ornamented, cursive Bengali.

The chowkidar looked her up and down, suspiciously. 'What's your business here?' he said, placing himself in front of her, rapping his stick on his thigh.

Urmila pushed him aside, barely pausing in her stride. 'You don't need to concern yourself with my business,' she said. 'You stay where you are and think about your own business.'

She marched off, down the driveway towards the covered porch that led into the house. The chowkidar gave chase, waving his stick and shouting: 'Stop! You can't go in.'

'Tell me something,' Urmila threw back at him, over her shoulder. 'Did the fish-seller come here today?'

'What fish-seller?' said the chowkidar. 'We don't have any fish-sellers coming here. Do you know whose house this is?'

'Yes,' said Urmila.

With a sudden burst of speed, the chowkidar ran around her, trying to block the driveway. But Urmila was used to forcing her way past doorkeepers and secretaries; he was no match for her. She stepped around him, unimpressed. He followed, mouthing imprecations.

The chowkidar's shouts caused a stir inside the house. An elderly man appeared on the porch, pen in hand, dressed in a starched white kurta and dhoti. 'What's the matter?' he demanded, peering irritably down the driveway.

He spotted Urmila and a frown appeared on his forehead. 'Yes, what is it?' he said, looking her over distastefully. 'What do you want? No appointments today—all appointments have been cancelled.'

Urmila ignored him. 'I want to see Mr Romen Haldar,' she said.

The secretary glowered at her, over the rim of his spectacles. 'What business do you have with Mr Haldar?' he asked.

'I want to ask him about a fish-seller who came to my flat this morning,' Urmila said defiantly.

The secretary's jaw dropped. 'Fish-seller?' he said. 'What fish-seller?'

'A young man,' Urmila said. She tried to describe him but all she could recall of his appearance was a fading T-shirt and a big, gap-toothed grin. 'He sells fish here regularly,' she said. 'He was on his way here right now, he told me so.'

She lifted up the packet of fish and held it out towards the secretary. 'Look: he sold me this just this morning.'

The secretary recoiled. 'Keep that filthy thing away from me,' he cried, snatching back a spotless, cotton-clothed arm. 'What nonsense is this? No fish-seller has set foot in this house for years.'

'He told me that he sold fish to Mr Haldar.'

'He was lying,' said the secretary.

Urmila stared at him, her head reeling. 'But the man told me . . .' she began.

The secretary made an impatient gesture. 'Enough,' he said. 'You can be off now.'

Urmila's tone hardened. 'No,' she said. 'I will not leave until I see Mr Haldar himself.'

'I see,' said the secretary. Raising a hand, he made a sign to the chowkidar, who was standing at the door. 'Shyam Bahadur,' he said. 'Show this lady the way out.'

Amitav Ghosh

Urmila pointed a finger at him, looking him directly in the eyes. 'I don't think you know who I am,' she said, in a firm, cool voice. 'Let me tell you: my name is Urmila Roy and I am a *Calcutta* reporter. Perhaps you should think a little before you do anything.'

The secretary's scowl deepened and he launched into a threat-laden diatribe. Urmila listened quietly; she had become all too used to situations like these over the last couple of years. In her own way she had even come to relish them.

She waited impassively until he ran out of breath. '*Now* will you please take me to Mr Haldar?' she said, silkily. 'Quickly please; I don't have much time. In a short while I have to be at the Great Eastern Hotel, for a press conference with the Minister of Communications.'

The secretary began to splutter. 'You don't understand,' he said, wiping his forehead with the sleeve of his spotless kurta. 'I can't take you to Mr Haldar because I don't know where he is. He's disappeared. He's missed two appointments already.'

Urmila stared at him, open-mouthed. 'But he's meant to come to our flat for dinner tonight,' she began to explain, meaninglessly. 'That's why I'm cooking this fish; that's why I'm going to be late for the press conference . . .' She shook the bag of fish under his nose once again.

The secretary sneered. 'You're either mad or dreaming,' he said. 'Mr Haldar is booked on a flight to Bombay this evening—he has to attend a meeting there. He had no plans to visit you or anyone else here.' With a gesture of dismissal, he turned to the chowkidar. 'Take her away,' he said. 'I'm not going to waste any more time on this nonsense.'

Urmila allowed herself to be led out of the room, but at the porch she broke suddenly free. 'You're lying,' she shouted, shaking off the chowkidar's hand. 'I don't believe you. You're not going to get away with this—you'll see . . .'

The chowkidar placed a restraining hand on her arm. Trying to evade his grip Urmila stumbled. And then the gravel path was flying up to meet her.

twenty-seven

When next she opened her eyes Urmila was lying in the shade of the pillared portico of the Haldar mansion. Her sight was blurred and her head was spinning. A large indistinct shape was hovering above her, and beyond it were about a dozen hazy faces, looking anxiously down at her. A voice was shouting in her ear; she couldn't tell what it was saying; the accent was odd. Someone was fanning her with a newspaper; someone else was offering her a glass of water. The chowkidar was somewhere in the middle distance, gesticulating and arguing with someone she couldn't see.

Gradually, as her vision cleared she saw that the large blur in front of her was a face, the face of a man, a man with a short, trimmed beard. He looked somehow familiar.

'Miss *Calcutta*!' he was shaking her shoulder. 'Come on, wake up. Where'd you get these? I've got to know.'

'Get what?' she said. He was waving something at her, but she couldn't see what it was.

'These,' he said impatiently. 'This stuff you brought with you; these papers.'

Brushing his hand away, she sat up. 'Who are you?' she said. 'Why are you shouting at me like this?'

He looked at her nonplussed. 'Don't you remember me?' he said. 'We met that day, at that auditorium.'

'What do you mean we met?' she said. 'I don't know your name, or who you are, or what you do or anything.'

'I'm L. Murugan,' he said. 'I work for LifeWatch.' Murugan took out his wallet and handed her a card. 'I know who you are,' he said. 'I don't recall the name exactly, but I know you work for *Calcutta* magazine.'

'That's all you need to know,' she said. 'Now kindly explain what you are doing here.'

'Me?' said Murugan. 'I wanted to ask Mr Haldar's permission to visit his Robinson Street property, so I thought I'd come and introduce myself.'

'And why were you shouting at me?'

'I've got to know where you found these.' He produced the crumpled bits of xerox paper she had found in the packet of fish. 'Can you tell me?'

'How dare you?' she cried. She lunged at his hand and snatched the papers away. 'These are mine. They belong to me.'

'They're not yours,' he said, grabbing at them. 'They have nothing to do with you.'

'They're mine and I'm going to keep them,' said Urmila. She screwed the papers into a tight little ball and tucked them into the front of her blouse.

Murugan gritted his teeth. 'Look,' he said. 'You've found something that just might be the key to one of the mysteries of the century, and all you want to do is start a custody battle?'

Urmila rose slowly to her feet. 'Why do you want them so much?' she said. 'They're just bits of waste paper.'

'Okay,' said Murugan. 'I'll tell you what: I'll save you the trouble of flushing them down the toilet. Give them back to me.'

'There is no need to get agitated,' she said coldly. She rose to her feet, and directed a look of enquiry at the faces around her. 'Where's my fish?' she demanded, of no one in particular. Someone handed the soggy packet back to her. Taking a firm grip on it she set off down the path, towards the gate.

Murugan ran after her. 'Wait up,' he said, trying to collect himself. 'Look, what is it that you want? Do you want money or something?'

She threw him a contemptuous glance and walked on.

'Then what?' said Murugan.

'I want to know what's in those papers.'

He caught hold of her elbow. 'Look,' he said, in as placatory a voice as he could muster. 'You haven't even told me your name. All I know about you is that you work for *Calcutta*.'

'My name is none of your business,' she answered, shaking his hand off. 'And kindly do not touch me.'

'Oh, so is that going to be your attitude?' said Murugan, his voice rising. 'So what shall I call you then, since I'm not going to be granted the honour of an introduction? Miss Calcutta? or perhaps even just Calcutta, or would that be too intimate? too affectionate, you think? your husband might begin to suspect some hanky-panky, some panking hankies, some altogether untoward hanking and panking . . .'

'I'm not married,' Urmila said coldly.

'Oh, better and better: you just made my day Calcutta, I'm going to count the seconds till the hanking ends and the panking begins, but before we start heaving our hanks let me tell you something Calcutta, let me feed a little factoid into your database: let me tell how this works: let me set your priorities a little more in line with the real world. You don't get to ask *me* the questions: you see what I'm saying? It's Dr Morgan who gets to decide what you deserve to know and when.'

She narrowed her eyes. 'Is that so?' she said.

'You want an explanation,' he said. 'You're going to get it. But I'm going to choose the weapons and the venue.'

He ran to the road and stopped a taxi.

'P.G. Hospital,' he said, to the Sikh driver. 'Quick; let's go.'

twenty-eight

A ntar shivered: he felt distinctly ill now. He would have to find a way of letting Tara know that he wasn't up to having dinner with her.

Fortunately she'd been wearing a beeper the last few weeks. Switching screens, he keyed in a few words: Regret must cancel dinner; explain later. He called up her number and dialled the message through.

The beeper had come with a new job Tara had found, a few weeks ago. The woman she was working for now was a stockbroker who often worked late: she liked to stay in constant touch with her four-year-old and had insisted that Tara carry a beeper.

The job was a good one, Tara said, much better than the one she'd lost: the pay was fair and better still, the boy was good-natured and his mother relatively undemanding. Tara never lost an opportunity to thank Antar for helping her find the job.

But the truth was that if Antar had helped at all, it was only in a rather roundabout way. One morning, about a month ago, he had noticed her hanging about her apartment at a time when she was usually out at work. Pushing up the kitchen window, he called out: 'What's the matter? Not going to work today?'

She stuck her head into the airshaft, and gave him a rueful smile. Her wispy hair was tied in an untidy knot and she looked as though she hadn't bothered to change after getting out of bed.

'I would if I could,' she said. 'But the job's not mine any more.'

'What happened?'

'Well,' she said. 'The gloss that was put on the matter was that I had rather reluctantly been allowed to depart. But the fact was they needed someone with the right papers so they could get a tax write-off.' She shrugged and made a face.

'Oh,' said Antar. 'Well, that's too bad.' It took him a moment to digest this bit of news.

'Haven't you found anything else yet?' he said. 'I thought babysitters were snapped up the minute they hit the market.'

Tara shook her head resignedly. 'The best jobs are posted on the Net,' she said. 'And I can't afford a susbscription. Come to think of it, I can't afford a computer and wouldn't know what to do with it if I could.'

'On the Net?' Antar was astounded. 'Babysitting jobs? You're joking. Surely?'

'I wish I were,' she said. 'But it's true. I've looked in the *Irish Echo* and *India Abroad*: not a thing in either.'

She gave him a bleak smile and a nod. 'I must go now,' she said. 'Or my tea will get cold. And the way things are going, I suspect it wouldn't be wise to waste a tea bag.' She ducked back inside.

The conversation resounded in Antar's mind through the day as he sat staring at Ava's screen: the precariousness of her circumstances weighed on him in ways he couldn't quite understand. The next morning he was in and out of the kitchen every few minutes until he spotted her, pottering around her apartment.

Leaning over the sink, he shouted: 'Listen: I have an idea.'

She gave him a wan smile. 'Yes?' He could tell she'd been up late, worrying.

'I have an old laptop in my cupboard,' he said. 'I could hook it up with Ava and run a cable through to you. You could have as much time on the Net as you wanted. I've upgraded it a couple of times and it can run the software. The

Council gives me twenty hours a week free, and I hardly ever use even a fraction of that. I've got at least a thousand hours coming to me. You can have them.'

Her thin, fine-boned face lit up. 'Really?' she said. 'Could you really do that?'

She hesitated, as though she couldn't believe her luck: 'Are you sure it would be all right? I don't want to get you in any trouble.'

Antar made an attempt at nonchalance. 'It's very irregular of course,' he said. 'The Council's paranoid about security. But I think I can rig it. If you're careful and you don't try to fool around we'll both be all right.'

'I'll be very careful,' she said earnestly. 'You have my word: I won't do anything that might get you in trouble.'

Antar set up the link later that day.

It gave him a twinge to leave his old laptop behind with her: it was an early nineties, Korean-made model, sleek and black, with beautifully rounded edges. He'd always loved it: the heft and weight of it in his hands, the muted click of its keyboard, its old-fashioned chrome detailing.

He offered to give her a few lessons but she declined. 'You've been to plenty of trouble already,' she said. 'I won't put you to any more. Lucky will show me: he knows a little about these things.'

'Lucky?' That was the name of the young man from the Penn Station news-stand. Antar tried to imagine him, with his fixed smile and his oddly spaced teeth, sitting in front of his laptop, trying to steer Tara around the Net. He had his doubts but he decided to keep them to himself.

As it turned out, Lucky was evidently a good teacher for Tara soon found her way around the Net. Antar monitored her closely for the first few days. Then he grew tired of following her around childcare bulletin boards and left her alone.

She got her new job within a few days and had been inordinately grateful ever since. That was why she had wanted to come over tonight. 'I can't afford to take you out,' she said. 'So the least I can do is make sure that you eat properly every once in a while.'

twenty-nine

On Lower Circular Road, halfway to the P.G. Hospital, Urmila found herself reading and re-reading the bright yellow lettering on the side of a crowded minibus that was jammed up close against her window. The taxi was idling in the traffic, imprisoned by the customary morning throng of cars and buses. Hesitantly Urmila raised her eyes to the windows of the minibus: a dozen people seemed to be staring at her. She turned quickly away.

This was probably the bus she would have been on right now, if she were on her way to work. They were probably on it, all the usual crowd: the old man in the dhoti who worked in the Accountant-General's office and was writing a book on something or the other; the railway clerk who carried a huge tiffin-carrier full of food to the Strand every morning; the woman from All India Radio, who had tried to get her to join the 'BBD Bagh Minibus Passengers Club' last week.

Urmila shrank into the seat. The crumpled sheets of paper were scraping uncomfortably against the tender spot between her breasts. She wanted to reach in and pull it out, but she couldn't, not with that minibus so close to her window.

What if they could see her now, the 'BBD Bagh Minibus Passengers Club'? What if they were to learn that she was on her way to P.G. Hospital with a complete stranger? What would they think? What would they make of it?

Suddenly she was furious. 'What does the P.G. Hospital

have to do with my pieces of paper?' she said, turning upon Murugan. 'Why are you taking me there? What are your intentions?'

'You wanted an explanation, Calcutta,' Murugan said. 'That was the deal. And I'm going to give you an explanation, but I'm going to begin exactly where I want to.'

'And you want to begin at the P.G. Hospital?' she said.

'That's right,' he said. 'That's why I'm taking you there.'

She noticed the taxi driver watching them in his mirror. She leaned over and waved her packet of fish under his nose. 'What're you looking at, you cabbage-head?' she snapped. 'Keep your eyes on the road.'

Chastened, the driver dropped his eyes.

'Wow!' said Murugan. 'What was that all about?'

'And you,' she cried, turning on him in fury. 'Who are you exactly?' Suspicion was raging in her mind now; she began to recall all the stories she had heard about foreign con-men and kidnappers and prostitution rings in the Middle East. 'I want to know who you are and what you are doing in Calcutta. I want to see a passport.'

'I don't have my passport with me right this minute,' said Murugan. 'But you can have this.' He took out his wallet and handed her his ID card.

She looked it over carefully, examining the lettering and matching the photograph with his face.

When they reached the Rabindra Sadan auditorium, Murugan tapped the driver on the shoulder and pointed down the road. 'Over there,' he said. 'Stop, over there.'

'Here?' Urmila found herself looking at a brick wall, across a narrow ditch. 'Why here? There's nothing here; we've left the hospital entrance behind: it's over there.'

'We don't need the entrance,' said Murugan, handing the taxi driver a fifty-rupee note. 'There's something I want to show you right here.'

'But there's nothing to see here,' Urmila said suspiciously. 'It's just a wall.'

'Look over there,' said Murugan, counting his change. He

pointed over his shoulder at the memorial to Ronald Ross. 'Did you get an eyeful of that?'

Urmila's eyes widened in surprise as they followed his finger to the marble plaque at the apex of the modest little arch. 'No,' she said. 'I've never noticed it before.' She began reading aloud: 'In the small laboratory seventy yards to the southeast of this gate Surgeon-Major Ronald Ross, I.M.S. in 1898 discovered the manner in which malaria is conveyed by mosquitoes.'

She shook her head. 'It's strange,' she said. 'I've changed buses here hundreds of times. I can't even begin to count how often I've walked past this wall. But I've never noticed that inscription up there.'

'No one notices poor Ron any more,' said Murugan. He set off towards a gate, a short distance down the road. 'Follow me,' he said, beckoning her on. 'I'll show you something else.'

A chain hung suspended from the gate-posts, just loose enough to let one person through at a time. Murugan went first and when Urmila caught up, he pointed across the hospital's busy compound to a graceful red-brick building set well back in the grounds.

'When Ronald Ross came to work here in 1898,' Murugan said, 'that building over there was all there was of the P.G. Hospital.'

'How do you know?' she said.

He laughed. 'It's simple,' he said. 'You happen to be speaking to the world's greatest living expert on Ronnie Ross.'

'You mean you?' she said.

'You said it.' He turned on his heel and set off down a path that was bustling with uniformed hospital staff.

'Look over there,' he said, pointing ahead at a complex of boxy new buildings all painted a drab, municipal yellow. 'None of those was here when Ronnie was doing his malaria research in Calcutta. It was just trees and bamboo and greenery around here—except for a couple of labs and outhouses where the servants and attendants lived.'

He held a handkerchief to his nose as they walked past an

Amitav Ghosh

open rubbish dump where crows, dogs and vultures were fighting over scraps of food and blood-soaked bandages. Nearby, a row of men stood lined up against a wall, unheeding of a notice that pleaded: 'Please do not urine here.'

Murugan came to a halt in an open space, between two wards, one of which bore a sign, 'Ross Memorial Ward'. He pointed to an old-fashioned red-brick bungalow that had been incorporated into one of the hospital's newly added wings. 'Look over there,' he said. 'That was Ross's lab.'

He went over to the bungalow and drew her attention to a marble tablet, set high in the wall. The tablet bore a stylized image of a mosquito, and under it an inscription.

'It's too far up to read,' Urmila said. 'Doesn't it say that it was in this laboratory that Surgeon-Major Ronald Ross made the momentous discovery that malaria is conveyed by the bite of a mosquito?'

'Something like that,' said Murugan.

Urmila pulled a quizzical face. 'What a strange little building,' she said. 'It looks so shut in on itself. It's hard to believe that anybody could discover anything in there.'

'What's even harder to believe,' said Murugan, 'is that this was once one of the best equipped research laboratories in the whole of the Indian subcontinent.'

'Was it?' she said, in surprise.

He nodded: 'That's right. And you know who set it up?'

'How would I know about that?' she snapped.

'But you do know,' said Murugan, 'as a matter of fact, you've got his name right there.' He pointed at the piece of paper that she had tucked into her blouse.

Turning her back to him, she took the ball of paper out of her blouse. 'Here it is,' she said. 'Show me.'

He pointed to one of the lines that had been marked in ink. 'That's him. Surgeon-Colonel D.D. Cunningham.'

'That's the guy who set up this place,' said Murugan. 'Like Ronnie Ross he was a doctor in the Indian Medical Service, which was a unit of the British Indian Army. But Cunningham was more or less a senior citizen, years older than Ross. And he was a research scientist too—a pathologist. In fact he was a Fellow of the Royal Society; he had an F.R.S. tagged to his name, which was one of the fanciest tags you could get those days. Cunningham did a lot of his work in Calcutta right here in this lab. He made it into the best equipped research centre in this part of the world. It was Ron who made it famous, but he couldn't have done it without old D.D.'

'I'll take your word for it,' said Urmila. 'But I still don't see how this makes those papers so special.'

'Patience, Calcutta,' Murugan said. 'I'm just getting started. Come on.'

He headed back the way they had come and led her through a passageway to the narrow dirt-filled space that separated the Ross Memorial Ward from the hospital's boundary wall. The memorial arch was now a few yards to their left, and over the top of the wall they could just see the clogged traffic on Lower Circular Road.

Murugan pointed to a couple of low, ramshackle tin-roofed structures, nestling in the mounds of earth and debris that were piled up against the wall. 'You see those outhouses over there?' he said. 'That's where Ronnie Ross's servants lived. One of them, a guy called Lutchman, was Ross's right-hand man. He used to breed the pigeons that Ross used for his research right over there.'

'Pigeons?' said Urmila distractedly, casting a distasteful glance at the little heaps of excrement that lay half-hidden in the debris. 'I thought you said he was working with mosquitoes and malaria.'

'Well, let me put it like this,' said Murugan. 'Ronnie Ross didn't always work with your usual plain-vanilla kinds of malaria. In Calcutta he began working with a related avian species, halteridium—you could call it a bird version of malaria.'

'Really?' Urmila looked up warily at the trees around them.

'Yes,' he said. 'And to keep him supplied with material for his experiments, his assistants, Lutchman and his crew, kept a

Amitav Ghosh

large flock of infected birds—right over there. And they released their entire flock here, in September 1898, just days after Ross finished his final series of experiments.'

He picked a stone off the ground. 'Let me show you something,' he said. He tossed the stone in the direction of the outhouse. It landed in the debris, and moments later, a flock of pigeons took to the air with clucks of alarm and a frantic beating of wings. Murugan stood back and watched the birds circling above.

'I wouldn't be at all surprised,' he said, 'if there were a couple of descendants of Lutchman's flock up there.'

thirty

S tanding on tiptoe, Urmila peeped over the boundary wall
at the office-going traffic, streaming down Lower Circular
Road, past the hospital. She was surprised by how sheltered
and self-contained the bungalow was, how far removed both
from the bustle of the hospital and the noise of the nearby
traffic.

'How quiet it seems here,' she said, glancing from the
outhouse to the Ross memorial. 'It's hard to believe that I go
past this place twice every day, at rush hour.'

'Exactly what Ronnie Ross thought,' said Murugan.
'Thought he'd found the lab of his dreams when he first got
here.'

Urmila stepped back from the wall. 'So how was it that
Ross came to be here?' she said. She ran her eyes over the
smoothed-out sheets of paper in her hands. 'Was it this man
D.D. Cunningham who invited him here?'

'No,' said Murugan. 'Exactly the opposite. Cunningham
did everything he could to make sure that Ross wouldn't get
here. Ronnie wrote him begging letters every couple of months,
and Cunningham's answers were always the same, short and
simple: no dice.'

'But still,' said Urmila, 'Ronald Ross did come here, didn't
he?'

'That's right,' said Murugan. 'Cunningham stonewalled Ross
for more than a year. And then one day, in January 1898,

right out of the blue, Cunningham caved. In fact he handed in his resignation and left for England in such a hurry he forgot to pack his boxer shorts. On January 30 the Government of India finally approved Ronnie Ross's transfer to Calcutta.

'The official story is that all this was just coincidence: old Cunningham was aching for the honeysuckled cottages of Ye Olde England. Well, where he ended up was in a boarding house in Surrey with a view of the municipal gasworks. You're going to tell me he left his cozy little set-up out here for that just because he was homesick for English muffins? Well let me tell you: I don't buy it.'

'So what are you saying then?' said Urmila. 'Why do you think he left?'

'I don't have the answer to that,' said Murugan. 'But it's clear that something happened round the middle of January 1898 that made Cunningham change his mind. And it was no accident either: somebody worked pretty hard to set it up.'

Urmila examined her papers again. 'Here, look at this,' she said, pointing at a line. 'It says here that D.D. Cunningham was granted five days' leave in the middle of January—from the 10th to the 15th of January. That's when it must have happened.'

'Right,' said Murugan. 'And look at the date on that railway reservation chart: on the 10th of January 1898 somebody called C.C. Dunn took a train to Madras.'

'And who was that?'

'No one,' said Murugan. 'That's just it. I think someone is trying to get the message across that D.D. Cunningham travelled to Madras under a false name on that day.'

'Madras?' said Urmila scowling at the papers. 'Why Madras? What could have happened there? I suppose there's no way of finding out since it happened so long ago?'

'So you'd think,' said Murugan. 'I mean it's not like you can look up something that happened in Madras in 1898 in the back issues of *Time*, right? But the fact is that I do happen to know about a guy called C.C. Dunn who was in Madras about that time. Only I'd never connected him with D.D.

Cunningham. Not until this morning, when I took those papers out of your hands. They were the missing link you see; they tie it all together.'

'And how did you learn about this C.C. . . . whoever he was?'

'Because someone wanted me to,' said Murugan. 'It's a long story. Are you sure you're up for it?'

Urmila nodded emphatically.

'A few years ago,' Murugan began, 'I was trying to update the malaria archive at the outfit where I work. I was three months into the North Africa and Middle East files when I came upon a weird report of a small, extremely localized epidemic in northern Egypt, about thirty miles south of Alexandria. The population of a tiny hamlet was wiped out in a period of a few days. There were no recurrences, no further outbreaks. This hamlet was settled by a family of migrants from the south—Coptic Christians. They didn't have much to do with their neighbours and they were a long way from the nearest village. When their bodies were discovered they were already in an advanced state of decomposition.'

'What sort of epidemic was it?' said Urmila.

'No one's sure,' said Murugan. 'There were no autopsies. In fact the only reason we know about it at all is because a British health officer wrote a short report on it. This was in 1950, soon after the war, and the British were basically still running the place. This health officer was a competent, no-nonsense guy from the sound of it: he'd spent his whole career in Egypt. By the time he visited the hamlet the bodies had been disposed of. But he reported two kinds of anecdotal evidence about the symptoms of the deceased: swollen neck glands and large numbers of tiny skin perforations, like insect bites. He thought it might be an exceptionally virulent strain of malaria but he had no way of confirming his hunch. People from the surrounding villages said that there might be a survivor: the body count left one fourteen-year-old boy unaccounted for. He was reported to have been seen at the railway station in a nearby town at about the time of the

Amitav Ghosh

outbreak. The health officer thought he might be a carrier, and he tried to find him. He thought an examination of the boy might yield a clue to what had happened. But he was never found.'

'So they had no idea what happened?'

'Basically, no. The health officer admitted he didn't know what the fuck had happened. He added that the only time he'd heard of similar symptoms was some twenty or more years before, down south, in Luxor. Someone had told him that the archaeology buff, Lord Carnarvon, had died of a mosquito bite that had led to a fever and swollen neck glands. He even quoted from a letter written by His Lordship's daughter, just before he bit the dust. "You know the mosquito bite on his (Papa's) cheek that was worrying him at Luxor, well yesterday quite suddenly all the glands in his neck started swelling and last night he had a high temperature and still has today."'

'I don't follow,' said Urmila. 'We were talking about something that is supposed to have happened in Madras in 1898. How did we end up in Egypt fifty years later?'

'That's exactly what I'm trying to explain,' said Murugan. 'That's what comes next. What happened was this: after I found the health officer's report, I began asking around to see if anyone had any leads on this. I even posted some queries on a couple of chat groups on the World Wide Web. One day I logged on and there was this long message waiting for me: pages and pages long. There was no return address or anything on it: it had been sent anonymously. I soon discovered that whoever sent it went to a lot of trouble to make sure that I wouldn't find out who they were: it had been routed and re-routed so many different ways I couldn't even begin to trace it.'

'And what did the message say?' Urmila asked.

'It was an excerpt from a book written by a Czech psycho-linguist. The excerpt was about a Hungarian high-society type, who became a distinguished amateur archaeologist and professional eccentric—one Countess Pongrácz. Towards the end of her life she moved to Egypt. The last time she was seen was in 1950: she was on her way to do a dig somewhere near this hamlet where the outbreak happened. No one knows what happened to her.'

'I still don't see the connection with Madras in January 1898,' said Urmila.

'I was just getting to that,' said Murugan. 'In her youth La Pongrácz was a kind of prototype of a sixties jet-setter, travelling around the world, picking up gurus and stuff. And in January 1898 she was nineteen years old, just starting on her long career. And where do you think she was?'

'Where?' said Urmila.

'In India,' said Murugan. 'Madras to be exact. Now you'd reckon that if a guru-groupie was down in that part of the world at that time they'd home in on Madame Blavatsky and the Theosophical Society like a heat-seeking missile seeks heat. But you'd be wrong. This Countess Pongrácz was a real guru-gourmet and she didn't go in for any of that heat-and-serve stuff. The guru she settled on was Mme Blavatsky's arch-rival—a Finnish number called Mme Liisa Salminen, who ran her own little outfit called the Society of Spiritualists. The Countess was Madame Salminen's leading disciple, and she noted down everything that happened to her guru.'

Amitav Ghosh

On the night of January 12, 1898, records the Grófné Pongrácz, a select few Spiritualists gathered, as was their custom, at a house rented by the Society for their weekly séance with Mme Salminen. Several independent sources attest that these séances were generally stately, highly regulated affairs. They usually began with a small reception, with Mme Salminen holding court and handing out cups of China tea. On this occasion however the solemnity of the tea-party was rudely interrupted by an unlikely and unexpected intruder. There were many in Madras who coveted invitations to join Mme Salminen's circle of intimates. Some had been known to go to considerable lengths to infiltrate the group. Thus it was not the mere fact of the arrival of an uninvited guest that took the assembled Spiritualists by surprise: rather it was because the man in question did not seem to be even remotely the kind of person who might wish to be associated with such a group. Quite the contrary. It ought to be noted that in general the Spiritualists, Theosophists and their fellow travellers looked upon British civilian and military officialdom with undisguised loathing—a sentiment that was reciprocated in more than ample measure. Such was their mutual revulsion that in the barrack-rooms of Madras's Fort St George, the phrase 'I would rather be a Spiritualist', when uttered by a cavalryman, was generally regarded as the equivalent, in connotative association, to such statements as 'I would rather be dead'.

Conversely, the sentence 'I would rather be a Lieutenant-Colonel' might be held to constitute a similarly firm statement of preferences amongst Spiritualists and their kin. Yet, it would appear from the Countess's brief but vivid description that the intruder in question was precisely a man of military affiliations. She describes him, in her inimitable Magyar way, as a portly ruddy-faced Englishman in his late fifties, with sparse hair and a Hussar's moustache. The man was clearly in a state of extreme emotional distress for he was observed to be wringing his hands and tugging his moustache, while his eyes were bloodshot and inflamed, as though he had not slept for several days. Yet, something in his bearing belied his overwrought state: the Countess for one, immediately took him to be an officer of high to middle rank, possibly in an infantry regiment. Imagine her surprise then, when the intruder made no mention of a rank or regiment while introducing himself. She took it as a rebuff, as a slight on her powers of observation: and it is worth remembering that the Countess Pongrácz claimed descent from no less a soldier than the great Attila himself, and moreover, was as accustomed to a place of honour in the courtly circles of Imperial Buda as she was to the taverns of soldierly Pest. She was unlikely to be mistaken in recognizing the attributes of a military man.

The Spiritualists' suspicions were further aroused when the intruder appeared to have some trouble remembering his own name, introducing himself finally (and not without some hesitation) as C.C. Dunn. No sooner had this cursory introduction been effected, however, than the self-styled Mr Dunn leant over towards the imposing head of Mme Salminen and began to whisper. The Countess happened to be close at hand at the time and now, without appearing to pay the slightest attention, she contrived to direct her hearing in this direction. But adept though she undoubtedly was at this rare aristocratic art, she managed to catch no more than a few disjointed syllables: 'Great distance . . . see you . . . dreams . . . visions . . . death . . . implore you . . . madness . . . annihilation.'

The Countess, like many others in the room, fully expected

Mme Salminen to give the stranger short shrift, as she had so many others before him. But here they underestimated the formidable Finn. Mme Salminen took a particular interest in people who exhibited signs of extreme emotion: it was her belief that violent passion, when efficiently channelled, can create the conditions for what she called 'psychic breakthroughs'. Thus, far from turning away the distraught Mr Dunn, she extended him a warm welcome and invited him to join the assembled company when they withdrew to the séance table.

It is worth emphasizing here that Countess Pongrácz's accounts of séances were not always entirely coherent. She would often jot down her impressions immediately after the session when she was herself in a state of considerable excitation. Often in these situations, the impeccable High German in which her accounts were composed would begin to show signs of strain; sometimes her beleaguered sense of syntax would yield altogether, and instead of complete sentences she would jot down strings of apparently disconnected syllables. Intensive computer analysis has demonstrated that these phonemic clusters were drawn from a mélange of Central European dialects such as Slovenian, and certain unusual Carpathian variants of Finno-Ugrian (all learned, no doubt, below stairs from the vast staff of the Kastély Pongrácz).

The point, of course, is that we cannot pretend that the Countess was a reliable witness or that an accurate narrative can be constructed from the skeletal word-associations of her diary. However, her accounts can frequently be corroborated with what is known of the protocols and procedures of Mme Salminen's séances, and these facts are not in general dispute. As a rule Mme Salminen and her little flock would withdraw after tea to a room that was lit with only one candle. Sitting around a heavy wooden table, the assembled company would join hands and attempt to bring their powers of concentration into focus, with Mme Salminen acting as a lens, so to speak, for the dispersed energy of their minds. To be counted as a success a session such as this would have to produce some of the 'manifestations' of psychic energy that were so dear to the Spiritualists—such phenomena as table-tapping, automatic writing, incorporeal voices and so on. On certain special occasions the lucky few were even rewarded with the most highly valued of psychic prizes, so to speak, that is to say a kind of light that was termed an 'ectoplasmic glow'. That 'manifestations' of this kind can very easily be manufactured in circumstances of collective hysteria has of course been repeatedly demonstrated and needs no comment here.

It must be noted however that the 'glow' phenomenon was a rare and unusual occurrence. It was usually produced only towards the end of a session, and was invariably preceded by other manifestations such as table-tapping, etc.

On the occasion with which we are currently concerned, it so happened that the Countess Pongrácz was chosen to sit beside Mme Salminen and opposite the uninvited guest—the self-styled Mr C.C. Dunn. Now it appears that, despite Mme Salminen's explicit instructions to the contrary, the Countess was in the habit of casting occasional glances around the table at these sessions. It was thus she noticed that after twenty minutes or so Mme Salminen and Mr Dunn appeared to have fallen into a kind of trance, with their heads slumped forward, almost touching the table. When this condition persisted for a considerable length of time, the Countess began to consider the otherwise unthinkable step of interrupting the proceedings (unthinkable because it was the current belief that an interruption would cause a 'spirit' to be trapped in inter-plasmic limbo).

However, even as she was considering this possibility, Mme Salminen's head was flung back against the chair, suddenly and violently, so that she was staring up at the ceiling, her hair flowing loose, her mouth slack and open, trailing ribbons of sputum. Then Mr Dunn was hurled backwards bodily from the table and flattened against the wall, his feet several inches off the ground. The next instant the single candle was extinguished and the room was suddenly plunged into an impenetrable, velvety darkness. The heavy table was upended with a violent crash, and Mr Dunn fell to the floor, screaming in what appeared to be Hindustani: Save me . . . from her . . . pursuit . . . beg mercy . . .'

The strangest aspect of these hallucinations, the Countess records, is that even in that darkness which was not merely the absence of light, but rather its opposite, an antithesis that can only be conceived in the inner eye of the mind: even in blank darkness they could see C.C. Dunn absolutely clearly, although not with the kind of vision that depends on exterior light; they could see him struggling; the agonies that passed over his face; they watched his futile attempts to fight off whatever it was that had tied him upon this rack of torment—all this they could see, but never once did they glimpse or even imagine the agent of his anguish, what arm or instrument, or whatever means it was through which these hideous agonies were effected. His face was livid with fear, and they saw him flailing his arms, fighting something off, a hand, or possibly an instrument. They saw him cowering on the floor, prostrate but not unconscious, but then just as suddenly the nature of his struggle changed, and he seemed instead to be grappling with an animal, fighting to keep its fangs from closing around his throat; shouting a repetitive string of invocations.

Then abruptly the noise ceased and the candle flared up again so that they were no longer in darkness. Opening their eyes they saw that the table was exactly where it had been, and that they were all sitting in their places, except the unannounced guest, who was cowering in a corner, stark naked.

And then Mme Salminen spoke her first words, in a whisper so soft as to be audible to none other than the Countess, who was seated beside her. All this while Mme Salminen had been sprawled in her chair, her head thrown back, her eyes blank and unseeing. When she spoke it was without properly regaining consciousness. The sentence that escaped her lips was: 'There is nothing I can do: the Silence has come to claim him.'

Having said these few words she collapsed on the table. Her alarmed acolytes removed her immediately to her bedroom, where she remained until well into the next day. On gaining consciousness her first act was to send for the Countess. The two women remained closeted together for several hours.

Unfortunately the Countess never provided a written account of their conversation of that day, but she is known to have described it as the turning point of her life on several occasions.

However, the actual influence of Mme Salminen on her disciple's subsequent career remains disputed. For instance, when she attributed her pioneering archaeological work in excavating early Manichaean and Nestorian sites in Central Asia, Nepal and Bengal to the influence of Mme Salminen, her friends assumed that this was merely a manner of speaking—a grateful acolyte's rendering of homage. But in her advocacy of the teachings of Valentinus, the Alexandrian philosopher of the early Christian era, they were more inclined to take her assertions at face value. When she asserted that it was Mme Salminen who had revealed to her the truth of the Valentinian cosmology, in which the ultimate deities are the Abyss and the Silence, the one being male and the other female, the one representing mind and the other truth, few disputed her account of the matter, for these beliefs clearly did not merit a prosaic explanation.

Yet, accustomed as her friends were to her eccentricities, they became seriously concerned when she moved to Egypt in the late nineteen forties to search for the most sacred site of the ancient Valentinian cult: the lost shrine of Silence. Some of them were to recall later, after her disappearance, that she had often spoken of a description that Madame Salminen had given her: of a small hamlet on the edge of the desert; of date palms and mud huts and creaking water-wheels.

thirty-two

U rmila shivered, despite the clammy heat.

'So do you think it's all connected?' she said. 'The message that was sent to you, and these bits of paper that the fish were wrapped in . . .'

'Are you kidding?' Murugan said. 'You bet they're connected. Your fish wrappings pull it all together. Look at it this way: Cunningham had the only lab on the continent where Ron had a snowflake's chance of making a breakthrough; Ron knew this and by late 1896 he was desperate to get his ass to Calcutta. But Cunningham just wasn't buying it: he'd set this lab up like his own backyard barbecue and he wasn't going to let some punk kid break up his party. *Ergo*: if Cunningham was the principal obstacle to Ron's moving to Calcutta, it follows that at this point in time—late 1897—he was the single greatest obstacle to the solution of the malaria puzzle. If someone was looking over Ron's shoulder at this stage, it wouldn't take them long to figure this out. So what do they do? They call a timeout and go into a huddle and when they go back on the floor, they've got a new gameplan: Cunningham's got to go. And sure enough, that's exactly what happens: suddenly in January 1898, Cunningham changes his mind; he throws the game and takes his tail off to England. In between he makes a pit-stop in Madras where he goes through some kind of psychotic episode. Those papers, that message on my screen—someone is trying to get me to make connections: they want me to know I was on the right track.'

'But wait a minute,' said Urmila. 'What do you mean wants you to know? It wasn't you who found the papers. It was me—and I met you by accident—because you happened to be at Romen Haldar's house when I . . . when I fainted.'

'Is that right?' said Murugan. 'Okay, now *you* tell me exactly how you happened to "find" those papers and we'll try and see if your accident theory holds up.'

Urmila began to tell him about the events of that morning, and the night before—the phone-call to her family, her promise to cook fish, and the providential ring of the doorbell at 7.15. And slowly, as she told the story her account grew more and more uncertain, so that when she got to the unknown fish-seller, her voice faded into a barely audible murmur.

'But why would anyone set about the whole thing in such a roundabout way?' she said. 'If they want you to know something why wouldn't they just tell you—why involve me and Romen Haldar and . . . ?'

Murugan paused to scratch his beard. 'The truth is,' he said, 'that I don't know. But a couple of things are clear enough. Someone's trying to get us to make some connections; they're trying to tell us something; something they don't want to put together themselves, so that when we get to the end we'll have a whole new story.'

'Why?' said Urmila. 'What purpose does it serve? What good will it do them if we get to the end or not?'

'I'm not absolutely sure,' said Murugan, 'but I guess I could sketch one possible scenario.'

'Go on,' said Urmila.

'All right,' said Murugan. 'Now suppose, just suppose you had this belief—don't ask me why or anything, this is strictly a let's pretend game—just suppose you believed that to know something is to change it, it would follow, wouldn't it, that to make something known would be one way of effecting a change? Or creating a mutation, if you like.'

Urmila made a doubtful noise.

'Now let's take this one step further. If you did believe this, it would follow that if you wanted to create a specific kind of change, or mutation, one of the ways in which you could get there, is by allowing certain things to be known. You'd have to be very careful in how you did it, because the experiment wouldn't work until it led to a genuine discovery of some kind. It wouldn't work, for instance, if you picked someone out of a crowd and said: "Yo here's a two and here's another; add them up and what do you get?" That wouldn't be a real discovery because the answer would be known already. So what you would have to do is to push your guinea pigs in the right direction and wait for them to get there on their own.'

'So what you're saying,' Urmila said, 'is that someone is telling you something, through me, in this very roundabout way, as a kind of experiment; because they're trying to change something?'

'I couldn't have said it better myself.'

'To change *what*?' cried Urmila. 'And why? What do they want to do with us?'

'We don't know,' said Murugan. 'We don't know what; we don't know why.'

'So you mean to say,' said Urmila, 'you and I are trapped in an experiment, and we don't know what it's for or why?'

'That's right,' said Murugan. 'Fact is we're dealing with a crowd for whom silence is a religion. We don't even know what we don't know. We don't know who's in this and who's not; we don't know how much of the spin they've got under control. We don't know how many of the threads they want us to pull together and how many they want to keep hanging for whoever comes next.'

'You mean,' said Urmila, 'they may keep the rest for someone else to put together—some time in the future?'

'I'd guess that's the case, yes,' Murugan said. 'These guys aren't going anywhere in a hurry. They've been planting carefully selected clues for the last century or so, and every once in a while, for reasons of their own, they choose to draw them to the attention of a couple of chosen people. Just because you and I happen to have been included doesn't mean they've closed the list.'

'So where is it all going?' said Urmila. 'Where will it end?'

'It won't,' said Murugan. 'Let me tell you how this works: they have to be very careful to pick the right time to turn the last page. See, for them, writing "The End" to this story is the way they hope to trigger the quantum leap into the next. 'But for that to happen two things have to coincide precisely: the end credits have to come up at exactly the same instant that the story is revealed to whoever they're keeping it for.'

'So what are they waiting for?' said Urmila.

'Could be any number of things,' said Murugan. 'Maybe they're waiting to find some previously unreported strain of malaria. Or maybe they're waiting on a technology that'll make it easier and quicker to deliver their story to whoever they're keeping it for: a technology that'll be a lot more efficient in mounting it than anything that's available right now. Or maybe they're waiting for both. Who's to say?'

He was cut short by a roll of thunder. Looking quickly around, Urmila noticed a sheltered spot under the overhanging roof of the derelict outhouse. She squeezed under it and seated herself on the ground, pulling her knees up against her chin. Murugan followed, crawling in beside her and creakily crossing his legs. Within minutes the rain was pouring down before them, off the edge of the overhang.

Urmila stared into the glassy wall of rain, hugging her knees. It was all so unclear now: the call from the Club, the fish-seller in the morning, Romen Haldar, Sonali Das. It was so hard now to know what was a part of it and what wasn't: the kitchen window which looked out over the Haldar house, was that a part of it? Her parents? her brothers? her sister-in-law? (no, not her.) Was it a part of it that she was dressed in this horrible, dirty saree, spattered with turmeric stains and fish-blood; was it a part of it that she'd knocked on the Gangopadhyayas' door and woken them up this morning? And so strange to think that all this had happened when the only thing she was thinking of was how she had to cook shorshe-ilish as soon as possible, so she would be able to catch the BBD Bagh minibus and get to the Great Eastern Hotel, on time for the Minister of Communications' press conference. Now, thinking of it, it seemed so long ago; she could hardly remember why the Minister of Communications and his press conference were so important, why she had been in such a hurry to get there, why the news editor had been so insistent: what would the Minister have said anyway? That Communications were good? that ministering to them was his life's mission? How odd it would have been to sit at a keyboard, trying to think of a good sentence to lead with: Today the Minister of Communications announced at a press conference that he believed strongly that communications were the key to India's future. In a way it seemed less odd to be here, almost, sitting on this leaky veranda, with the smell of shit everywhere, than to listen to some fat old man from Delhi talking into a screeching microphone; it was easier to understand why she was here, crouching in this damp corner of this decrepit outhouse than it was to know why she had been trying to cook a fish so that her brother could get into a First Division football team; it made more sense to be listening to Murugan going on about Ronald Ross than it did to be worrying about whether she would be able to fight her way into a BBD Bagh minibus so she wouldn't be late for a press conference at the Great Eastern. This even though she had never heard of Ronald Ross before, never met this man before, this man sitting pushed up against her now, his leg against hers. He wasn't like anyone she knew, but there was nothing wrong with that, of course, it was nice to meet someone new, and his beard was nice too, sort of like a stiff brush. What would it be like to touch it—his beard—she began to wonder, and then to her surprise, she realized, why yes, she was touching him, but not his beard—his thigh was against hers, pleasantly warm, not clammy. Out on the road the buses were still roaring by, in the rain; she could see people huddling behind the misted windows, hurrying along down the pavement, under their umbrellas, rushing into the Nandan cinema complex and the Academy of Fine Arts. How odd to think that all that separated them from her and Murugan was a paltry little wall, just one little wall, yet it did the job just as well as if it was the Great Wall of China, for they couldn't see her or him. In a way it was like being in a test-tube: that was probably what it felt like, to know that something was going to happen on this side of the glass but not on the other; that there was a wall between you and everyone else, all those people in the buses and the minibuses, hurrying to work from Kankurgachi and Beleghata and Bansdroni, after their morning rice, with the smell of dal still buried deep in their fingernails; they were so far away, even though they were just on the other side of the wall; they wouldn't know even if he had his shirt off and she were running her nails down his chest to his belly; they wouldn't know if he had his trousers down, around his ankles, and her hand was in his lap instead of her own, her forefinger picking through the curly hair of his groin; they wouldn't know if her blouse was off and his arm were around her shoulder, his hand cupping her breast and his thumbnail rubbing on her nipple; they wouldn't know, they wouldn't have the faintest idea, rushing past on their way to work, and actually, it wasn't so hard to imagine, his arm around her shoulder and his hand upon her breast. It would be like an experiment too; that was exactly what it would be like, the feel of him between her legs, his lips on her neck, the sense of something animated deep inside her. What other word could there be for it, but 'experiment', something new, something which she knew was going to change her even if it lasted only a few minutes, or even seconds; something that was happening in ways that were entirely beyond her own imagining, and which she was powerless to affect in any way.

thirty-three

———————————————

After making sure his message to Tara had gone through, Antar went to the kitchen to fetch himself a glass of water. Tara's apartment was still dark but her white lace curtains were billowing spectrally in the gentle evening breeze. She had left her windows open again, an inch or two at the bottom. Antar bit his lip: it was odd that he hadn't noticed before. He always worried when she did that. He still hadn't grown used to the idea that there was someone else living here now, opening her own windows, closing her own doors.

Another time when she left the windows open, a storm hit unexpectedly, in the afternoon. Ava warned Antar early, interrupting one of her interminable inventories to let him know that bad weather was on the way.

He went around his apartment, shutting the windows. It was when he got to the kitchen that he noticed Tara had left her windows open—not all the way, but a good four or five inches. The white lace curtains in her living room were flapping in the gale.

He checked again half an hour later, and the curtains were gone: the wind had torn them off the rails. The rain was pouring in, driven by the wind. Over the next couple of hours Antar found himself drawn to the kitchen window again and again. He felt somehow responsible; as though he were to blame.

It was too dark to see what the wind and the rain were doing to the interior of the apartment. But he could imagine it all too well: the water streaming over the bare wood floor, collecting in puddles around the rush mats she had laid out, so carefully and precisely.

Tara's friends, Lucky and Maria, had helped carry her things up the stairs when she first moved in, a few months ago. Antar had marvelled at how few things she had: a futon, some sheets and mats and a couple of tables and chairs that looked like they'd come off the street. The only things on the walls were a few calligraphed scrolls. And now the scrolls were ruined: he could see them flapping on the walls of her living room in ragged flurries of white, torn to ribbons by the wind.

What was worse was that he had no way of letting her know. This was before her beeper: she was still working at her other job then and he didn't have her phone number. All he could do was wait. The storm was over by the time the lights came on in her apartment. Antar hurried into the kitchen to tell her what had happened and discovered that it wasn't Tara who'd come in. It was Lucky, and he'd already got busy cleaning up. Antar kept a discreet eye on him over the next hour or so: he didn't seem to know that he could be seen. He took off his T-shirt and his trousers and wrapped a dishtowel around his groin, like a loincloth. Then he got down on his knees and mopped the floor, not once but twice. Antar watched worriedly, wondering whether he'd do any damage. Lucky was notoriously clumsy, always dropping trays and spilling tea: 'all thumbs' as Tara often said.

Shortly afterwards Antar heard Tara's door banging shut. He went into the kitchen to see if she'd come home at last.

He was in time to see her tiredly unslinging her handbag and dropping it to the floor. Then Lucky came hurrying out of another room—to greet her, as Antar thought. But instead he did something that amazed Antar. He flung himself down on the floor in front of Tara and touched his forehead to her feet.

Tara's first, instinctive response was to look up, across the apartment, in the direction of Antar's kitchen window. She was very embarrassed when she saw Antar standing there. She gave him an awkward wave and then muttered something to Lucky who pulled himself up, looking sheepish.

Antar was embarrassed too, but he managed a smile and a wave. He had always assumed that they were just friends; he'd even wondered if they were lovers—though Lucky did seem a bit young for her. But Tara explained later that they were related in some complicated way: thus the greeting.

And now she'd done it again: left her window open. Antar shrugged: well, at least it wasn't raining today. He lowered his sweating face to the sink and sluiced water over it.

He was on his way to his bedroom when the phone rang. He took the call in his living room, dropping into the chair that faced Ava's screen.

It was Tara, sounding a little breathless.

'You got my message?' Antar said.

'I did indeed,' she answered. 'You sounded so mysterious; I had to find out what you were up to.'

'Oh, nothing important,' said Antar. 'Just some routine stuff that's going to take longer than it should.'

'Oh really?' she said. 'Sounds frightfully important.'

'Also I don't feel well.'

'Can I help?' her voice was immediately full of concern. 'Is there anything I can do?'

'I'll be all right; I've been through this before.'

'I could come by,' she said. 'Just say the word.'

'No. Thank you.' He decided to change the subject. 'Where are you calling from?' he said.

'The playground at 97th and Riverside,' she said. 'My little monster's trying to climb a fibreglass dinosaur.'

'You're at the playground?' Antar said in surprise. 'But I don't hear any children.'

She laughed. 'No. Most of them are down with the sprinklers, getting soaked to the skin.'

Antar paused, in puzzlement. Something didn't seem quite

right. 'Do they have public phones at the playground?' he asked.

'No,' she said. 'Or at least I'm not using one if they do. One of the sitters lent me her—what do you call them?—those portable thingummyjigs. I suppose I'd better let you go now. Let me know if you change your mind about dinner. I can be over in a couple of minutes.'

'Did you say a couple of minutes?' Antar said. 'But surely it'll take you at least half an hour to get here from 96th Street. Even by taxi . . .'

'Just a manner of speaking . . .' she said quickly.

At exactly that moment Ava emitted a ping, to warn him that she was about to go into standby mode. An instant later Antar heard the same sound relayed down the telephone line.

'I'd better get off,' Tara said.

Antar started. 'Wait a minute . . .' he cried into the telephone. But the line had gone dead.

Antar stared at the receiver, not quite sure of what had happened. For a moment it had sounded as though Tara were in the room with him and her mouthpiece had picked up Ava's ping.

He put the back of his hand against his forehead and wasn't surprised to find it very hot. He knew he was really feverish now.

He decided it was time to lie down.

thirty-four

With his pocket diary resting on his knee, shielded from the splashing rain by a protective arm, Murugan began to draw on an empty page with a ballpoint pen. When he had finished, he tore the page out of the diary and passed it to Urmila. It was a sketch of a figurine, a semi-circular mound with two painted eyes. On one side of the mound was a tiny pigeon, and on the other a small semi-circular instrument.

'Ever seen anything like this before?' he said.

Urmila examined the drawing minutely, frowning in concentration. 'I probably wouldn't have noticed if I had,' she said. 'It's like so many temple images—except for that thing over there. What is it?' She pointed at the instrument.

'My guess is that it's a version of an old-fashioned microscope,' Murugan said.

'So who or what is it an image of?'

'If I had to take a guess, I'd say that that was the demi-urge of Ron's discovery,' he said. 'My guess is that she's the one behind this whole experiment.'

'You think it was a woman?' said Urmila.

Murugan nodded.

'Where did you find it?' Urmila asked.

'Over there,' said Murugan, pointing his pencil at the wall: it was raining so hard now that the alcove was barely visible, even though it was no more than a few yards away. He began to explain how he had found the little figurine there the night before. Urmila listened intently, and when he had finished, she gave a little nod, as though confirming something to herself.

'It's strange,' said Urmila. 'Just the other day, I was reading a book of Phulboni's essays—you know, the writer who was given the award at Rabindra Sadan yesterday? What you were saying reminded me of something he wrote a long time ago. I remember the passage almost by heart. "I have never known," it begins, "whether life lies in words or in images, in speech or sight. Does a story come to be in the words that I conjure out of my mind or does it live already, somewhere, enshrined in mud and clay—in an image, that is, in the crafted mimicry of life?"

'Apparently,' Urmila continued, 'Phulboni wrote a story many years ago: about a woman, bathing . . .' Her voice deepened in tone, in imitation of the writer's: '". . . A woman no different from the hundreds of women you see every day, from the windows of your cars and buses, a woman washing off the day's dirt in the dank, weed-rich water of a pond, in a park—a pond like so many in our city, like Minto Park, or Poddopukur, or any one of a dozen others. The woman kneels, in the soft, glutinous mud, the water rises in a dark curtain to her throat, allowing her to momentarily slip the top of her mud-browned saree off her shoulders, and run the tips of her fingers over her breasts, scrape a sliver of soap across the hardened skin of child-bitten nipples, then run her hand down, below, past the folds of a wasted belly, and even further, down, down, scraping that foaming sliver past the parted lips that have vomited a dozen children into her husband's bed, and further still into the velvet dampness of the mud, the soap clinging to her fingers, and then, without warning her foot slips, and she finds herself, for one panic-stricken moment, clutching at the mud which is suddenly as soft, as pliant and yielding as death itself, her hands clawing at that depthless murk, and then, when the face of extinction seems to be looking unsmiling into her eyes, the edge of a fingernail scrapes suddenly upon something solid, something abrasive, something with redeeming, saving, life-giving edges, something blessedly hard, something that can give her the moment's handhold she needs to claw her way back to the surface and seize a breath of our city's dankly sustaining humours.

'"And when her torso rises above the water, her breasts bared, her hair hanging black to her knees, her arms fling an arc of water high into the air, and she screams: 'She saved me; she saved me', and at once all the other bathers plunge in, their feet churning the silky brown water into a frothing bog, and taking her by the arms, they drag her ashore, while she goes on screaming, through mouthfuls of water: 'She saved me, saved me.'

'"When she is lying on the grass, they pry open her fist and see that it has fastened upon an object, a polished grey stone with a whirl of white staring out of its centre like an all-seeing eye. She screams, spluttering through jets of swallowed mud and water, she will not part from that tiny shape that gave her the handhold she needed to keep from drowning, but the others tear it from her, for they know that the rock that saved her, that the small, life-giving, lump of stone was none other than a miraculous manifestation of . . . of what? They do not know; believing only in the reality of the miracle . . ."'

Pausing to catch her breath, Urmila turned to Murugan.

'And then,' she said, 'one day, many years later, Phulboni was going past a park and what did he see but a little shrine, decorated with flowers and offerings. He stopped to enquire, but no one could tell him whose shrine it was and how it had come to be there. Determined to find out he went to Kalighat, to one of the lanes where these images are made. And there he found someone who told him a story that was very much like his own, yet the man had never heard of Phulboni and had never read anything he had ever written, and by the time he had finished, it was Phulboni who was no longer sure which had happened first or whether they were all aspects of the coming of that image into the world: its presence in the mud, the writing of his story, that bather's discovery or the tale he had just heard, in Kalighat.'

Murugan ran a fingernail through his goatee. 'I don't get it,' he said.

Urmila put out a hand to test the rain. It had thinned to a light drizzle now. She gave Murugan a sharp prod in the ribs. 'Come on,' she said, 'let's go.'

'Go where?' said Murugan.

'To Kalighat,' she said. 'Let's go and see if we can learn anything about that image you saw.'

thirty-five

———————

On the way to Kalighat, watching the rain-slicked streets through the misted glass of the taxi's window, Urmila had a vivid recollection of the lane they were going to: she remembered a narrow alley, winding through low, tin-roofed sheds, pavements that were lined with rows of grey-brown clay figures, some just torsos, full-breasted but headless, with tufts of straw blossoming out of their necks, some legless, some without hands, some with their arms curved in phantom gestures around invisible objects—weapons, sitars, skulls.

She had an aunt who lived nearby, in a big, old-fashioned house that towered above the lanes around it. As a child she had often walked through the lane, to visit her aunt. She had watched in amazement as breasts and bellies took shape under the craftsmen's kneading fingers, wondering at the intimacy of their knowledge of those spectral bodies. At her aunt's house she would go to the balcony and look down on the lane and its rows of clay images, watching the image-makers at their work; noting details of the different ways in which they modelled heads and hands; observing how the images changed with the seasons; how phalanxes of Ma Shoroshshotis appeared in January, each embellished with the goddess's swan and sitar; Ma Durgas in autumn, with the entire pantheon of her family ranged around her and Mahishashur writhing at her feet.

The taxi came to a halt at the corner of the lane, and they stepped out into the fine, fog-like drizzle. Murugan paid and then Urmila led him quickly towards the low, bamboo-walled workshops at the end of the lane. Hundreds of beatifically smiling faces floated by them as they hurried past, some draped in tarpaulin, their eyes unpupilled, their arms outstretched in immobile benediction.

Urmila laughed.

'What's up?' said Murugan.

'I often had a dream when I was a child,' Urmila said, with a laugh in her throat. 'I dreamt I would open the front door of our flat one day and find a small group of gods and goddesses outside, ringing the bell with the tips of their clay fingers. I would open the door and welcome them, hands folded, and they would float in on their swans and rats and lions and owls, and my mother would lead them to the little formica-topped table where we eat. They would seat themselves on our chairs while my mother ran in and out of the kitchen, making tea and frying luchis and shingaras, while we watched in awe, our hands joined in prayer. We would offer sweets to the swan and the owl, and Ma Kali would smile at us with her burning eyes, and Ma Shoroshshoti would play a note or two on her sitar and Ma Lokhkhi would sit cross-legged on her lotus, holding up her hand, looking just as she does on the labels of ghee tins.'

She paused at the open door of a workshop. 'Let's try this one,' she said, leading him in. They stepped through the open doorway, into the workshop's dimly lit interior and found themselves staring into a teeming crowd of smiling, flesh-coloured faces.

Urmila spotted a moving figure somewhere among the stationary images. 'Is somebody there?' she called out.

'Who is it?' the figure vanished as quickly as it had appeared, behind a six-foot dancing Ganesh.

'We just wanted to talk to you,' Urmila said.

An elderly man materialized suddenly in front of her, detaching himself from a pantheon on a plinth. He was wearing a dhoti and a string vest and his thin, ill-tempered face was screwed into a scowl. Stepping away, Urmila very nearly impaled

Amitav Ghosh

herself on a spear, upraised in the hands of a serene Ma Durga.

'Careful,' the man snapped. He looked her over suspiciously as she straightened her damp, dirt-streaked saree. 'What do you want?' he said. 'We're very busy right now, no time to talk.'

Urmila stiffened, falling immediately into her professional manner. 'I am a reporter for *Calcutta*,' she said, in a crisp, firm voice. 'And I'd like to ask you a question.'

The man's frown deepened. 'What question?' he said. 'Why? I don't know anything. We're not involved in politics.'

'It's not about politics.' Urmila thrust Murugan's drawing into his hands. 'Can you tell me what kind of image this is?'

The man narrowed his eyes, directing a sharp glance at Murugan. 'I've never seen anything like this in my life,' he said, handing the drawing back. 'I know every divine image there is and I've never seen one like this.'

Urmila turned to Murugan to translate, but he cut her short. 'I got that,' he whispered. 'But something tells me he's in denial mode.'

'You don't know anything about this image then?' Urmila said to the man in the dhoti. 'Are you sure?'

'What did I tell you?' the man said, his voice rising. 'Haven't I said "no" already? How many times do I have to say it?'

A couple of younger men had gathered around them now. Urmila held the drawing out to them but the older man cut her short.

'What can they tell you?' he said. 'They're just boys.' He herded Urmila and Murugan quickly towards the door, muttering under his breath. He saw them to the door and shooed them impatiently off: 'Go on, go on, there's nothing for you here.' He watched them leave and then disappeared into the interior of the workshop.

'Well,' said Murugan, dusting his hands. 'I guess that's as much as we're going to get from him.'

Urmila was about to walk away when Murugan pulled her to an abrupt halt. 'Look!' he said, with a sudden intake of breath. 'Over there.' His finger was pointing at a child, a six-

or seven-year-old girl, who was sitting by the roadside playing with a doll.

'At what?' said Urmila.

'Look at what she just put into her doll's hands,' Murugan whispered into her ear.

Now, looking closely, Urmila noticed that the girl was trying to push a tiny semi-circular object into the unyielding grasp of her sightless plastic doll. 'What is it?' she said, 'I can't tell.'

'Don't you see?' said Murugan. 'It's a little stylized microscope, just like the one I saw.' He gave her a nudge: 'Go on, ask her, ask her where she got it.'

Urmila took a step forward, and as her shadow approached, the girl glanced up, her eyes widening warily. Urmila gave her a reassuring smile and sank slowly down to her knees, beside her.

'Why, how beautiful,' she said, speaking softly, in a child's Bengali, pointing at the tiny microscope, now firmly lodged in the doll's hands.

'It's mine,' the girl said defensively, closing her fist upon the doll's hand.

'Yes of course it's yours,' said Urmila. 'Your father gave it to you, didn't he?'

The girl nodded, moving her head slowly up and down. She cocked her head at the workshop. 'My father is in there,' she said. 'He's made a lot of them.'

'Oh?' said Urmila, nodding encouragement.

'He made them for the big puja tonight,' the girl offered.

'Really?' Urmila smiled. 'I didn't know there's a puja tonight.'

'There is,' the girl nodded vigorously. 'Today is the last day of the puja of Mangala-bibi. Baba says that tonight Mangala-bibi is going to enter a new body.'

'And whose is that?' Urmila said.

'The body she's chosen of course,' the girl said. 'No one knows whose it is.'

Murugan hissed into Urmila's ear: 'Ask her about Lutchman.' But before Urmila could say another word a man burst out of

Amitav Ghosh

the workshop. Picking up the girl, he took her inside. Then the elderly man in the dhoti appeared again, carrying a stick.

'Why are you still here?' he shouted at Urmila. 'Why were you talking to that child? Are you kidnappers? I'm going to call the police, right now.'

'Don't bother,' said Urmila, rising to her feet. 'We're going.' She tapped Murugan on the arm and set off briskly down the lane.

thirty-six

A ntar was drifting off to sleep when Ava began to emit an urgent summons. It wasn't very loud and Antar felt it before he heard it, in his belly, reverberating through the floor.

Antar made his way gingerly into the living room, and spotted the outer nimbus of a package, deep inside Ava's delivery slot. It was a folder from the personal terminus of the Council's Assistant-Secretary General for Human Resources. It began by thanking him for the time and effort he had already invested in the L. Murugan case. Then, in polite but uncompromising language it informed him that since he was already 'cognizant of the details' it had been decided that he should proceed with a further investigation of the matter. He was thus given authority to open up a direct line to the Council's representative in Calcutta, in order to conduct whatever interrogations were necessary (there followed a lengthy sequence of codes and clearances).

Antar spent a few minutes lashing together a raft of commands to take Ava through to Calcutta. When he was ready he went into the kitchen and splashed water over his face.

Tara's apartment was still dark, except for a light in the living room, which she always left on, night and day. As Antar was patting his face dry something shot up out of the airshaft and began to knock furiously on the glass windowpane. Antar recoiled, throwing his arms up: it was a pigeon, flapping against the glass. Its beady red eyes fixed on him for an instant, and then it was gone.

Antar poured himself a glass of water and carried it into his living room. Then he began the process of arming the raft.

It took exactly 5.65 seconds before the raft came to a stop at the personal terminus of the Director of the Council's office in Calcutta. It ran up against a barrier and began to thrash about, like a fish at a lock, sending back frantic signals: there was no one in the office and the only person who was directly connected was the Director himself. And the Director was at his residence, with the privacy controls in his surveillance system activated. Ava wouldn't be able to get through without a Shatter Command.

Antar looked up the code in his list of clearances and fed the command in. It took Ava just an instant to break through, and a moment later a holographic projection of the Director appeared in Antar's living room, half-size. He was standing under a shower, a tall paunchy Peruvian. His eyes were closed and he was crooning to himself and scratching his balls.

Resisting the temptation to say 'boo!' Antar cleared his throat with a gentle cough.

The Director opened one eye very slowly, looking around in disbelief. When he saw what was happening, his hands flew down to cup his genitals. He began to scream, his voice rising from a soundless wheeze into a high-pitched shriek. He dropped to all fours and began crawling furiously, dripping soap and water on the floor. Antar guessed he was heading for a towel, but he couldn't see the rest of the bathroom: to him, the Director looked frantically stationary, in the middle of his living room, as though he were crawling on a conveyor belt.

The Director jumped to his feet, grabbed a towel and wrapped it around his middle. 'You fucking son-of-a-bitch,' Ava translated, into gleefully demotic Arabic, as the Director began to scream at Antar. 'You can't do this! I'll have you brought to book! I'll see you pay for this! You'll go to gaol, you wait . . .'

Antar tried to explain but he wouldn't listen. So Antar hit

the bathroom with the Alert signal until he quieted down and went to look for his clothes.

He went on grumbling while he dressed. 'You don't know what it's like here,' he muttered, pulling on his trousers. 'I have to run the whole office myself.'

'Is it hard work?' Antar said, trying to sound sympathetic.

'Hard work!' cried the Director laughing sarcastically. 'That's the problem; there's no work at all, now that the river doesn't flow through the city any more. I have to make work for the office. I keep recommending projects but the people here won't let the Council touch a thing: I've never seen anything like it. In the last year they've only let us start one project. And you know what that is?'

'What?' said Antar.

'A shelter!' said the Director, throwing up his hands. 'A shelter for the needy is how we describe it. They have a big fort here, called Fort William. It was built by the British in the eighteenth century. The Council requisitioned it, but then couldn't figure out what to do with it. The only thing everyone could agree on was the shelter idea. So that's what I do now, I run a shelter.'

He had finished dressing and was sitting at his terminus, looking through his files. 'All right, what was it you were asking about?' he said, looking over his shoulder. 'An ID card in an inventory? That's easy—there's only one place it could have come from.'

He made a couple of short-sighted jabs at his keyboard. 'Yes,' he said. 'I thought so. It was in an inventory that came from the Fort William Shelter.'

'Go on,' said Antar.

'Well,' said the Director, 'it seems to have been found in the Department of Alternative Inner States . . .'

He gave Antar a wink, over his shoulder. 'What we old-timers used to call asylums,' he said. 'It says here it was entered into the system this morning. They found it while registering an inmate. They always do a strip search when they bring someone in.'

Peering into the panel, he gave Antar a sly grin. 'From what I can see here,' he said, 'I would say the guy you're looking for is experiencing an inner state that is about as alternative as it can be.'

'Who was he?' asked Antar.

'He wouldn't give a name,' said the Director.

'Where was he found?'

The Director peered at his panel again. 'It says here,' he said, 'that he turned himself in at a railway station—a place called Sealdah.'

'When can I talk to him?' said Antar.

'You want to talk to him?' groaned the Director. 'You realize I'll have to bring him here? This is the Council's only secured communications facility here—right in my home. What if he experiences an alternative inner state while he's here? What if he wrecks the place? What if he wrecks the terminus?'

'I'll make sure you're insured,' said Antar. 'Just have him here: as soon as you can.' He cut the Director off before he could protest.

Then he stumbled back to bed.

thirty-seven

Walking past the pavement stalls on Shyama Prasad Mukherjee Road, Urmila caught a whiff of the irresistible smell of fish cutlets and dhakai parotha wafting through the doors of the Dilkhusha Cabin.

'I'll die if I don't eat soon,' she remarked to Murugan. She lost no time in propelling him into the eatery. Leading him to a curtained booth, she slid on to a bench and signalled to Murugan to seat himself opposite her. A waiter appeared almost immediately, with two limp menu cards in his hand. Urmila ordered for them both, and as soon as the waiter left, she pulled the curtain shut.

'Tell me,' she said, leaning across the table. 'Who is this Lachman you keep talking about?'

'You mean Lutchman,' Murugan corrected her. 'That's how Ronnie Ross would have said it; that's how he spelt it anyhow.'

'But the name must have been Lachman,' said Urmila. 'Ross probably just spelt it in a British kind of way.'

'Same difference,' said Murugan. 'Who knows what his mother called him? We weren't there. Anyways, Lutchman was this young guy who walked into Ronnie Ross's life on May 25, 1895 at 8 p.m., offering himself as a guinea pig. He ended up spending the next three years doing everything for Ron, from slicing his breakfast bagels to counting his slides. Every time Ron went running off in the wrong direction, Lutchman was waiting to head him off and show him the way to go. He claimed to be a "dhooley-bearer" by trade but my guess is that he was leading Ronnie by the nose.'

'But,' said Urmila, 'how would he have known about where to lead Ronald Ross?'

'It's a long story,' he said. 'I'll cut it short for you: a few years ago I found a letter that was written in Calcutta, by an American missionary doctor called Elijah Farley. Before he got religion Farley was doing medical research back in the States, at Johns Hopkins. As a student he'd worked with some of the biggest names in malaria research.

'Well, the last thing he ever wrote was this letter in which he described a visit to Cunningham's laboratory in Calcutta. He saw some stuff there that was—oh, maybe three or four years ahead of the state of play in the international scientific community. None of it made any sense to him of course, because it didn't fit with anything he'd ever been taught.'

'Don't talk so fast,' said Urmila. 'I'm not sure I understand what you're trying to tell me. Are you talking about Cunningham's own research?'

Murugan laughed: 'No. Cunningham didn't have a clue.'

'So who was doing this work then?'

'The way Farley saw it,' said Murugan, 'it was the people in the lab, Cunningham's servants and assistants.'

'But surely,' said Urmila, 'Cunningham's assistants would have told him what they were doing?'

'It's like this,' said Murugan. 'Cunningham's assistants were a pretty wild mix. You see, he didn't want educated college kids from Calcutta messing around in his lab, and asking questions and stuff. So what he did instead was he'd train his own assistants.'

'Who were they?' Urmila asked. 'And where did he find them?'

'In the last place anyone would think of looking,' said Murugan. 'At Sealdah railway station. The station hadn't been around that long, but if you wanted to find people who were pretty much on their own, down and out with nowhere to go, that was the place to look. Cunningham used to check out the whole station every once in a while and when he saw a likely-looking kid he'd offer them room and board in exchange for work—nothing fancy, just a minimum-wage kind of job around the lab, sweeper, "dhooley-bearer", that sort of shit. They'd jump at it of course: what did they have to lose? They'd live in those outhouses near the hospital wall, and help around the lab. It was a nice, cozy little set-up.'

'So he taught them?' said Urmila. 'And trained them and so on?'

'Not really,' said Murugan. 'He may have taught them how to read a little English and he probably showed them a couple of things—but just monkey-see, monkey-do kind of stuff. They probably didn't give a shit anyway. But there was this one person, a woman, who took to the lab like a duck to water. My guess is that within a few years she was way ahead of Cunningham in her intuitive understanding of the fundamentals of the malaria problem.'

'But who was this woman?' said Urmila. 'And what was she called?'

Murugan smiled: 'The way Farley tells it,' he said, drawing his sleeve across his damp forehead, 'her name was Mangala.'

Urmila gasped. 'Mangala?' she cried. 'You mean like Mangala-bibi—like the name the girl said?'

'I guess you could call her a prototype,' said Murugan. 'And as for who she was—who knows? The only indication we have that she even existed was in this letter written by Elijah Farley. And even that letter isn't around any more: at least it's untraceable in the catalogues.'

'What did Elijah Farley say about her?'

'Not much,' said Murugan. 'All he knew was what Cunningham told him—which was that he found her at Sealdah station, that she was dirt poor and that she probably had hereditary syphilis. But then the big question is: did Cunningham find her or did she find him? Anyway, Farley saw things happening in the lab that left him in no doubt that she knew a whole lot more about malaria than Cunningham could ever have taught her.'

'Really?' said Urmila, her forehead wrinkling in disbelief. 'Is it possible that she could have taught herself something as technical as that?'

Murugan shrugged. 'Similar things have been known to happen,' he said. 'Think of Ramanujan, the mathematician, down in Madras. He went ahead and re-invented a fair hunk of modern mathematics just because nobody had told him that it had already been done. And with Mangala we're not talking about mathematics: we're talking about microscopy which was still an artisanal kind of skill at that time. Real talent could take you a long way in it—Ronnie Ross's career is living proof of that. With this woman we're talking about a whole lot more than just talent; we may be talking genius here. You also have to remember that she wasn't hampered by the sort of stuff that might slow down someone who was conventionally trained: she wasn't carrying a shit-load of theory in her head, she didn't have to write papers or construct proofs. Unlike Ross she didn't need to read a zoological study to see that there was a difference between Culex and Anopheles: she'd have seen it like you or I can see the difference between a dachshund and a doberman. She didn't care about formal classifications. In fact she didn't even really care about malaria. That's probably why she got behind Ronnie Ross and started pushing him towards the finish-line. She was working towards something altogether different, and she'd begun to believe that the only way she was going to make her final breakthrough was by getting Ronnie Ross to make his. She had bigger things in mind than the malaria bug.'

'Like what?' said Urmila.

'The Calcutta chromosome.'

With a discreet cough, the waiter parted their curtain, and placed their orders on the table. Urmila waited till he had left.

'What was that you just said?'

'The Calcutta chromosome,' said Murugan. 'That's my name for what she was working towards.'

'Now I'm really lost,' said Urmila. 'I've lived here all my life and I've never heard of this thing you're talking about.'

'And who knows if you ever will?' said Murugan. 'Or whether I will. Or whether it exists or has ever existed. At this point in time it's still all guesswork on my part.'

'But you must have something to found your guesses on,' said Urmila.

Murugan made no answer. 'Go on,' Urmila prompted, almost pleading. 'We're caught in this together, after all. I have a right to know.'

Murugan hesitated. 'Are you really sure you want to know?'

She nodded.

'Okay, I'll tell you what started me off,' said Murugan reluctantly. 'It seemed to me from Farley's letter that Mangala was actually using the malaria bug as a treatment in another disease.'

'What disease?'

'Syphilis,' said Murugan. 'Or to put it more precisely, syphilitic paresis—the final paralytic stage of syphilis. From Farley's account it seems there was an underground network of people who believed that she possessed a cure. Remember that we're talking about the 1890s—long before the discovery of penicillin. Syphilis was untreatable and incurable: it killed millions of people every year, all around the world. These people who came to see Mangala may have believed that she was a witch or a magician or a god or whatever: it doesn't matter—the conventional medical treatments for syphilis at that time weren't much more than hocus-pocus either. Let's just stick with that old saying about no smoke without a fire. If a whole crowd of people believed that Mangala had a cure, or a halfway effective treatment, it must have been because she had a certain rate of success. People aren't crazy: if they travelled long distances to see her they must have thought she offered some kind of hope.'

'What do you think that treatment was?' said Urmila.

'I'm just guessing wildly here, okay? But if you twisted my arm, I'd say that she'd stumbled upon some variant of a process that got a guy called Julius von Wagner-Jauregg the Nobel in 1927. Guess what that treatment was?'

Amitav Ghosh

Urmila looked up from her plate. 'You know perfectly well I have no idea,' she said. 'What was it?'

Murugan poked a finger into the crisp, rounded top of his dhakai parotha, releasing a puff of steam. 'All right, I'll tell you,' he said. 'What Wagner-Jauregg showed was that artificially induced malaria often cured, or at least mitigated, syphilitic paresis. What he'd do is, he'd actually inject malarial blood into the patient by making a little incision. It was a pretty crude process, but the weird thing is that it worked. In fact, until antibiotics, the Wagner-Jauregg process was pretty much a standard treatment: every major VD hospital had its little incubating room where it grew a flock of anopheles. Think about it: hospitals cultivating disease! But on the other hand, what could be more natural than fighting fire with fire? You could say vaccines work on the same sort of principle really, but what they do is to prime your immune system against themselves. This is the only instance known to medicine of using one disease to fight another.

'To this day no one really knows how the Wagner-Jauregg treatment worked. Not that anyone's losing any sleep over it. It was a scientific scandal and medicine was almost grateful to turn its back on it once antibiotics came along. Old Julius didn't worry too much about how it worked either. He was no biologist remember: he was a clinician and a psychologist. He thought the process worked by raising the patient's body temperature. It didn't seem to bother him that no other fever had the same effect.

'But it's quite possible that malaria worked on paresis through a different route: the brain for example. One of the things that syphilis does is that it muddies up the blood/brain barrier. Malaria works on the brain too, in different ways: that's why falciparum malaria is also called cerebral malaria. But other kinds of malaria have weird neural effects too. A lot of people who've had malaria know that: it can be more hallucinogenic than any mind-bending drug. That's why primitive people sometimes thought of malaria as a kind of spirit-possession.

'Enter Mangala: it looks like she hit upon this treatment too, at about the same time as the Herr Doktor. But she added a little twist to it. From what we know of her technique, it sounds like she was working with some weird strain of malaria—that is, by some kind of primitive horse-breeding method she had developed a strain that could actually be cultivated in pigeons. My hunch is that she found some way of making the bug cross over, so that the bird could be used like a test-tube, or an agar plate.

'Now here's the really wacky stuff. I'll just stick my neck out and say it: I think what happened was that somewhere down the line Mangala began to notice that her treatment often produced weird side-effects—what looked like strange personality disorders. Except that they weren't really disorders but transpositions. She began to put two and two together and found that in fact what she had on her hands was a cross-over of randomly assorted personality traits, from the malaria donor to the recipient—via the bird of course. And once she saw this she became more and more invested in isolating this aspect of the treatment, so that she could control the ways in which these cross-overs worked.'

'I'm not sure I follow,' said Urmila. 'What exactly are you trying to say?'

'What am I saying? Well, what I'm saying is this: I think Mangala stumbled on something that neither she nor Ronnie Ross nor any scientist of that time would have had a name for. For the sake of argument let's call it a chromosome: though the whole point of this is that if it is really a chromosome, it's only by extension so to speak—by analogy. Because what we're talking about here is an item that is to the standard Mendelian pantheon of twenty-three chromosomes what Ganesh is to the gods; that is, different, non-standard, unique—which is exactly why it eludes standard techniques of research. And which is why I call it the Calcutta chromosome.

'One of the reasons why the Calcutta chromosome can't be found by normal methods is because, unlike the standard chromosomes, it isn't present in every cell. Or if it is, it's so deeply encrypted that our current techniques can't isolate it. And the reason why it isn't present in every cell is because unlike the other chromosomes it's not symmetrically paired. And the reason why it's not paired is because it doesn't split into eggs and sperm. And guess why that is? I'll tell you: it's because this is a chromosome that is not transmitted from generation to generation by sexual reproduction. It develops out of a process of recombination and is particular to every individual. That's why it's only found in certain kinds of cells: it simply isn't present in regenerative tissue. It only exists in non-regenerating tissue: in other words, the brain.

'Let me put it like this: if there really is such a thing as the Calcutta chromosome only a person like Mangala, someone who's completely out of the loop, scientifically speaking, would be able to find it—even if she didn't know what it was and didn't even have a name for it. For what we have here is a biological expression of human traits that is neither inherited from the immediate gene pool, nor transmitted into it. It's exactly the kind of entity that would be hardest for a conventional scientist to accept. Biologists are under so much pressure to bring their findings into line with politics: right-wing politicians sit on them to find genes for everything, from poverty to terrorism, so they'll have an alibi for castrating the poor or nuking the Middle East. The left goes ballistic if they say anything at all about the biological expression of human traits: it's all consciousness and soul at that end of the spectrum.

'But if you think about it, it figures that certain kinds of traits would have a biological correlate. But who said they have to be determined by biology? Maybe it even works the other way around—that they leave their imprint on biology. Who knows?

'And just because those biological correlates aren't transmitted by sexual reproduction, it doesn't mean that they can't be transferred between individuals by other methods. And that's where Mangala comes up to bat. Remember that she started at the deep end, by stumbling upon the process of transmission, rather than the chromosome itself—after all she didn't know what a chromosome was. No one did back then. Remember that it was malaria that led her to it. Remember that one of the extraordinary things about the malaria bug is that it has the capacity to "cut and paste" its DNA—unlike any creature we know of except the trypanosome. Remember that's one of the reasons why it's been so hard to develop a malaria vaccine. Because what's special about the malaria bug is that, as it goes through its life cycle, it keeps altering its coat-proteins. So by the time the body's immune system learns to recognize the threat, the bug's already had time to do a little costume-change before the next act.

'Perhaps what Mangala chanced upon was just this: that the malaria bug, because of its recombinatory powers, can actually digest this bit of DNA by splitting it up and redistributing it. Then, when it's reintroduced in a patient whose blood/brain barrier's been made spongy, perhaps it can carry the information back and make some tiny little re-wirings in the host's wetware.

'I reckon that once she stumbled on the process she dropped everything else and began to concentrate on refining it—in two directions. One was in trying to figure out some way of side-stepping the syphilis step. And the other was in trying to stabilize the chromosome during the process of transference. Because what was happening till then was that the bug was breaking it up in the weirdest ways and she wanted to be able to control the kinds of traits that were being transmitted.

'It's my guess that by about 1897 Mangala had run into a dead end, and she'd come to the conclusion that the existent strains of malaria wouldn't let her go any further. That's why she was so desperate to have Ronnie figure the whole thing out and publish it. Because she actually believed that the link between the bug and the human mind was so close that, once its life cycle had been figured out, it would spontaneously mutate in directions that would take her work to the next step. That was what she believed, I think: that every time she reached a dead end, the way ahead was by provoking another mutation.'

Amitav Ghosh

Pushing away her empty plate, Urmila said: 'How?'

'By trying to make certain things known.'

'So did she succeed?' she asked.

Murugan smiled. 'I think we're going to find out.'

'How?'

'My guess is that that's what this experiment is about.'

'But why in this way? Why not . . . ?'

'Don't you get it?' said Murugan. 'She's not in this because she wants to be a scientist. She's in this because she thinks she's a god. And what that means is that she wants to be the mind that sets things in motion. The way she sees it, we can't ever know her, or her motives, or anything else about her: the experiment won't work unless the reasons for it are utterly inscrutable to us, as unknowable as a disease. But at the same time, she's got to try and tell us about her own history: that's part of the experiment too.'

'Why are you talking about her as if she was still alive?' said Urmila. 'Are you really trying to say that she is? That she somehow managed to . . . ?'

Murugan smiled. 'Well,' he said. 'What do you think?'

Crossing her arms, Urmila hugged herself, suddenly cold. 'I don't know what to think,' she said. She took hold of the booth's curtain and tweaked it back.

The moment she looked into the cabin, everything seemed to stop; it was as though everyone in the room had turned to stare—the other customers, the waiters, the dishevelled college students at the next table—as though they had been waiting all along to see her face.

She pushed the curtain quickly shut.

'But what about Lutchman?' she said. 'Nothing you've told me proves any connection between Mangala and Lutchman. For that matter who was Lutchman? What was his past?'

'You've got me there Calcutta,' Murugan said. 'That's where I keep coming up short. All I have is bits and pieces—no beginning, no middle and definitely no end.'

'Give me examples,' said Urmila. 'What are these bits and pieces you're talking about?'

'Farley's letter is the main source,' said Murugan. 'Farley says there was another guy working with Mangala at Cunningham's lab. He seems to have been about the same age as Lutchman and he fits the same general profile.'

'That's not much to go on,' said Urmila.

'That's true,' Murugan acknowledged, 'except that a couple of references in the letter seem to suggest that this assistant was the same guy who turned up at Ross's door on May 25, 1895.'

'Like what?' said Urmila.

'Well, one thing we know about Lutchman, from another source, is that he was digitally challenged—that is, his left hand was missing a thumb. It doesn't seem to have made any difference to his manual skills. He was probably born that way, because his index finger seems to have re-trained itself to do the thumb's job . . .'

Something stirred in Urmila's mind, a distant memory.

'What's up?' said Murugan. 'Why're you frowning?'

She bit her lip: 'I thought I'd remembered something, but I can't place it. Anyway, go on. Does Farley say anything about the assistant's hand?'

'Nothing explicit,' said Murugan. 'But there's a sentence where he says: "he was surprisingly deft given the circumstances". Something like that anyway. My guess is that the "circumstances" he's referring to had something to do with the guy's hand.'

'Is that all?' Urmila said in disappointment.

'There's just one other thing. At the end of the letter Farley said that the assistant had been using an assumed name.'

'So what was his real name then?'

'I wish I knew,' said Murugan. 'But I don't. Farley didn't mention it in his letter. He left Calcutta the same day he posted the letter. He was seen boarding a train at Sealdah station and a young man who fits the assistant's description was carrying his luggage. They were also seen getting off the train together later, at a deserted little station. Farley was never seen again. A few months later, in May 1895, "Lutchman" walked into Ronald Ross's lab in Secunderabad.'

'That could just be a coincidence,' said Urmila.

'Could be,' said Murugan. 'But there's another coincidence left to account for.'

'Yes?'

'It's just this,' said Murugan. 'I've established from a different source that Lutchman's name wasn't a real name either.'

'What was it?' said Urmila.

'Laakhan,' said Murugan.

Urmila's hands flew to her mouth. 'Tell me,' she said. 'Quick: what was the name of the station where Farley and the assistant were last seen?'

'Renupur,' said Murugan.

She stared at him soundlessly.

Murugan took hold of her hand and shook it. 'Hey wake up,' he said. 'What's up?'

'It's just that I think I may be able to fill in a part of the picture,' Urmila said.

'How come?'

'Last night I went home with Sonali-di and she told me something: a story she'd heard from her mother, about something that happened to Phulboni many years ago.'

thirty-eight

In 1933, soon after he got his first and only job, Phulboni was sent on a trip to the remote provincial town of Renupur.

Phulboni was working for a well-known British firm, Palmer Brothers, which made soaps and oils and other household goods. The company was famous for its extensive distribution network, which reached into the smallest towns and villages. Every new recruit to the company had to spend a couple of years travelling within a region, visiting village shops, getting to know the local merchants, sitting in tea-stalls, visiting fairs and fairgrounds.

Being new to the job, Phulboni had never heard of Renupur. Upon making enquiries he was pleasantly surprised to discover that, tiny though it was, the town boasted a railway station. A train that connected Calcutta to the cotton market of Barich passed through it every other day.

As the crow flies, Renupur was no more than three hundred miles from Calcutta but the journey was a slow and rather tedious one, meandering as it did through Darbhanga and a wide swathe of the great Maithil plain. But far from being dismayed at the thought of spending two days on a train, Phulboni was delighted: he loved everything to do with the railways—stations, engines, Bradshaws, the acrid, creosote smell of teakwood sleepers. There was nothing he liked better than to daydream by an open window with the wind in his face. He was particularly enthusiastic on this occasion because he had been told that the forests near Renupur offered good hunting. Typically, he had spent his first month's salary on a new .303 rifle. Now he was looking forward to the prospect of putting the gun to use.

It was mid-July. The monsoons had set in and the whole of eastern India was awash in rain. Several of the famously restless rivers of the region had burst their banks and swept across the broad, flat plains. Those waters, so full of menace to those they nourished, presented an entirely different aspect to a casual spectator in a train, watching from the safety of a tall embankment. The still waters, lying in great silver sheets under the lowering monsoon skies, presented an enchanting, bewitching spectacle. Phulboni, raised amidst the hills and forests of Orissa, had never seen anything like this before: this majestic, endless plain mirroring the turbulent heavens.

Before leaving Darbhanga Phulboni had asked the guard on the train to let him know before they arrived in Renupur. The journey took eight hours, but to the young writer it seemed to pass in a matter of minutes. Long before he had slaked his appetite for the landscape, the guard appeared to tell him that they were almost at Renupur.

Phulboni was astonished: looking out of the window all he could see were flooded fields, the still waters broken only by the careful geometry of bunds and embankments. An occasional, distant curl of wood-smoke spiralling out of a thicket of trees, suggested a village or a hamlet but he could see no sign whatever of habitation on a scale that might earn entitlement to a railway station.

On expressing his surprise to the guard Phulboni learnt, to his alarm, that the town (or rather village) of Renupur was some three miles distant from the station that bore its name. Renupur was by no means large or important enough to merit a deviation in the tracks that linked Darbhanga to Barich. Those of Renupur's villagers who wished to avail themselves of this facility were expected instead to make the journey to the station in a bullock cart. Indeed, the station of Renupur owed its existence more to the demands of engineering than to the requirements of the local population. Railway regulations decreed that single-track lines such as this were required to have sidings at regular intervals, so that oncoming trains could pass each other in safety. It was thus that Renupur came to boast of a station: it was really little more than a signboard and a platform attached to a siding.

It was all just red tape and regulations of course, the guard said. There was no real need for a siding on this line. This was the only train that ever used this length of track. It went chugging along, stopping wherever the slightest pretext offered itself, until it came to the end of the line. And then it simply turned around and headed back. It never encountered other trains until it reached Darbhanga.

The guard was an odd-looking man. He had a grotesquely twisted face: his lower jaw was so much out of alignment with the upper that his mouth was perpetually open in a crooked, leering grimace. Now he began to laugh, in his dry, rustling voice. Leaning out of the window he pointed to a length of track that ran alongside the main line for a couple of hundred yards before rejoining it. The tracks were so rusted and overgrown as to be barely visible.

'And there you see the Renupur siding,' he said thrusting his face close to Phulboni's and showering him with blood-red paan-spittle. 'As you can tell, it's not used. They say it's only ever been used once, and that was many, many years ago.'

Phulboni paid no attention: he was too busy wiping the paan-stains off his face.

The train ground to a halt and the guard flung a door open and scurried down carrying Phulboni's gun-bag and portmanteau. Before Phulboni could tip him, he was back on the train waving his green flag.

'Wait a minute,' Phulboni cried, taken aback.

With a blast of its whistle the train pulled slowly away. Phulboni looked around him and saw, to his considerable surprise, that he was the only person who had disembarked at Renupur. He cast a last, lingering glance at the train and saw the guard watching him from a window, his mouth hanging maniacally open. Then the train gave another blast of its whistle and the strange twisted face vanished into a cloud of smoke.

Phulboni shrugged and bent down to pick up his luggage. He was impatient to be on his way to the village and instinctively he held up a hand, to summon a coolie. It was not till then that he noticed that there were no coolies anywhere in sight.

The station was the smallest Phulboni had ever seen, smaller even than those tiny village stations that sometimes loom unexpectedly into view as one drowses in a speeding train, only to disappear again, just as quickly. For even the smallest stations usually have at least a platform, and often a few wooden benches too. But the platform at Renupur was a length of beaten earth, its surface covered in weeds and a few cracked paving stones. Two creaking signboards hung beside the track, separated by a hundred yards, each bearing the barely legible legend: 'Renupur'. Halfway between them, serving as a signal-room-cum-station-house, was a ramshackle tin-roofed brick structure, painted the usual railway red. There were no houses or huts anywhere in sight, no villagers, no railway guards, no staring rustics, no urchins, no food-vendors, no beggars, no sleeping travellers, not even the inevitable barking dog.

Phulboni realized, looking around him, that the station was empty—absolutely empty. There was nobody, not a single human being anywhere in sight. The spectacle was so startling as literally to provoke disbelief. Stations, in the young writer's experience, were either crowded or less-crowded. They were less crowded when you could walk through them unimpeded, without having to push people aside. On the rare occasions when that happened you said, in surprise: 'Why, the station's empty today!', using the term metaphorically, conjuring away the coolies and the vendors and the dozing passengers and the waiting relatives and so on who, without actually impeding your progress, were still undeniably present. That, as far as the young writer knew, was what the word empty meant when applied to a station. But this? Phulboni, for all his gifts was at a loss to think of a word to describe a station that was literally uninhabited and unpeopled.

The young man's heart sank as he contemplated that desolate spot. He had no idea where to go next or how. There was no road or pathway in sight. The station, perched on the railway embankment, was a little island in a sea of shimmering floodwater.

Phulboni had been led to believe that someone would meet him at the station: a shopkeeper or stall-owner or some other person who dealt in Palmer's products. But here he was, in Renupur, and so far as he could see, he was the sole occupant of the station. Picking up his bedding-roll, he slung his gun over his shoulder, and set off for the signal room to see if he could find the station-master. No sooner had he taken his first few steps than he heard a voice behind him, calling out 'Sahib, sahib'. Turning around, Phulboni saw a tiny, bandy-legged man, scrambling up the embankment. He was dressed in a mud-stained dhoti and a railwayman's coat and he was holding a brass pitcher by its lip.

Phulboni was so relieved to see another human being that he would gladly have embraced him. But mindful of his status as a representative of Palmer Brothers he stiffened his back and raised his chin.

The man caught up with Phulboni and took the bedding-roll out of his hands.

'Arrey sahib,' he said, panting. 'What to do? Every time the rains start it's like this with me: back and forth, out to the fields and in again. If I eat so much as one banana it goes shooting right through and out again like a cannonball. It's an affliction. The-one-who's-at-home always says to me, she says, Arrey Budhhu Dubey, if you were a cow instead of a station-master at least I would be able to do all my cooking with your dung. And I say to her, woman, think a little before you speak. Just ask yourself, if I was a cow instead of a station-master why would you need to cook for me?'

Phulboni's mouth twitched, but being new at the job he

was not quite sure of the tone that was expected of a representative of Palmer Brothers in situations like these. Sensing his hesitation, Budhhu Dubey was already the picture of contrition.

'Oh sahib,' he said. 'Budhhu Dubey is a fool, telling a big sahib like you about his dung. Forgive me, forgive me . . .'

He threw himself at Phulboni's feet. Now it was all the writer could do to keep him from buffing his shoes with his forehead.

Phulboni pulled him up, brusquely. 'Enough of that,' he said. 'Tell me, how can I get to Renupur?'

'That's the thing,' the station-master said, apologetically. 'Even if you had a boat you would not be able to get to Renupur today.'

Phulboni was aghast. 'But where will I stay?' he said. 'What will I do?'

'Nothing to worry about sahib,' said the station-master. He gave Phulboni a wide grin. 'You will stay with me.' He explained that a shopkeeper had sent word from Renupur asking him to look after Phulboni.

Phulboni pondered this proposition at some length. 'Where do you live?' he asked finally.

'Right there,' said the station-master, 'behind those trees.' He pointed at a distant mango grove, perched upon a gentle rise. To Phulboni the spot seemed to be separated from the station by some two or three miles of waterlogged plain.

'It won't take a moment to get there,' said the station-master. 'We'll leave your bags in the signal room and then we'll start walking. You'll see, by the time we get there, the-one-who-is-at-home will have something special ready for you.'

He picked up Phulboni's bedding-roll and started towards the signal room, swaying on his bandy legs. Phulboni followed close behind, carrying his canvas gun-bag. Pushing the door gingerly open the station-master ushered Phulboni in. As they stepped in a gust of wind blew the door shut. Suddenly they were enveloped in cobwebbed gloom.

The room was very small, with only the one door and a

single shuttered window. In one corner, there stood a dusty desk. Otherwise the room seemed abandoned and unused.

It was only when Phulboni's eyes had grown accustomed to the darkness, that he spotted a string bed, pushed up against the far wall. It was an old charpai, covered with torn matting. Phulboni went over and gave the mat a slap, raising a cloud of swirling dust. 'Whose is this?' he asked the station-master.

'Oh that's been here forever,' said the station-master dismissively. 'It belongs to the snakes and rats.' He pushed the door quickly open and stepped out. 'Let us go now sahib: it will soon be dark.'

Phulboni cast another glance around the room. This time his eyes fell upon a small alcove in the wall. Standing inside it was a signal lantern. Phulboni went over to take a closer look and was pleasantly surprised to see that the lantern had been recently cleaned and polished. The tin body was gleaming clean and the circle of red glass in the lantern's window shone bright red in the reflected sunlight. Phulboni put out a finger to tap on the glass, but the station-master stopped him, hurtling across the room and pushing his hand away.

'No, no!' he cried. 'Don't do that.'

Phulboni jumped in surprise, and the station-master said vehemently: 'No, no, it's not to be touched.'

'But don't you touch it?' said Phulboni, even more surprised now. 'Then who cleans it? Who polishes it?'

The station-master dismissed the question with a wave of his hand, muttering something about railway property. 'We should set off now sahib,' he said trying to steer Phulboni to the door. 'It's getting dark; we have to be quick now.'

The writer shrugged and bent down to pick up his bedding-roll. 'No,' he said, throwing it on the charpai. 'No. I am going to stay here tonight.'

The station-master's mouth fell open and a look of alarm descended on his jovial, slightly doltish face. 'No, no sahib,' he said, his voice rising. 'You can't do that—that cannot happen. It cannot be done.'

'Why not?' he asked. Dilapidated though it was, the prospect of a night in that room seemed vastly preferable to that of wading through two miles of floodwater.

'No, no,' the station-master cried. 'No: put it out of your mind.' There was a note of panic in his voice and his forehead was beaded with sweat.

'But I'll be fine here,' said Phulboni.

'No sahib, you mustn't stay here,' the station-master implored him. 'Come home with me; I won't let you stay here all by yourself.'

This made up Phulboni's mind. 'I'll be very comfortable here,' he said. 'Don't worry about me.' He set about unstrapping his hold-all before the station-master could answer.

Like all train travellers of the time, Phulboni was wholly prepared for an eventuality such as this: packed in his bedding-roll were a thin mattress, a pillow, and several sheets and towels. When he unstrapped it, the bag fell open like a ready-made bed.

'Look,' he said with a triumphant gesture. 'I'll sleep very well here.'

'No,' the station-master said, tugging ineffectually at his hold-all. 'You can't: it's not safe.'

'Not safe?' said Phulboni. 'Why? What could happen to me here?'

'Anything,' said the station-master. 'This is not the city after all. All sorts of things happen in lonely places like this: there are thieves and brigands and dacoits . . .'

Phulboni burst out laughing. 'With so much water around,' he said, 'dacoits will need boats to get here. And if they did, this is what they'd have to face.' He tapped his canvas gun-bag.

'And snakes?' said the station-master.

'I'm not afraid of snakes,' said Phulboni with a smile. 'Where I grew up people used pythons as pillows.'

The station-master cast a despairing glance around the room, at the grimy, belittered desk and the massed cobwebs hanging from the ceiling in sooty honeycombs. 'But what will you eat sahib?' he said.

'Since your house is so close,' Phulboni said equably, 'I hope it will not be too much trouble for you to bring me something from your kitchen.'

The station-master sighed. 'All right sahib,' he said reluctantly. 'Do what you like; but just one thing: don't blame Budhhu Dubey later.'

'Don't worry,' said Phulboni. He prided himself on his knowledge of village folk, and knew that rural people often had set ideas about certain things. 'If I'm attacked by snakes or dacoits,' he said with a smile, 'I'll be the one to take the blame.'

The station-master left and Phulboni busied himself unpacking his things and settling in. He forced open the shuttered window and left the door swinging wide. Soon, with a little dusting and cleaning, the room began to look much more cheerful.

Encouraged, Phulboni decided to dust and clean the charpai too. He pulled the hold-all off the bed and carried the frayed old mat outside and gave it a vigorous shake. A cloud of dust rose out of it, and once it had cleared Phulboni spotted a strangely shaped mark upon the mat; a fading, rust-red stain. He laid the mat on the ground and took a closer look.

It was an imprint of two large hands, placed next to each other. But there was something puzzling about them, something that did not quite fit. Phulboni had to turn his head this way and that before he worked out what it was: the imprint of the left hand showed four fingers and no thumb.

There was something just a little eerie and menacing about that strange outline, imprinted on the yellowing rush. He rolled the mat up and put it away, out of sight. He went back in, heaved the hold-all up to the bare strings of the charpai and made a comfortable bed for himself. Then he put out his nightclothes and laid his shaving things in a neat row on the alcove, beside the signal lantern, in preparation for the morning. Standing back he looked around the room: everything was in order now, but somehow he still had a bad taste in his mouth. He decided to go for a walk.

Amitav Ghosh

It was late afternoon now. The clouds had parted and the sun was shining brightly through the rain-washed skies, touching everything in sight with an iridescent brilliance. Phulboni walked along the tracks, hopping from sleeper to sleeper, watching the parallel rails shoot away towards the horizon, slicing through the flooded, shimmering fields that flanked the tall embankment.

When he came to the point where the tracks separated he turned to look at the overgrown siding. He noticed fleetingly that the steel point-tongues that joined the siding to the main tracks were stiff and rusty with disuse. Then his eyes fell on a family of egrets that were using the weed-covered rails of the siding as a perch, to hunt from. Captivated, he walked stealthily towards the birds and seated himself on a rail, at a safe distance. A mound of raised earth—possibly once a platform— ran between the parallel rail tracks. The writer sat lounging, with his back against the mound, and spent the better part of an hour watching the egrets as they foraged amongst the frogs that were skimming the surface of the flooded fields below.

At last, filled with a sense of peace and well-being, he stood up and stretched. He was doubly glad now that he had decided to stay in the signal room instead of going to the station-master's house: this was the kind of place in which solitude was its own reward.

He got up and walked on, balancing on a rail. It was almost sunset now, and the scudding flat-bottomed clouds above were shot through with streaks of scarlet and magenta. When he came to the points-switch that joined the siding and the main line into a single track, Phulboni decided to turn back. He stopped to cast one last glance over the spectacular sight of the flooded fields glowing in the sunset. Inadvertently his eyes fell upon the red handle of the switching lever. He noticed, to his surprise, that the mechanism looked well-cared for. There was no trace of rust on the lever and nor were the wires that connected it to the point-rails at all overgrown, even though they ran very close to the ground. On the contrary, the deep grooves in the grass under them suggested regular maintenance and use.

Phulboni had an instinctive interest in machinery. He liked the feel of cold metal, took pleasure in a good, well-crafted piece of iron or steel. He crossed the rails and went over to cast an appreciative eye at the gleaming iron lever: it gave him an obscure sense of satisfaction to see a well-cared for piece of machinery in these unlikely surroundings.

As he leaned over, arm extended, he heard a shout. Straightening up, he saw the station-master struggling up the embankment. He was waving frantically, making signs to Phulboni to step back from the switching lever. He had a cloth bundle in one hand and an earthen pitcher in the other. Phulboni realized suddenly that he was ravenously hungry. He waved and went hurrying back along the tracks.

The station-master was waiting for him a hundred yards down the track. He had an angry frown on his forehead. 'Look,' he said to the writer. 'You may be a big sahib and all that but if you know what's good for you, you won't meddle with anything around here.'

He added, as an afterthought: 'This is government property, it belongs to the railways.'

Phulboni had been intending to compliment the station-master on his maintenance of the station's switching gear. He listened now in abashed silence, unable to think of an appropriate response.

The station-master thrust the cloth bundle and the earthen pitcher into his hands. 'Just put them in a corner after you've finished,' he said abruptly. 'I'll take care of them in the morning.' He shuffled quickly to the embankment and went scrambling down the side, towards the water-logged field below.

Recovering himself, Phulboni shouted: 'Why don't you stay a minute? Eat something with me before you go.'

'I'll be back in the morning,' the station-master answered, over his shoulder.

There was something about this hurried departure that disquieted Phulboni. Going to the edge of the embankment, he called out: 'Masterji, is there something you have not told me?'

'Tomorrow,' called back the station-master. 'Tomorrow . . . everything . . . it's getting dark . . .' Hurried splashes drowned out the sound of his voice.

Phulboni felt oddly forlorn now, standing by the deserted rail tracks in the dying daylight. He made his way slowly back to the signal room and pushed the door open. It was dark inside, but a metallic glint led his eyes to the floor. It was the curved blade of his razor: lying beside it were the pot of shaving soap, the brush and the lump of clear alum that he had placed in the alcove before leaving for his walk.

Phulboni placed the food and water on the desk and looked around to see if the window had blown open to let a draught or a gust of wind into the room. But the window was still firmly shut. For want of a better explanation, he decided that the objects must have been blown off when he opened the door. He picked them off the floor and arranged them neatly in the alcove once again, next to the signal lantern.

He decided to eat outside while there was still some light. Carrying the food and water to the door, he sat cross-legged on the ground and opened the cloth bundle. He found a stack of parathas, a generous helping of mango achar and a heap of golden-yellow potatoes thickly encrusted in masala. The food smelt better than anything he could ever remember and he fell upon it with gusto.

He was halfway through his third paratha when he heard something fall, in the room behind him. He looked over his shoulder, startled. Through the open door, he spotted his razor and shaving things lying on the floor. Nothing had gone into the room and the wind had died down. He had a moment of unease but then his hunger reclaimed him and he went on with his meal.

After he had eaten he washed his hands, drank a copious draught of water and sat back, picking his teeth contentedly with a twig. His sense of well-being returned now, as he sat in the gentle breeze, listening to the chorus of frogs and crickets that came welling up from the flooded fields below. It was so restful, so tranquil, that something special was called for, he decided: it was an occasion that demanded one of his rare cheroots.

Phulboni was not much of a smoker, but once or twice a week after a good meal he took pleasure in lighting up a good cheroot or cigar. He remembered packing some for the trip, but he wasn't sure exactly where he had put them.

The signal room was pitch dark now, but he had kept a match-box handy. He struck a match and at once his eyes fell on the signal lantern, gleaming in its alcove. An idea flashed into his mind. He picked up the lantern and shook it. The sound of sloshing oil told him that the tank was full. He flipped back the glass window and fumbled for the screw that operated the wick. Giving it a couple of turns, he raised the wick an inch or so and lit it. When he snapped the window back into place a bright red light filled the room.

Pleased with himself, he went over to his hold-all and began to rifle through its pockets, looking for his tin of cheroots. He had just found it when there was a metallic snap behind him and the light went out. Phulboni clicked his tongue, irritated with himself for not having shut the door before lighting the lantern. He made his way over to the desk and lit another match. But then he took a closer look and discovered that he had been mistaken: the flame had not been extinguished by a gust of wind. Rather, the wick had been lowered back into its socket with a turn of the screw. He fiddled with the screw, frowning, wondering whether it had come loose. It was hard to be sure, and in the end he just turned the wick up and lit it again. This time he made sure to put it in a corner that was well sheltered from the wind.

Then he lit his cheroot, sitting cross-legged in the doorway, listening to the myriad insects of the monsoon. Halfway through the cheroot, he heard the screw in the lantern turning once again. Casting a glance over his shoulder he saw that the light had gone out. Phulboni froze; a chill ran down his spine. Then he remembered his gun and settled back reassured. There was nothing he knew of that was proof against a .303. He went on puffing at his cheroot.

He smoked the cheroot right down to the stub and then rose to his feet. It was something of an effort to go back into the signal room, but now he had no option. He knew he would not be able to find his way to the station-master's house on his own, in the dark. Phulboni set about preparing for the night very calmly and deliberately. He changed into his night-time pajamas in the dark, rationing his matches. Then he pulled his stout leather belt off his trousers and used it to fasten the door. He took the gun out of its bag and placed it on the floor beside his bed, within easy reach. Then he lay down on the bed, facing the door. He had half-expected that he would find himself lying awake a long time. But it had been a long day and he was very tired: within a few minutes he was fast asleep.

He was awoken by the touch of rain upon his face. He sat up, startled, and reached instinctively for his gun. The door was open, flapping in the wind, and the rain was blowing into the room in great billowing gusts.

He struggled out of bed, cursing himself under his breath for not having made sure of the door. The belt was lying by the entrance, still buckled. He picked it up, pulled the door shut and tied the belt around the doorpost again, as tightly as he could. Stepping back he lit a match to see if the belt would hold.

That was when he noticed that the signal lantern was no longer in the corner where he had last placed it. He looked around at the desk and then at the alcove: the lantern was nowhere to be seen. It had vanished. Phulboni was groggy with sleep and the first thought that came into his mind was that the station-master must have come in and taken the lantern while he was asleep; maybe there was an emergency somewhere down the track. He undid the door and looked out into the driving rain. Sure enough, there it was: a little circle of red light, bobbing up and down, some fifty yards down the track.

'Masterji, masterji!' Phulboni called out after him, shouting at the top of his voice, through cupped hands. But the light went on its way, and little wonder: the wind was howling, driving the rain before it.

Phulboni gave himself no time to think. He pulled his shoes on, wrapped a heavy towel around his body, and ran out. For an instant he toyed with the idea of taking his gun. But then, thinking of what the rain and mud might do to it, he changed his mind. Squaring his shoulders he walked out on to the track, narrowing his eyes against the buffeting wind. It was not till he was halfway to the siding that he began wondering how the station-master had let himself into the signal room when the door was fastened from inside.

Phulboni stumbled on, lengthening his stride to match the gap between the sleepers. The wood was slippery with the rain, and he had to struggle to keep his footing. He had trouble keeping the red light in sight, but he had the feeling that he was gaining on it. Every time he caught a glimpse of it the light seemed to be just a little closer than it was before.

Then, between two furious gusts of rain, he saw the light change course and veer off towards the right. He wasn't sure of his bearings any more, but he guessed that the station-master had reached the point where the tracks forked off towards the siding. He was amazed: whatever the emergency, it was hard to imagine why the station-master would come all this way in a storm to go to the siding.

Now he lost sight of the light and slowed down a little. Dark as it was, he fixed his eyes on the track, trying to make sure that he didn't miss the turn to the siding when it came. But in the end he found the turn only because he happened to stumble upon the curved point-rails. He began to feel his way ahead with his feet, following the tracks as they veered off to the right.

After a few steps he stopped and looked ahead, shading his eyes. Somewhere within a swirl of pouring rain he spotted the bobbing red light. It seemed much closer now and it seemed to be almost stationary.

Amitav Ghosh

After a few more steps he was certain. The light had stopped moving: it was on the ground, beside the track—probably very near the spot where he had been sitting earlier that day, watching the egrets as they fished in the water below. He was sure the station-master had seen him and was waiting for him to catch up. Cupping his hands around his mouth he shouted once again, at the top of his voice: 'Masterji, masterji.' The light seemed to bob in encouragement and he began to run faster, as fast as he could, eager to catch up. Then suddenly, when the light was no more than twenty feet away, he tripped. He fell face forward but managed to throw his hands out in time to save his forehead from smashing into the cold steel.

He paused, in relief, to catch his breath, holding himself up with stiffened arms, his hands clutching the rails. And then, just as his breath was beginning to return he felt a tremor in the rail. He placed both hands on the rail. There could be no doubt of it: the rail was shaking, vibrating under an approaching train.

Phulboni was stunned: the chances of there being a train anywhere nearby were close to nil. The train he had taken was not due back from Barich until dawn, and there were no other trains running on that line. And even if there were, why would they be diverted to that siding—and who would switch the tracks? He had been following the station-master for the last several minutes, and he knew that he had been nowhere near the switching mechanism.

And yet there was no denying the evidence of his senses: the rails were shaking under his hands, and the vibrations were getting steadily stronger. He laid his ear upon the rail and listened carefully. He heard the unmistakable rumble of an approaching train. It was thundering towards him, very close at hand. At the last minute he flung himself sideways over the embankment and went tumbling down towards the water.

Phulboni was still falling when the lights of the train flashed across the flooded fields. Clutching wildly at a bush, he managed to bring himself to a stop, his head inches from the water. At that very moment he heard a scream, a raging, inhuman howl that tore through the stormy night. It hurled a single word into the wind—'Laakhan'—and then it was silenced by the thunder of the speeding train.

Phulboni was clinging to the embankment, head downwards, facing the water. He could not see the siding from that position, but he saw the train's lights, very clearly, skimming across the floodwater, he felt its weight shaking the embankment, he heard the anguished pant of its engine and smelt the coal in its boiler. But all the while the only thing he could think of was how narrowly he had escaped death.

He lay there for a few minutes shaking in fear and relief. It was still pitch dark but the storm had let up a little. Once his hands had steadied he pushed himself to his feet and began to scramble up the embankment.

When he felt the ground levelling out under him, he called out: 'Anyone there?' just in case whoever it was that had screamed was still within earshot. There was no answer, so he sank to his knees and began to pat the earth around him, trying to find the rails. He knew he would not be able to find his way back to the signal room without the tracks to guide him. After several minutes he felt a cold glancing touch on one of his hands. Breathing a sigh of relief, he fastened both hands upon the rail.

Disoriented as he was, it took a few minutes before Phulboni realized that the rail, which had come so vividly alive under his hands a short while ago, was now absolutely still, motionless. He knew that rail tracks carry the sound of trains for miles, in either direction. It was only a short while since the train had passed over the siding: it could not be more than a mile away. He put his ear to the rail and listened carefully. The only sound he heard was the pattering of raindrops falling on metal. Then one of his hands touched some weeds growing over the tracks. He began to run his hands frantically along the rail in both directions. He discovered that the undergrowth that he had seen earlier that day, growing over the tracks, showed no signs of having been disturbed by the passage of a train.

Phulboni was frightened now, more than he had ever been in his life, frightened in a way that left his brain numb, his vision blurred. He was standing on the rail, looking around in a daze, when he saw the red light again. It was about a hundred yards away and it was coming slowly towards him.

Phulboni greeted it with a shout of relief: 'Masterji, masterji, I'm right here . . .'

The shout went unacknowledged but the lantern began to move a little faster. As he stood there watching the light Phulboni's head cleared a little; he peered at the lantern, trying to catch a glimpse of the face behind it. He could see nothing; the face remained wrapped in darkness.

Phulboni turned and ran. He ran faster than he had ever run, gasping for breath, fighting to keep his footing on the slippery tracks. He glanced over his shoulder once and saw the lantern running after him, closing the gap. He ran still faster, pushing himself on, moaning in terror.

Then he saw the signal room taking shape in front of him, looming out of the darkness. He flung one last glance over his shoulder. The lantern was no more than a few paces behind him now, a hand clearly visible upon the steel handle.

With one final, desperate effort Phulboni flung himself at the signal room and stumbled through the doorway. The gun was where he had left it, beside the bed. He snatched it up and turned, aiming the barrel at the door.

He was fumbling with the safety-catch when the lantern appeared in the doorway. It stepped in and began to approach him; a hand appeared, bathed in the red light of the lantern. The face was still in darkness but suddenly that inhuman voice rang through the room again. It said just that one word, 'Laakhan'.

And then Phulboni fired, point-blank, into the window of the lantern. The report of the gun filled the room like dynamite exploding in a cave: the recoil of the barrel caught the writer on the chin and knocked him hard against the bed.

thirty-nine
_____

The next thing Phulboni knew, it was dawn and he was staring into the station-master's grinning face. He was no longer in the signal room: it was dawn and he was outside, lying on his back on something soft.

'I told the-one-who-is-at-home,' said the station-master. 'I told her, you'll see there's no need to worry, he'll be all right.' Phulboni closed his eyes. Such was his relief at finding himself unharmed and safe that his whole body went limp.

'I had such a time pulling you out of there sahib,' the station-master said. 'You would think that huge frame of yours is made of brass. I had to pull and pull and pull: all on my own too. But I said to myself, "Budhhu Dubey, whatever happens you have to get him out of this terrible place; even if you hurt your own back. As long as he's inside here; there's no hope for him. You have to get him out."'

'What happened?' asked Phulboni. 'Where was I when you found me?'

'I came as early as I could,' the station-master said. 'The-one-who-is-at-home woke me while it was still dark and said, "Go now, and see if the poor man is all right." I came hurrying as quickly as I could. I found you lying on the floor with your gun across your body. At first I thought you were dead: but then I found you breathing so I pulled you out.'

'And the lantern?' said Phulboni. 'I fired at it: did you see any glass in the signal room?'

The station-master frowned: 'Which lantern?'

'The signal lantern,' said Phulboni. 'The one that was in the room yesterday.'

'It was in the same place,' said the station-master. 'All polished and clean: no one ever touches it. It's always like that, always in the same place: always clean, never any dust on it.'

The station-master fanned Phulboni's face vigorously with a banana leaf. 'This station is a terrible place,' he said. 'No one in any of the villages around here comes within a mile of this station after dark. You couldn't make them come if you gave them all the gold that is hoarded in the heavens. I tried to tell you but you wouldn't listen.'

'I'll listen now,' said Phulboni. 'I want to know what happened.'

The station-master sighed. 'I don't know what to tell you,' he said. 'A big sahib like yourself. I can only tell you what people say in these parts: simple village people like myself . . .'

Phulboni, listening with his eyes closed, ran his hand over his forehead. 'What is it that people say?' he said. 'I want to know.'

And then as luck would have it, one of his hands, reaching back, brushed against a rail, a length of cold, vibrating steel. He opened his eyes, and found himself gazing at an uninterrupted view of leaves and trees, outlined against a rosy dawn sky. There was no sign of the station-master or anybody else. He looked around and discovered that he was lying on the siding, across the tracks, on a mattress. Hesitantly he stretched out his arm and touched the rail.

And then once again Phulboni threw himself off the tracks. But this time he managed to halt his fall so that he was just inches away when the train went hurtling over the siding, over the mattress that he had just been lying on, tearing it to shreds. This time the train was all too real: he saw the horrified faces of the stokers and engineers as the train thundered past; he heard the screech of its brakes and the shriek of its whistle.

He scrambled up the siding and began to run. He caught

up with the train a mile or so away where it had finally ground to a halt.

The stokers and engineers were examining the points and switches, trying to work out how the tracks had been switched. Incomprehensible, said the Anglo-Indian Chief Engineer; that siding hadn't been used in decades, the mechanism had been dismantled years ago. The train had almost been derailed, it was a miracle that it hadn't, with all the debris on those rusty, overgrown tracks.

So Phulboni said to the Chief Engineer: 'Maybe the station-master pulled the switch by mistake?'

The Chief Engineer was a grizzled old veteran, an Anglo-Indian. He gave Phulboni an odd smile and said: 'There hasn't been a station-master at Renupur for more than thirty years.'

Then the guard appeared, obsequious as ever, and led Phulboni to an empty first class carriage. Later, when the train had started off towards Darbhanga, he sidled up and whispered in the writer's ear: 'You were lucky, at least you are still alive.'

'Why?' Phulboni demanded. 'Have there been others who . . . ?'

'The year I first began this job,' the guard said. 'In '94, there was another who was not so fortunate: he died there—in just that way, lying on the rails, at dawn. The corpse was so mangled that they never discovered exactly who it was, but it was rumoured that he was a foreigner.'

He gave Phulboni a melancholy smile. 'No one ever goes near that station at night,' he said.

'Why didn't you tell me this before?' said Phulboni.

'I tried to,' said the guard, with a crooked smile. 'But you would not have believed me. You would have laughed and said, "these villagers, their heads are full of fantasies and superstitions". Everyone knows that for city-men like you such warnings always have the opposite effect.'

Acknowledging the truth of this Phulboni apologized and asked the guard to sit and recount everything he knew.

For many years, the guard said, the signal room had been home to a young lad called Laakhan. The boy had drifted in from somewhere up the line soon after the station was first built. He was a stray, orphaned by famine, with a thin, wasted body and a deformed hand. The signal room was empty then, because no railway employee would agree to live in such a lonely, isolated place. So Laakhan made it his home. The guards and stokers who passed through taught him how to use a signal lamp and work the switches. He made himself useful to the railways and they let him stay.

The boy was in his teens when a station-master was finally found for Renupur. As it turned out this station-master was an orthodox, upper-caste man: he took an instant dislike to the lad, looking on him as an affront to himself. He told the villagers that Laakhan was worse than untouchable; that he carried contagion; that he was probably the child of a prostitute; that his misshapen left hand was a mark of hereditary disease. He tried his best to drive the boy away from the station, but Laakhan had nowhere to go. The boy built a bamboo shack on the tracks of the unused siding and tried to keep out of sight.

This drove the station-master into an even greater fury. On a moonless Amavasya night, during a storm, the station-master tried to kill the boy by switching the points and leading him before a train. But no one knew the station better than Laakhan and he managed to escape. Instead it was the station-master who tripped on a rail and fell before the train.

That was the last time that Renupur had a station-master.

Phulboni's mind was full of questions: having escaped a similar death he was consumed with curiosity about the boy's fate. 'Tell me more,' he begged the guard. 'What became of Laakhan? I must know; you must tell me.'

'There is not much else to tell,' the guard said. 'What people say is that he hid himself on a train and went to Calcutta. They say he was living at Sealdah station when a woman found him and gave him a home.'

'Is that all?' Phulboni persisted. 'Who was the woman? What happened to Laakhan?'

The guard pulled an apologetic face. 'That's all I know,' he said. 'Except . . .'

'Except what?'

'The man who was my predecessor at this job once told me something. He said that he had talked to the foreigner—the one who died at Renupur. He, the foreigner, had come up to him on the platform, just as he was about to flag the train out. He said that he had been travelling with a young man, a native of Renupur. As a sahib, naturally, the foreigner was in first class while this other man was in third. But now he could not find the young man: he had disappeared. My predecessor could not help him; he hadn't noticed anyone else getting off at Renupur. The foreigner was very annoyed and said he would wait at the station. The guard, my predecessor, told him that whatever happened he should not stay the night at the station. He did everything he could to make him leave, but the sahib only laughed, and said, Oh, you villagers . . .'

forty

'Oh my God!' Urmila cried suddenly, tugging at the booth's plastic curtain.

'What?' said Murugan.

'Sonali-di,' Urmila replied. 'I have to find a telephone.'

She darted across the restaurant to the manager's desk at the back and picked up the telephone. Murugan waited to pay the bill and then followed her over.

She was staring at the receiver in shock when he caught up with her.

'Sonali-di's disappeared,' she said. 'She's not in her office, and she's not at home. She missed a staff meeting this morning and they've been trying to contact her. She hasn't been seen since last night. No one's answering the phone at her flat. Apparently I was the last person to talk to her.'

'What time was that?'

'About ten thirty I think,' Urmila said. 'We went to her flat together, and I left about then.'

'I've got news for you Calcutta,' Murugan said. 'I saw her after you did.'

'What?' Urmila cried. 'But you don't even know her.'

'But I still saw her,' said Murugan. 'I went out to my balcony at about one o'clock last night, and I saw her getting out of a taxi: she went into number three Robinson Street . . .'

With a wail of despair Urmila pushed him aside: 'Why didn't you *tell* me?' She ran to the road and flagged down a taxi. 'Come on,' she called out to him, over her shoulder. 'We have to hurry.' Murugan climbed in after her and slammed the door shut.

'Robinson Street,' Urmila said to the taxi driver. 'Between Loudon and Rawdon.'

Then she turned to Murugan. 'We have to find Sonali-di,' she said. 'We have to try and warn her.'

'Why her?' said Murugan.

'Don't you see?' Urmila said. 'Because she's in it too: she told me that story.'

The evening rush hour was just beginning and traffic was very heavy once the taxi got to Chowringhee. Urmila sat hunched over the front seat, urging the driver on.

When Murugan spoke to Urmila again it was in a voice that was unaccustomedly quiet. 'Listen, Calcutta,' he said. 'You've been on the move since this morning; maybe you should give yourself a time-out here, just to think things over.'

'Think what over?' said Urmila distractedly. They were on Theatre Road now, beside the Kenilworth Hotel, and the air was fragrant with the smell of kababs.

'About whether you want to get any deeper into this,' said Murugan.

'What else could I do?' she said, in surprise.

'We could stop the taxi right here,' said Murugan. 'And you could get out and go home; go back to whatever you were doing.'

A shadow fell over Urmila's face.

'Go back home?' Urmila said to herself, under her breath, resting her eyes on the neat, bright buildings of the British Council. If she went home she would have to buy fish on the way. Her mother wouldn't believe her if she said Romen Haldar wasn't really going to come to their house in the evening, to offer her brother a First Division contract. She could hear her already; 'Oh, you don't care about us at all: your family means nothing to you; all you care about is yourself and your career; that's why no one will marry you; that's what Mrs Gangopadhyaya said the other day . . .'

Amitav Ghosh

Urmila turned to Murugan with an emphatic shake of her head. 'No,' she said. 'I don't want to go home.'

'It's your life Calcutta,' Murugan said philosophically. 'You know best.'

A build-up of traffic at the Loudon Road crossing brought the taxi rattling to a halt. Urmila turned away from the Pierre Cardin boutique at the corner. Her eyes were brimming with curiosity as they settled on Murugan.

'What about you?' she said to Murugan. 'Why are you going on with this? What's kept you at it so long?'

'Can't you tell?' Murugan said.

Urmila shook her head: 'No.'

Murugan gave her a grim smile. 'It's not me,' he said. 'It's what's inside me.'

'Do you mean malaria?'

'That too,' said Murugan.

'What else?' said Urmila.

There was a brief pause, and then in an undertone, Murugan said: 'Syphilis.'

Urmila flinched, making an involuntary shrinking movement. Murugan turned on her, eyes narrowed. 'You don't have to worry,' he said. 'It's not contagious: I was officially cured a long time ago.'

'I'm sorry . . .' Urmila could not trust herself to say any more.

Murugan kept his eyes on the shops, food-stalls and travel agencies that flanked the road. With his face averted, he said: 'I guess it started somewhere over there.' He made a vague gesture at the skyline. 'On Free School Street. I was fifteen: I'd been to see a film at the Globe, after school. I was walking past New Market, on my way home, when a guy came up to me and whispered in my ear. I guessed he was a pimp: I'd been reading a lot of American detective novels. I was in my ink-stained school pants and a sweaty end-of-the-day shirt, with my textbooks and classnotes slung over my shoulder. He was wearing a green, checked lungi, and he had a thin, pencil moustache and tiny, bloodshot eyes. He winked before he whispered in my ear and gave me this toothy little grin. I could smell the paan and stale liquor on his breath. It was irresistible. All I had was five rupees but that was enough. He led me down one of those tiny alleys around Free School Street, just around the corner from the Armenian school, where William Thackeray was born. We went up a dark, stinking staircase that looked like it led to the anus of the earth. But then we got to the top and suddenly there was this great sunburst of light and noise and voices and music: it was like walking into a fairground—a huge room, with little curtained cubicles all around it, and vendors selling paan and tea, and all these women sitting on chairs lined up against the wall, with flowers around their wrists. I never looked back; I was hooked. I loved them; I loved everything about them, even the way they laughed behind my back when I was running down the stairs, afterwards, my pants half-unbuttoned.'

He fell silent, smiling to himself.

'And then,' he said, 'the lesions began to appear: scabs and sores and loosening teeth. I changed the way I dressed; I wore a lot of clothes, more and more, even on those June days when the heat is like a jackhammer waiting to hit you in the face. I managed to hide the scabs for, oh, I don't know how long, for months anyway—even though it hurt by then, god, it hurt. And when it was finally caught there was no disguising it. That was why my family had to leave the city: the shame.'

'But syphilis is curable now, isn't it?' Urmila said. 'With antibiotics?'

'Sure,' said Murugan. 'I got cured. They can cure it now—except for what it does to your head.'

It was the rain, blowing in through the flapping shutters, that roused Sonali. Her eyes were gummy and swollen; she had trouble prying her eyelids open. She was lying on her side, staring at a ribbon of dust that had gathered along the edge of a wooden floor.

She had no idea where she was, the wall could have been any wall, anywhere; she did not know how long she had been there or what she was doing on the floor. Her first instinct was to go rigid, to keep absolutely still, lizard-like, to make herself invisible.

Lying motionless on the floor, she began to listen, concentrating her mind on her hearing. Slowly she began to pick up the sound of cars on a road nearby, a Vividh-Bharati jingle on a transistor radio; bicycle bells, a backfiring engine, all the usual street-noises, but somewhere in the distance. But here in her immediate vicinity, there were no sounds at all; she could hear nothing—nothing that gave her any clues about where she was or whether there was anyone else in the room.

And then she heard something, not so far away as the sounds of the street: a metallic creak, the sound of an unoiled hinge, of a heavy gate swinging slowly open. A moment later she heard footsteps, crunching on gravel: they seemed to be getting closer, coming towards her.

She turned over, slowly, and discovered that she was lying on the floor of a narrow, wooden gallery. Pushing herself up she inched to the edge and looked over.

She found herself looking down upon an enormous, empty room. A fading, twilight glow was shining through a broken skylight. She spotted a small pile of ashes and half-burnt twigs at the far end of the cavernous room. Now it started to come flooding back: the staircase, the noise, the smoke, the crowd of people, gathered around a body. With a gasp she leaned over again, looking all around her: there was no sign of anyone; the room was empty.

The footsteps were inside the house now, they were downstairs, probably somewhere near the staircase. Sonali drew her head quickly back, and lay still, her breath pumping torpidly in and out of her lungs.

They were climbing up the rotten staircase; she could hear their shoes on the steel scaffolding. She heard the sound of a voice—a man's voice, somewhere outside. Then there was a woman's voice too; still muffled, although their footsteps were somewhere beneath her, very close to the reception room.

She heard the feet entering, pacing back and forth. Then all she could hear was the sound of the blood pounding in her ears. She closed her eyes, biting her lip, trying to summon the courage to look down.

'There's no one here,' a voice said. It was a woman speaking—someone familiar, someone she knew.

She raised her head, very slowly and inched forward, to the edge. Then a cry burst from her lips: 'Urmila!'

'Sonali-di!' Urmila gasped, spinning around. Simultaneously Murugan shouted: 'She's up there, come on.'

Sonali allowed her head to sink to the floor, in relief. Then they were up beside her, in the gallery, helping her down the ladder, holding her hands, and she was crying, fighting for her breath, and between her sobs she heard herself trying to speak, struggling to say something coherent, but the words came out all wrong, all mixed up, in a meaningless jumble.

'Calm down Sonali-di,' Urmila said. 'It's all right; we're here now. Tell me: why are you here? When did you come?'

Sonali tightened her grip on Urmila's hand.

'I came late last night,' she said. 'I came to look for Romen; somehow I knew he would be here.'

'Did you find him?' Urmila asked.

Sonali began to sob again.

'That's the strange part Urmila,' she said, 'I don't know.' Sonali began to tell them about the taxi to Robinson Street, climbing the stairs, the smoke, the people, finding the gallery, the boy, the woman in the saree, the fire, the body . . .

'And then she put out her hands,' said Sonali, 'and touched the body that was lying in front of the fire and called him Laakhan. Just before I passed out I managed to see who it was.'

She choked.

'Who was it?' said Urmila.

'It was Romen.' Sonali began to sob.

'And the woman,' Murugan broke in, 'who was she? Did you know her?'

Sonali shook her head, from side to side, wiping her tear-streaked face on her blouse.

'I'm not sure,' she said. 'She looked so familiar, but I couldn't remember.'

Then Urmila took her hand, elbowing Murugan out of the way. 'Try, Sonali-di,' she said. 'Try and remember. Who was it?'

Sonali's eyes widened as she looked into Urmila's face. 'It was someone you know Urmila,' she said. 'I'm sure of that: that's why she seemed familiar—someone I've heard you talk about, someone I haven't seen in years.'

Suddenly, Urmila rocked back on her heels, dropping Sonali's hand. 'No,' she whimpered, her hands flying to her mouth. 'No, not Mrs . . .'

'Yes,' said Sonali. 'That's who it was—Mrs Aratounian.'

forty-two

Antar woke up to find his bedclothes drenched in sweat and his throat burning. He stumbled to the door, and looked down the corridor: the kitchen seemed to slide away from him, receding into the distance. He felt his knees weakening and had to lean against the wall to keep himself upright. He turned his head to look at the palm of his hand, and saw that it was trembling, shimmering against the flat whiteness of the wall. In rising panic he clapped his hands against his cheeks, his chest, his sides, only to discover that he was shaking all over.

He took one step towards the kitchen, still leaning against the wall. It seemed a little easier now; he was just a couple of feet from the open doorway of his living room, halfway down the corridor, between the kitchen and the bedroom. Leaning forward, he reached for the edge of the doorway, trying to pull himself along.

His fingers found the doorway and took a grip on it. Then a shiver ran through his outstretched arm and he snatched his hand back, recoiling, as though from an unexpected touch. He could feel the hairs bristling on his face as he stood leaning on the wall, biting his knuckles: it was as though something were in that room, a presence that his body had sensed before he knew it was there.

He edged forward, slowly, pushed himself away from the wall and stepped through the door. He stood there transfixed, disbelieving. His knees buckled and he fell to the floor.

Sitting gnome-like in the middle of the living room was a naked man. A blanket of matted, ropy hair hung halfway down a swollen, distended belly; his upper body was encrusted with dead leaves and straw, and his thighs were caked with mud and excrement. His hands were resting in his lap, bound together by a pair of steel handcuffs.

He was staring at Antar with bloodshot, grime-caked eyes; his lips drawn back in a grin, baring yellow, decaying teeth.

'What's the matter?' a voice cried out suddenly, filling the room through Ava's concealed sound outlets. 'You wanted to see me, didn't you? I'm just a little early, that's all.'

Antar picked himself up and made his way slowly towards Ava's control panel. He found himself skirting around the edges of the room, with his back to the walls, keeping as far away from the figure as possible, as though it were a real presence.

'Where have you been?' the figure shouted after him. 'Why have you kept me waiting so long?'

Antar's eyes fell on the mud-caked thighs and he turned away, with an involuntary shudder. Reaching for Ava's keyboard, he rewrote the vectors of the image.

There was a tremor in the image and the man's torso vanished. Now only his head remained, vastly enlarged, much larger than life-size, blown up to the scale of a piece of monumental statuary.

'Guess you couldn't bear to look at my body any more,' said the man, laughing again.

Now Antar could see the maggots in his hair; the sight was so grotesque that he reached for the control panel and tilted the head away. But then, as the flat cross-section of the neck hove slowly into view, he discovered that Ava had done such a realistic job of severing the head that every artery and vein was clearly visible. He could see the throbbing capillaries; even the directional flow of the blood was reproduced, in motion, so that the neck looked as though it were spouting gore.

Antar choked: the head was startlingly like a vision that

often recurred in his worst nightmares; an image from a medieval painting he had once seen in a European museum, a picture of a beheaded saint, holding his own dripping head nonchalantly under his arm, as though it were a fresh-picked cabbage.

The man began to shout as his head tilted further and further back.

'Put me down you bastard,' he shouted. 'Look me in the eye.'

Antar tilted the image again, with a signal, and the red glaring eyes fastened upon him. 'So you want to know what happened to Murugan?' he said.

'Yes,' said Antar.

The man erupted into another burst of manic laughter.

'Let me ask you again,' he said. 'Are you quite sure?'

Amitav Ghosh

forty-three
_____

It was raining hard when they got down to the pillared
portico of the tumbledown old mansion. The neon lamps
on Robinson Street were glowing fuzzily greenish, like aquarium
lights. Urmila and Sonali drew their sarees over their heads as
they stood under the portico, looking into the pouring rain.
Murugan started down the gravelled driveway at a run. At the
gate he stopped to look back at the two women, who were
still waiting uncertainly under the portico.

'Come on,' he shouted, at the top of his voice, urging them
on. 'Let's move it, let's go.'

His voice came back to the portico disembodied, buffeted
by the wind, and softened by the rain. Urmila gave Sonali's
arm a tug and they began to run, hesitantly at first, and then
faster, following Murugan as he sprinted down the road,
towards the entrance of number eight.

Turning blindly through the gate of Mrs Aratounian's
building Murugan ran straight into something that was standing
in the narrow driveway. He picked himself up and saw that
two bamboo pushcarts were standing in the driveway, blocking
the entrance. Tents of translucent tarpaulin rose out of them,
stretched tight over jumbled heaps of objects.

He was rubbing his knees, swearing, when Sonali and Urmila
caught up. Urmila edged quickly past the carts, made her way
to the entrance and started towards the lift. Halfway through
the dimly lit hall she noticed two men in lungis and vests,

squatting by the staircase, smoking biris. Standing beside them was a large piece of furniture, a heavy mahogany sideboard.

Urmila stopped dead, shifting her gaze from the two men to the sideboard and back again. The men stared back in unruffled calm, the biri-smoke rising above them in widening spirals.

Sonali came to a halt beside her: 'What's the matter?'

'That's Mrs Aratounian's,' said Urmila, pointing at the sideboard. 'She used to have it in her dining room. I remember it.'

'You're right,' said Murugan. 'I saw it there last night.'

Speaking to the two men in Hindi, Urmila said: 'Where did you get that?'

One of the men flicked a thumb over his shoulder, pointing up the staircase. A moment later they heard a loud clatter, followed by shouts and grunts. Three bare-bodied men came around the bend in the stairs carrying a huge chintz-printed sofa.

'Hey!' said Murugan. 'That's Mrs Aratounian's too; I was sitting on it last night, watching TV.'

Raising her voice, Urmila said: 'What's happening?'

One of the men took aim with the butt of his biri and flicked it away, into a corner. Then he rose unhurriedly to his feet, and stretched. 'Someone's leaving,' he said with a yawn, putting his shoulder to the sideboard. 'And we're carrying away the furniture.'

'Who's leaving?' Urmila said.

The man shrugged and lowered his shoulder to the sideboard. 'How am I to know?'

Urmila went running over to the lift and opened the door, motioning to Murugan and Sonali to follow. They squeezed in beside her and she pressed the button for the fourth floor. None of them said a word as the ancient lift ascended slowly upwards through the hollow centre of the staircase.

The lift came to a halt and Urmila stepped out. Her eyes fell on Mrs Aratounian's door and she froze.

The door was wide open, held in place by a brick. Light

was pouring out of the flat, gilding the scarred, dusty planks of the landing. On the wall beside the door where the nameplates had once hung, there were now two discoloured rectangular spots.

Their eyes were drawn irresistibly past the door. The hall beyond was empty; the clutter and the bric-à-brac were gone. The walls were absolutely bare. As they stood there staring, two men came out with jute sacks slung over their shoulders: both were full to bursting.

Murugan was the first to move. Running through the empty drawing room he darted into the room he had slept in the night before. Urmila followed, walking as though in a trance, with Sonali close behind her.

A moment later a howl echoed out of Murugan's room: 'My things are all gone. Everything: my laptop, my clothes, my Vuitton suitcase, everything . . .' Murugan came running back, wild-eyed: 'Even the bed and the mosquito net are gone—everything . . .'

Footsteps sounded somewhere behind them, along the corridor that led to the kitchen. All three of them turned in unison and found themselves facing a thin, bespectacled man, in a fraying shirt and trousers. He had a pencil behind his ear, and he was holding a clipboard and a sheaf of stapled papers in one hand. In the other he had a fistful of peanuts.

He glared at them, his eyes hugely enlarged by his spectacles. 'Who are you?' he said, with an uncomprehending blink. 'What are you doing here?'

'Who are *you*?' snapped Urmila. 'And what are *you* doing in Mrs Aratounian's flat?'

The man stiffened and a frown appeared on his forehead. His eyes flickered angrily from Urmila's face to Murugan's. Then he looked at Sonali and suddenly his face went slack. His arm rose slowly upwards, trembling, scattering peanuts on the floor. His mouth dropped open and his eyes grew larger, spilling out of the rims of his spectacles.

'Why,' he stammered, stabbing his index finger in her direction. 'Why, but you . . . you are . . . you are Sonali Das.'

Sonali gave him a nod and a distant smile. He swallowed convulsively, his Adam's apple bobbing like a fisherman's float.

'Do you know who she is?' he said to the others, spluttering in excitement, spraying a fine plume of spit in their direction. 'She is Sonali Das . . . the great actress . . . I never dreamed . . .'

He was hopping on his toes now, his face flushed with pleasure and excitement.

'Oh Madame,' he said to Sonali, 'we see your films at least twice every year at the Bansdroni Film Society. At my insistence if I may say so—I am treasurer, co-founder and member-secretary. You can ask anyone in Bansdroni and they'll tell you: Bolai-da won't let a year go by without showing each of Sonali Das's films at least twice. Once there was even an impeachment motion on this score, but . . .'

He paused, at a loss for words, his eyes filling with tears. 'Oh Madame Sonali,' he said, 'for me you are greater than Anna Magnani in *Open City*, greater than Garbo in *Camille*, greater even than . . .'

He swallowed as though gathering his courage. 'Yes,' he said, with an air of recklessness. 'I will say it, why not? greater even than the incomparable Madhabi in *Charulata*.'

Sonali gave him an embarrassed smile.

Murugan could contain his impatience no longer. 'Can we leave this fan-club stuff till later?' he exploded, shaking a fist.

The man flinched, and knocked his knuckles on his skull, as though to awaken himself from a dream. 'I am sorry,' he said. 'I should not permit myself to become so excited.'

Urmila patted him gently on the shoulder.

'It doesn't matter,' she said. 'You are quite right about Sonali-di. But at the moment we have something else on our minds. We came here to see Mrs Aratounian. Can you tell us where she is?'

'Mrs Aratounian?' the bespectacled man said dreamily, his eyes drifting back to Sonali. 'She has gone.'

'Gone where?' said Murugan.

'Just gone.' The man shrugged, losing interest in the

conversation. Suddenly a thought struck him and he turned to Sonali, his face brightening. 'Perhaps you will consent to make an appearance at our Society?' he said. 'Is it possible Madame?'

Sonali answered with a practiced gesture that indicated neither confirmation nor disavowal.

Murugan took hold of the man's arm and shook it, hard. 'Later,' he shouted. 'You can talk about that later. First tell us, where's Mrs Aratounian? And where's her stuff—her furniture, and plants and everything? And *my* stuff—my suitcase, laptop and all the rest?'

The man flicked Murugan's fingers off his arm with a fastidious sniff. 'By the way,' he said. 'There is no need to raise your voice.'

'Sorry,' said Murugan. 'I just wanted to get a grip on your attention before it escaped again. As I was saying: where is everything—my things, her things.'

The man gave him a look of puzzled enquiry, spectacles glinting. 'Don't you know?' he said. 'She sold everything. To the New Russell Exchange. That is why I am here: I am the head clerk in charge of collections and evaluations.'

'But it was all here this morning,' Murugan cried breathlessly. 'I mean, I stayed here last night. Everything was here when I went out this morning. She couldn't have sold it all today.'

The clerk gave him a pitying smile. 'Of course not,' he said. 'Such a sale cannot be arranged in a day! The legal formalities alone . . . there is the registration of sale to consider and the affidavits and the stamp duty.'

He thrust his clipboard in Murugan's direction. 'Here look,' he said, pointing with his pencil. 'This is the contract.'

Peering over his shoulder, Murugan and Urmila found themselves looking at a carbon copy of a long typewritten document. The letterhead said: 'New Russell Exchange, Auctioneers and Valuers.' The margin of each page was covered with a patchwork of legal stamps, initials and signatures.

The clerk hummed as he flipped through the document. He stopped at the end, with a triumphant cry. 'Here,' he said. 'Do you see? The contract was signed and sealed exactly a year ago, to the day. Mrs Aratounian sold everything on these premises on an as-is-where-is basis, subject to the stipulation that collection would occur exactly a year later.'

He flipped the pages back and tapped on the document with the rubberized butt of his pencil.

'Everything is accounted for in this list,' he said. 'Mrs Aratounian personally showed me the location of every item on that list, this morning. Everything in this flat was entered here at the time of evaluation, just before the flat was sold.'

Urmila gave a disbelieving cry: 'The flat was sold!'

'Yes,' said the clerk. 'The new owners will be taking possession today.'

Murugan stared at him flabbergasted. 'But,' he began, 'but my things can't be on that list: I wasn't even here.'

The clerk directed a glance of enquiry at Murugan. 'Are you attempting to establish a claim to certain articles?' he said. 'I should inform you that according to this contract we have an absolute legal right to remove everything on these premises.'

'I'm not attempting to claim anything,' said Murugan. 'I just want to know what happened to my things.'

'What were they?' said the clerk. 'Can you describe them?'

Murugan nodded: 'A suitcase, a laptop—that kind of stuff.'

The clerk ran his pencil through the list, humming to himself. 'Here!' he said, pointing to a line. 'Suitcase, leather, plus miscellaneous travel articles and imported electronic equipment.'

Murugan fell silent, staring at the clipboard, shaking his head in incomprehension. 'But this is insane,' he said. 'I mean—being here today wasn't even a glimmer in my eye a year ago.'

The clerk handed Murugan the clipboard and wandered off in Sonali's direction. He produced a piece of paper from his trouser pocket and handed it to her. 'Please Madame,' he said, 'if you could just give me your autograph . . . just to show the Society . . .'

Sonali took the paper and the proffered pencil. She scribbled her name and handed the paper back. He received it with both hands, cupping it reverently between his palms. 'You do not know what this means to me,' he breathed, 'two famous people in one day—it is more than I could ever have imagined.'

Murugan reappeared, thrusting himself between them. 'I have another question for you,' he said. 'Did Mrs Aratounian leave any papers behind? Any xeroxes, old newspaper cuttings, anything?'

The clerk cocked his head, regarding Murugan with a puzzled frown. 'It is interesting that you ask,' he said. 'Usually when we clear out a flat there's a lot of waste paper lying around. But here there was nothing. No newspapers, old books, nothing. I looked because I wanted to put these in some paper.' Unfurling his fist he showed them his last remaining peanuts. 'But I couldn't find a single bit of paper in the whole house. That is why for Madame's autograph once again I had to use the paper that Mrs Aratounian gave me just before she left.'

'What paper?' said Murugan.

The clerk parted his hands slowly to reveal the slip of paper that Sonali had just autographed.

'When did Mrs Aratounian give you that?' Murugan demanded. 'And why?'

'She said if anyone came here to tell them . . .'

'Tell them what?'

The clerk squinted at the little slip. 'That she was going to catch a train at eight thirty,' he said. 'To Renupur, from Sealdah.'

'What!' cried Murugan. 'Quick: what time is it now?'

Grabbing the clerk's wrist, Urmila looked at his watch. 'Seven forty-five,' she said. 'We might just get there in time, if we find a taxi right away.'

She dropped the clerk's hand and said: 'Why didn't you tell us this before?'

'I didn't know,' he replied, sheepishly. 'I thought she meant someone else.'

'Who?' said Murugan.

'Phulboni,' said the clerk.

'Phulboni!' Sonali cried.

'Yes,' said the clerk. 'Phulboni himself. The great writer, he was here just a short while ago. He said that someone had gone to his house very late last night and left a note telling him to come here. Look . . .' He flipped the paper over and pointed to another scrawled autograph.

Murugan started for the door. 'Come on,' he said to Urmila. 'Let's move it.'

Urmila and Sonali followed him at a run, leaving the clerk momentarily stunned. They were halfway down when he shouted after them, hanging over the stairwell: 'Madame . . . my invitation . . .' There was no answer.

At the bottom of the stairs, Urmila stopped for a moment, to regain her breath. 'Sonali-di,' she said, panting. 'Why are you coming with us? You don't have to come.'

Sonali burst into laughter. 'Of course I'm coming with you,' she said.

'But why?' said Urmila. 'You don't know anything about this business.'

'There's something you don't know either,' Sonali said.

'What?'

'That Phulboni is my father,' said Sonali. 'With Phulboni and Romen gone, what will I stay for?'

A startled cry came floating down the stairwell. 'Oh my god!' the clerk's voice breathed. 'Phulboni is your father Madame? Oh my god! What will they say at the Film Society?'

They heard his footsteps pounding down the stairs and went running out to the street.

Murugan had already stopped a taxi. 'Quick,' he said to the driver. 'Sealdah—jaldi, as quick as you can.'

forty-four

_____

As the taxi lurched around a corner, on to Park Street, Murugan reached for Urmila's hand and sandwiched it between his.

'I want you to promise me something Calcutta,' he said.

'What?' said Urmila. 'What are you talking about?'

Murugan tugged urgently at her hand. 'Promise me Calcutta,' he said. 'Promise me that you'll take me across if I don't make it on my own.'

Urmila's eyes widened. 'Make it where?' she said.

'Wherever.'

She laughed out loud, throwing back her head: 'I don't know what you're talking about.'

'But promise anyway,' Murugan insisted. 'Promise you'll take me, even if they want you to leave me behind?'

'Why would anyone want to leave you behind?' said Urmila. 'You're the only one who knows what's happened, what's happening. You said yourself that someone had gone to a lot of trouble to help you make connections.'

'That's just the problem,' said Murugan. 'My part in this was to tie some threads together so that they could hand the whole package over in a neat little bundle some time in the future, to whoever it is they're waiting for.'

'And how do you know it's not you they've been waiting for?'

'It can't be me,' said Murugan flatly. 'You see, for them the only way to escape the tyranny of knowledge is to turn it on itself. But for that to work they have to create a single perfect moment of discovery when the person who discovers is also that which is discovered. The problem with me is that I know too much and too little.'

'But who is it then?' said Urmila.

'I wish I could tell you,' said Murugan. 'But I can't. In fact, I should be asking you that question.'

'What do you mean?' said Urmila.

'You still don't get it?' Murugan asked her, with a rueful half-smile.

'No,' said Urmila. 'I don't know what you're talking about.'

Murugan looked her in the eyes. 'Don't you see?' he said. 'You're the one she's chosen.'

Urmila gasped. 'For what?'

'For herself.'

Suddenly, taking Urmila by surprise, Murugan fell to his knees, squeezing himself into the narrow legspace of the backseat. Bending low he touched his forehead to her feet. 'Don't forget me,' he begged her. 'If you have it in your power to change the script, write me in. Don't leave me behind. Please.'

Urmila laughed. She put a hand on his head and an arm around Sonali's shoulders. 'Don't worry,' she said. 'I'll take you both with me, wherever I go.'

Then she caught a glimpse of the taxi driver, craning his neck over the back of the seat, grinning salaciously.

'And you keep your eyes on the road,' she snapped. 'This has nothing to do with you.'

Amitav Ghosh

forty-five

'Guess you don't remember me huh?' the Head said to Antar. 'Your old pal from the Thai restaurant?'

'Murugan!' Antar cried.

'You said it,' said Murugan. 'It's me.'

'Is that really you?' said Antar.

'Sure is,' said Murugan. 'I've waited a long time to get in touch with you. I figured nothing would be quite as quick as that ID card.'

'But people have been looking for you for years,' said Antar. 'Where have you been?'

'I've asked you this before,' said Murugan. 'And I'll ask again. Are you sure you want to know?'

'Yes,' said Antar.

'Okay Ant,' Murugan said with a laugh. 'It's your funeral. All you've got to do to find out is pick up that gadget over there.'

The disembodied chin wagged in the direction of Antar's Simultaneous Visualization headgear.

'You mean it's in there?' Antar gasped. 'But it can't be: nobody has access . . .'

'Guess we got in while the going was good,' said Murugan. 'Anyway it's all in there, waiting for you to hit the button.'

Slowly and deliberately, Antar reached for the headgear, slipped it on and clicked the visor into place, in front of his eyes. He tapped a key and suddenly a man appeared, walking down a wide road, beside a grey cathedral. He was wearing khaki trousers and a green baseball cap. It was Murugan. He stopped to look over his shoulder: dark threatening clouds were approaching across a wide green expanse. A minibus shot by, sending a plume of water shooting up from a puddle. Murugan began to run.

Antar shot a quick glance at the 'Time of Conversion' prompt, at the bottom of the three-dimensional, wraparound image. It said: '5.25 p.m.' Antar gasped: that could only mean that someone had started loading the Sim Vis system at about the time that Ava stumbled upon Murugan's ID card.

Now Murugan was standing in the lobby of a large auditorium and two women were running up the stairs. They came closer and suddenly Antar recognized Tara—except that she was in a saree. She was talking to Maria who was wearing a saree too.

He felt a cool soft touch upon his shoulder and his hand flew up to take off the Sim Vis Headgear. But now there was a restraining hand upon his wrist, and a voice in his ear, Tara's voice, whispering: 'Keep watching; we're here; we're all with you.'

There were voices everywhere now, in his room, in his head, in his ears, it was as though a crowd of people were in the room with him. They were saying: 'We're with you; you're not alone; we'll help you across.'

He sat back and sighed as he hadn't sighed in years.

I am very grateful to Raj Kumar Rajendran of the Dept of Computer Sciences, Columbia University for his advice on certain details. I am especially indebted to Alka Mansukhani of the Dept of Microbiology, New York University Medical Center: her ideas and support were essential to the writing of this book.